HOT ON THE TRAIL MIX

HOT ON THE TRAIL MIX

AUNTIE CLEM'S BAKERY #15

P.D. WORKMAN

ISBN: 9781774680551 (IS Hardcover)

ISBN: 9781774680568 (IS Paperback)

ISBN: 9781774680544 (IS Large Print)

ISBN: 9781774680513 (KDP Paperback)

ISBN: 9781774680520 (Kindle)

ISBN: 9781774680537 (ePub)

pdworkman

ALSO BY P.D. WORKMAN

Delusions of the Past

Fairy Blade Unmade

Web of Nightmares

A Whisker's Breadth

Skunk Man Swamp (Coming Soon)

Magic Ain't A Game (Coming Soon)

Without Foresight (Coming Soon)

Zachary Goldman Mysteries

She Wore Mourning

His Hands Were Quiet

She Was Dying Anyway

He Was Walking Alone

They Thought He was Safe

He Was Not There

Her Work Was Everything

She Told a Lie

He Never Forgot

She Was At Risk

Kenzie Kirsch Medical Thrillers

Unlawful Harvest

Doctored Death (Coming soon)

Dosed to Death (Coming soon)

Gentle Angel (Coming soon)

AND MORE AT PDWORKMAN.COM

To those still searching
for their place in the world

CHAPTER 1

*E*rin pushed Orange Blossom to the side with her foot, ignoring his meows of protest, so that she could get into the pantry cupboard for the food she had set aside for Vic. In order to keep him from getting into something that would make him sick, Blossom was not allowed in the pantry, even though it had now been determined that he hadn't gotten sick from getting into something he shouldn't have, but had been intentionally poisoned. It was still safest if she only fed him cat food she knew to be safe. Or meat that she prepared for him while making her own meals.

"I made you some sandwiches too, they're in the fridge."

Vic, a slim transgender woman, Erin's best friend and employee at the bakery, opened the fridge. Orange Blossom hurried over to her to see if Vic would be more cooperative about feeding him. Erin grabbed what she needed and shut the pantry.

"I made these granola bars. See what you think. I made some of them with certified gluten-free rolled oats, and some with buckwheat flakes. So the people who can't tolerate oats still have an option as well. If you can't really tell the difference, I'll just make the buckwheat, so I don't have to make two different kinds."

Vic nodded. "They look good. No nuts?" Vic knew that Auntie Clem's didn't sell anything containing nuts. But of course, granola bars frequently had nuts.

"No. I put in some pumpkin seeds and sunflower seeds. And some raisins and goji berries. And I made this trail mix." Erin put a baggie down on the counter. "Sunflower seeds, hemp seed, and chia—loads of protein."

Vic swept her long, blond hair out of her face as she leaned over and packed the goodies into her backpack. "Sounds great. This should be more than enough to get us through the day."

"Make sure you have plenty of water."

"We do." Vic pulled the zipper of the pack closed. "You sure you don't want to come along with us?" she teased.

Erin flashed back to being trapped underground—no light, no water, bound hand and foot with no idea how to get out of the labyrinthine caves. She had been terrified she was going to die there, injured and alone. No one would be able to find her. She wouldn't be able to find her own way out. The oxygen had been thin and she had been dehydrated.

"No," she told Vic firmly. "I am never going into a cave again."

Vic squeezed her arm. "And you never have to," she assured Erin. She gave Erin a mischievous smile. "But I'm going to keep asking. Spelunking is so much fun."

"It's just not for me."

It amazed Erin that Vic was still into spelunking. After having been trapped in a collapsed mine, Vic should have hated dark, enclosed spaces as much as Erin. But she had bounced back quickly and, as soon as she and Willie had their casts off, they were back at it again. Maybe it was because she was so young, just barely an adult, that she had bounced back so fast.

"You can keep asking. As long as you don't think I'm going to change my answer."

Vic nodded. She shouldered the pack. "We're off, then." She looked at the clock. While early, it wasn't nearly as early as when they usually had to get up to bake the day's goods and open up Auntie Clem's. Considering their usual schedule, it was a relaxed morning.

"Say 'hi' to Willie for me."

"Will do."

～

Once Vic and Willie were on their way, Erin sat down to work on her plans for the day and consider the upcoming week. In an effort to get control over the clutter in her purse and on her desk, she had actually purchased a planner. It had been a lengthy process. First, looking over the planners available at the stationery store in the city and considering all of the possibilities of size, layout, and binding type. And, of course, the price point. She didn't want something that would become a craft, with all kinds of stickers and accessories and time required to decorate it. Just somewhere she could keep her lists, plans, and appointments together and organized.

After finally settling on a book that would fit in her purse, she had started to use it. Breaking the habit of years of writing on scrap pieces of paper, napkins, and an assortment of notepads was not easy. She had to train herself to reach for her book instead and write her lists and thoughts in the appropriate place. Where hopefully she would be able to find them again later when she wanted them.

But she was growing to love her little planner. She didn't waste as much time searching for lists and notes that she had written and then 'filed' in her purse, wallet, or pocket for later reference. Her purse, while still full, was a lot less cluttered.

Erin sat on the couch with her feet curled under her. In a few minutes, Orange Blossom jumped up beside her and cuddled up.

She enjoyed the peace and quiet of the morning. Terry was still sleeping and could continue to sleep for however long his body let him. He didn't go on shift until the afternoon. If he got up in good time, they would have some couple's time together and maybe go out for lunch.

Everything was finally calm and peaceful in Erin's life.

CHAPTER 2

When Erin heard Terry stirring in the bedroom, she looked at the time on her phone. She had promised Vic that she would check on her new dog, Nilla, and make sure that he got a break and a bit of exercise. That would hopefully keep him from destroying Vic's loft apartment over the garage.

She went down to the bedroom and poked her head in to look at Terry. "Morning."

Terry stretched and groaned. He scratched the stubble on his cheek and smiled. Not enough to show the dimple in his cheek, but it warmed Erin's heart to see him happy in the morning instead of worn out and miserable because he hadn't been able to get any sleep and had a migraine.

"Mmm. Come here."

Erin obliged, going around to his side of the bed and giving him a good morning hug and kiss. His body was warm, his hair mussed, and he smelled faintly of sweat. Erin buried her face in the hollow of his shoulder, enjoying their closeness and the looseness of his body.

"I'm just popping out for a few minutes to take care of Nilla."

There was a whine from K9 in his kennel.

"Yes, you can come too," Erin agreed. "Come on."

K9 jumped out of his kennel, tail wagging excitedly. He stopped to give

4

Terry a nuzzle and get his ears scratched, then headed out the bedroom door, leading the way for Erin.

"See you in a few minutes," Terry told her.

Erin blew him a kiss and followed K9 to the back door. She disabled the alarm and followed him out.

⁓

Once in the yard, Erin could hear a frantic yipping coming from the direction of Vic's apartment.

"Uh-oh."

K9 was on his way to his dog run in the corner of the yard. He looked back at Erin with a comical eye roll. Sometimes his expressions seemed very human. Erin left him to his business and went up the stairs to the loft apartment. She unlocked the door, calling out to the little dog.

"Nilla! Come here, boy! What's the matter?"

The apartment was a mess and Erin knew it wasn't because Vic had left it that way. When Nilla got into a mood, he could be a little tornado of destruction. Kind of like the Tasmanian devil in the cartoons.

The yipping continued. Erin tried to home in on him.

"Nilla? Where are you? What are you doing?"

She was afraid at first that he had gotten himself into trouble and was stuck somewhere. But she found him in Vic's bedroom, wrestling with a pair of leggings.

"Nilla! No!"

Nilla turned on her, growling. If he'd been a big dog, Erin might have been concerned, but the little white fluff-ball was not very intimidating. Although he threatened, when the critical point was reached, he would run, not attack.

"No," Erin repeated firmly and bent down to pick up the leggings. She didn't want to start a tug-of-war, which might cause worse damage to the clothes than just leaving them on the floor. "Shoo. Get back." She waved her hands at the dog. Nilla remained, growling fiercely until the last minute, and then he ran away. Erin picked up the leggings and any other clothes that Nilla had pulled to the floor. She folded them and put them into the top drawer where they would be safe. She made sure to shut the drawer tightly so that he wouldn't be able to open it, and pushed the others closed, making sure they were all tight so that hopefully Nilla wouldn't be able to drag any more out.

"Do you want to go for a walk?" She called out to Nilla. "Outside? Walk?"

Nilla growled, but when Erin left the bedroom and headed back toward the front door, he immediately dropped all pretense of being threatening and jumped at the doorknob. It was amazing the height that the little dog could achieve.

There were scratches on the door already from the past few weeks that Nilla had lived there. Erin should probably have told Vic no, no pets allowed, but since Erin had taken in two pets of her own and K9 also spent most of the week there, it was pretty hard to deny Vic the privilege.

It wouldn't have been a problem if Nilla had been better behaved.

She thought about texting Vic to let her know that Nilla was causing problems once more, but decided against it. Vic wasn't likely to have cell coverage where she was. Even if she did, there wasn't anything she could do to fix the problem and Erin didn't want her worrying about it the whole time she was away.

Erin managed to hold Nilla still long enough to get his walking harness on him, then took him outside and down the stairs. She always worried with how hyper and excited Nilla got that he was going to end up getting hung falling down the stairs, or falling off the side through the railing. The dog seemed incapable of moving in a straight line. But using a harness instead of a collar helped allay her worries. He didn't have something around his neck that was going to strangle him.

She managed to get down the stairs without getting tangled up in the leash and gently encouraged him toward the dog run. Unlike K9, Nilla seemed resistant to the idea of training to one area of the yard and always wanted to sniff and pee everywhere.

"Come over here. Come on. This is where you're supposed to go. Watch K9. He knows what to do. Don't you want to be a big dog like K9?"

By the time she got him over to the dog run, she suspected he was empty, but she stayed there with him for a little while, encouraging him to make use of the run.

K9 was sitting watching them patiently, but Erin knew he wanted to go for a walk to stretch his legs. He was a big dog and needed a lot of exercise.

"Okay, you done, Nilla? Let's walk."

Nilla allowed himself to be coaxed toward the gate. He knew that walking was next, and though he was slower than K9 and easily distracted, he was pretty good for his walks.

"Come on, K9," Erin called. K9 bounded after her, quickly falling in at her heel and showing the little dog proper behavior. Nilla gave him a little growl, pretending that he could take K9 on if he had to, and went on with his explorations, ranging out on the leash as far as Erin would let him go.

~

Even though Nilla was just a little dog, Erin was always tired after walking him. He pulled and moved erratically and she was always worried about what he was going to do next, so the emotional effort took more than the physical. Nilla was also tired, and Erin was able to pick him up and carry him up the steps so that she didn't have to worry about him shooting off the side or between the slats. She took him to his kennel and shunted him inside. She shut the door while she got him some food and water. He was chill enough after his walk that he didn't whine or try to get out. She gave him his bowls and left, locking up behind her.

Terry had already let K9 into the house, and he opened the door for Erin as she approached. "How was it?"

Erin shook her head. "About usual! I'm sure glad that K9 is so well-trained and calm."

"Yeah. Vic really needs to get that dog trained."

"She's trying. And I think he's improved in the time that she's had him. But Beryl obviously didn't know anything about training."

Terry nodded. "Some people shouldn't have pets. Did you put him in his kennel?"

"Yes. But Vic doesn't want him to be kenneled all day."

"Won't hurt him for a while."

"If he was better-behaved, then I would just bring him over here. He gets along with K9. They could hang out together and Nilla wouldn't be lonely."

"After seeing the destruction that little dog can cause, I would not want to see how he would treat a cat or a rabbit."

"They're both bigger than him. He would probably end up with the wrong end of the stick. But I don't want to try it. I don't want any of them to end up hurt."

"No," Terry agreed. "We can try introducing them gradually but, since Orange Blossom still hasn't made friends with K9, I don't know how that would go over."

Erin sighed. "They're as bad as people. I wish that everyone would just get along."

CHAPTER 3

t had been a productive day. Erin had run some errands, gone through her projects and plans for the next week, taken Nilla out for another round of exercise, and made an early supper that involved more than just opening a can of soup or making sandwiches. All in all, she had gotten a good amount done.

Terry was just scraping the last of the pasta sauce from his plate when his phone buzzed with a message. He looked at Erin, raising his brows. She made a motion for him to go ahead and answer it. Supper was over, so he might as well. Besides, it could be a work call, and he should take it. He wasn't on call with the dispatcher yet, but the sheriff could still call him if they needed all hands on deck.

He looked down at his screen and his brows lowered into a scowl. He looked back at Erin.

"Looks like Vic and Willie ran into some trouble."

Erin's heart sank. Her stomach tightened with worry. "What kind of trouble? Are they okay?"

"They are fine. But I've got to go in."

Erin shook her head, wondering what kind of problem might have occurred that would cause that kind of response. Most things could wait until the morning. But Terry wasn't likely to tell her what was going on. He normally wouldn't even have said that Vic and Willie were involved. He was good about keeping everything quiet, even from her.

"They're not hurt? Sick?" she persisted.

"They're okay," he reassured her. "No cave collapse. They haven't been injured. But I need to go out and help take care of things. I'm sorry. You're going to be on your own tonight."

"Okay. That's fine, of course." They didn't need to be together all the time. In fact, when he had been off work, it had been very stressful to have him home all the time. Of course, a lot of that might have had to do with his irritability and PTSD. *Thanks for that, Theresa Franklin.* "But you won't stay out too long, will you? You'll be careful?"

He wasn't yet putting in full-time hours and Erin was constantly afraid that he would do too much and end up with a week-long migraine or other relapse symptoms. He wasn't yet fully healed. The sheriff needed to understand that.

And Terry himself needed to understand that. He was probably the one who expected the most from himself. It had been too long since he had been injured. He felt that he should have been able to heal in that length of time. And that he should certainly not still be having any PTSD. That should all be behind him.

"I only put in a half shift this afternoon. I'm fresh as a daisy."

"But you won't be if you work all night. Be careful. Tell the sheriff if it's too much and you have to go home."

He scowled at her and didn't answer. Erin knew there was no way that he was going to tell Sheriff Wilmot that he was tired and wanted to go home. Even though the sheriff would send him home. Terry wanted too much to show that he had recovered and was just as tough as ever.

Even though Terry had said that Vic and Willie were unhurt and everything was okay, Erin was still worried. The entire Bald Eagle Falls police department would not be called out there for nothing. It didn't matter that the department consisted only of Terry, the sheriff, young Stayner, and Tom Banks, who was part time. There were few occurrences in Bald Eagle Falls that required all of them to be on site. And if something else happened and they needed to attend to another call, they would all be out at the cave. Or wherever it was that they had gone to take care of Vic's and Willie's problem.

Something had happened. Something serious.

A few hours went by. Erin busied herself in the little attic room reading through Clementine's genealogy files and books, learning more about the history of Bald Eagle Falls and her father's family. It was hard to stay focused and not let her mind wander to the call. But thinking about it wasn't going to solve anything, so she did her best to just dive deep into the pages of history and lose herself in the stories and genealogies.

She saw the flash of headlights out back and looked out the window to see Willie's truck pull into the pad beside the garage. She left all of her papers and books scattered around and hurried down the stairs to see them.

Erin keyed the burglar alarm and stepped out the back door, arriving in the yard as Vic and Willie were climbing down from the cab of the truck.

"Hey, are you guys okay?"

"We're all right!" Vic assured her. "See? All in one piece."

Erin looked them both over. They looked tired, but unharmed. Willie went to the back of the truck to unload Vic's spelunking gear.

"Great granola bars and trail mix," he told Erin. "They came in very handy when we had to stick around longer than expected."

"You liked them?" She allowed herself to be distracted for just a moment. "That's great. Both kinds?"

"Yes, everything. All good. I couldn't tell the difference between the two kinds of granola bars."

"Perfect." Erin turned to Vic. "You too? You liked them?"

"Yes, they were good."

That was one question checked off of her list. Erin raised her brows and spread her hands out in a query. "So…?"

Vic looked over at Willie, but he seemed very intent on the gear. She sighed. "Well… let's just say… Erin Price isn't the only one who can find human remains around here."

CHAPTER 4

$\mathcal{E}$rin felt her eyes go wide. "What? Are you serious?"

Vic nodded. Her eyes were amused and tired, and just a little strained around the corners. She had been acting happy and relaxed for too long and was ready to crash, maybe have a glass of wine, and put it all behind her.

"Tell me about it!"

"Why don't we go inside? I'm about dead on my feet. You'll be okay with the gear?" she asked Willie.

"If it will get me out of the recap," Willie grumbled. "I'll take mine home and unload, I don't want to leave it in the truck overnight. Then I'll be back."

Vic shrugged and rolled her eyes. "Okay, then. I'll leave you to it. Erin and I will go set a spell."

She and Erin walked into the house together. Orange Blossom began yowling as if he'd been left alone all day. With no food, even. Vic laughed at him as he complained noisily and rubbed her legs.

"Really? Has it been that awful? Well, I'll definitely have a word with her." She looked at Erin for permission. "Can I give him a couple of treats?"

"Of course."

Vic knew where everything was. She used the kitchen as much as Erin did, even though she had her own kitchenette in the loft. It was just more natural for her and Erin to cook together or that she would get tea for both of them in Erin's kitchen rather than her own. She got out the can of kitty treats and slid a few across the floor for Orange Blossom to chase and consume. Vic also called Marshmallow in to get a carrot. Then she and Erin made their way to the living room and sat down.

"So spill," Erin commanded. "Tell me all about it."

"Well, what's to tell? You know what it's like…" Vic teased.

"Just tell me. Who? What happened? I can't believe you didn't call me earlier and tell me about it."

"Earlier, we were talking to the police and under strict instructions not to call anyone until we had given full statements and been questioned individually about it. And you know how they have to ask the same question ten different ways to make sure that they got a complete answer and to see if you trip over your own story. It takes forever."

"Yes." Erin nodded sympathetically. She knew all about that. But she wanted to hear about what had happened.

※

"So, it was just a normal day spelunking. Get all of the gear set up, work out your plan, and into the cave you go."

Erin shuddered at that. She was okay with the 'getting ready' part. And with the going home part. It was everything else in between that was the problem.

"Where were you? Or can you even tell me that part?"

"I'll show you on a map later. It's not a popular spot, just one Willie knew about."

Erin nodded. She waited for the punchline. Vic raised her brows as if she didn't know what Erin was waiting for. Then she finally went on.

"We'd been exploring another cave. But Willie wanted to show me this one before we went home, and it was just on the other side of the hill. Well, we got in about fifty feet, where there's an underground spring and pool. Dark as pitch, but we had our lights, so we were okay. I wanted to see what wildlife we could find, so we had on the red lights rather than the big white ones. The white ones would just scare everything away."

Erin thought of bats hanging from the ceiling, dark things scuttling in the dark, and pale blind fish swimming silently in the underground pool.

Not her idea of a romantic getaway. She would do her hiking and sight-seeing above ground, thank you very much.

She swallowed, turning her thoughts back toward Vic and Willie and what they had seen. She tried not to envision what they had come across down in that dark, damp cave.

"You okay?" Vic checked.

"Yeah. Go ahead."

"So we had just these dim lights on, and we were scouting around, seeing what we could see before we scared anything away. Some pretty bizarre critters live underground. You just won't see them anywhere else."

"I'm okay with that."

Vic laughed. "I was looking into the pool, and down where it was deeper, I could see something white. Red, in the light, but I still knew it was white. Figured maybe it was a cave fish, so I leaned in for a closer look."

Erin really hoped that she hadn't ended up going into the pool face-first, leaning over too far. She thought about the scene in Harry Potter, where the dead people started coming out of the underground lake, trying to pull them under.

"When I leaned closer, I could see more white things. Maybe a whole school of fish. Or salamanders or something else that might congregate and not disperse very quickly. But then I started to realize that they were *arranged*. And... well, arranged in the shape of a skeleton."

"Ugh."

"And of course, that's exactly what it was. A skeleton in the pool."

"Just bones?" Erin asked. That might not be so bad. It wasn't bloody and gory. Unsettling, of course, but the bones might have been in that pool for hundreds of years. They might even be fossilized.

"That's all I could see with the red light on, because it's very dim, and only white stuff reflected back. I called Willie over, and he had a look, and then we turned on our white headlamps to get a better look at what we had found. It was *mostly* skeletonized. Like, you could see the fingers and the ribs and everything. There was still some..." Vic hesitated, and Erin thought she decided not to say what she had been planning to. "We could see that there was clothing around parts of it. So it was, you know, modern. And besides, Willie has been there before, so he knew it wasn't something that had been there for years."

"That sounds horrible. Are you okay?"

"Yes, I'm fine." Vic rolled her eyes. "It's all been very surreal. We went back outside, called the police, waited for them to get out there, led them to it, and answered all of their questions. It didn't really feel real, if you know what I mean."

Erin nodded. She understood that feeling of unreality. Like maybe it was just a mannequin, or a joke, or some student film project. Her mind always went to other explanations, something to indicate that it wasn't really real.

"So, that's all," Vic said. "I know it sounds like a big, exciting thing, but it really wasn't. There wasn't much to see, and when we saw it, we had to get the police involved and then spend half the night dealing with them."

"Did you see Terry out there?"

"Sure. Officer Terry Piper was on duty. Everyone was on duty. I talked to him. He was very good. Very professional."

Erin knew his professional face and manner. She nodded. "Yeah. He's good at what he does. Did he look okay? Not like he'd been there for too long?"

"He was fine when I saw him. I don't think you need to worry about him."

"I always worry about him."

"I know. And maybe you should ease up a bit on that. He's a big boy. He can take care of himself."

"I just know that he doesn't always do that."

"No one *always* does. We all let ourselves get a bit overtired sometimes, or don't eat right away when we should. Or do things that we know aren't good for us. It's normal. And men are like that. They don't want to look weak. They want to tough it out. Show everybody what a good protector they are."

Erin nodded. She knew that. She'd had plenty of experience with it the last few months. She squeezed Vic's arm. "So, you're okay?"

"I'm okay. Willie's okay. Terry's okay. The only one who isn't okay is the poor guy in the pool."

"And you didn't... recognize him."

"How could I? He had no—" Vic cut herself off. "No, I couldn't tell who it was. It was mostly just bones. And the clothes could have been anyone's. Blue jeans, plaid flannel shirt. Practically a uniform in the wilds around here."

"Yeah. I don't know anyone who has been declared missing lately, do you? I mean… no one since Joshua."

"Nope. No one I know about. He was probably from out of town. Maybe even out of state. Just came here to explore caves…"

"You think so? No one we know?"

"Nah. After what happened to Josh, I think we would have heard if anyone else disappeared. We're kind of a bit paranoid about that right now. If rumors started going around town about someone else being missing, we would have heard about it, I'm sure."

"Yeah. That makes sense. We would have heard about it."

"So he must have been someone from out of town. Another spelunker or a miner. Shouldn't have been exploring by himself. You should always take a partner, at least. File a plan to make sure that people know where you're going to be."

"Yeah. I worry even when it's you and Willie. I know you are together, and he's experienced and good at first aid care, but… like with the mine collapse…"

"At least we were stuck together. If we didn't come back, you'd come looking for us sooner or later. And you and Terry would get us out. Just like before."

Erin hadn't really done anything to get them out when the mine collapsed. She had called it in, and the police department and search and rescue had taken over. All she had done was sit there waiting for someone else to do all of the work.

CHAPTER 5

They only spent a few more minutes visiting. Vic stretched and massaged the back of her neck and excused herself.

"I'm going to need some time to unwind if I'm going to be at Auntie Clem's in the morning."

Erin hadn't even thought about that. "I can call someone else in. Do you want me to do that?"

"No. I'd rather be working. Keep my mind off of things."

"You're not going to be able to do that," Erin warned, thinking about how many people would be at the bakery the next day to gossip and get all of the details.

"Well… no, not most of the time. But work makes it go faster. I'll take a sleeping pill. But I want some time to just decompress first."

Erin nodded. "Sure. Of course. I'll see you in the morning. But if you do have a bad night and want to sleep, just let me know so I can call someone."

"I'll be fine." Vic leaned toward her and gave her a hug goodbye. "See you tomorrow. You should be heading to bed soon."

Erin tried to sleep, but her brain was whirling and she couldn't settle her thoughts. She couldn't help thinking about the bones in the underground pond. She had a feeling they were going to figure into her dreams that night. If she ever got to sleep.

Terry gave her a bear hug in greeting and looked at her face. "I thought you and Vic would still be talking."

"We talked. But we're both on at the bakery tomorrow, so I was hoping to get some sleep."

"She told you all about it?" Since Terry wasn't allowed to tell Erin anything about his investigations, he couldn't really talk to her about anything but what she already knew from other sources.

"Yes. I can't believe it! What a shock it must have been for them."

"I imagine so. That's not one of the things that you expect to discover when you go exploring caves. Although, there have certainly been remains discovered in other caves. Sometimes they were used as natural tombs by the native peoples or early settlers. A lot easier than digging a hole."

"But this one that Vic and Willie found… it's not an Indian or early settler."

"Oh?" He raised his brows.

"Not if it was wearing blue jeans."

"No," he agreed.

"And Vic said that Willie has been in there before and he wasn't there. So it's not even someone in one-hundred-year-old Levis. It's… recent."

"Contemporary, anyway," Terry agreed. "Willie said that he hasn't been there for a couple of months. And even when he was there last, he didn't take a careful look in the pool. It could have been deeper in the mud at that point. Maybe spring rains stirred things up a little to reveal it."

"So, you think it's older?"

"No. There are just other possibilities. It's important not to jump to immediate conclusions."

"Like that it could be someone we know?"

"It's not someone we know," he assured her.

"Does that mean you've already identified the… remains?"

"We have some initial leads to follow up. Probably won't take long, though we'll have to send them to the city to have them make the official identification. Don't want to misidentify them, you know."

Erin thought about her father. "No," she agreed. It would probably take weeks or months before the city had the official identity for them. If the remains were skeletonized. Erin knew it took longer than on TV, when an episode of *Bones* was completed in an hour and things like facial reconstructions or DNA analysis were instantaneous. "And it wasn't… Vic said it probably was someone from out of town, since there hasn't been anyone reported missing in Bald Eagle Falls."

Terry didn't agree or disagree. He shrugged and gave a head wobble that could have been yes or not. Noncommittal.

"You think it *was* someone from Bald Eagle Falls?"

"We'll have to see. But you don't know everybody in Bald Eagle Falls."

"Well, no," Erin agreed. And there were a lot of outlying farms and shacks. Someone could be local and still unknown to her. She'd only lived there for a short time as an adult, though she'd been there as a child before her parents had died.

"Is it someone *you* know?" she pried.

"Can't give you that kind of information."

"No, I guess not." Erin relaxed back into her pillow. "I don't suppose you're ready for bed."

He rubbed his forehead, considering. "I'm tired, but I don't think I'm ready for sleep. If I lay down now, I'm going to be tossing and turning and keeping us both awake."

Erin nodded. They'd been through it enough to know what didn't work.

"I'll need some time to relax and veg out before I'm ready for bed," Terry said.

"Okay… well, come in once you're ready, if you can."

"Sure. I don't want to wake you, though."

"You won't."

Erin wondered if she would wake him. Her brain was still whirling and she had a feeling that she was going to have a night filled with restless nightmares. "Do you want to cuddle for a little while?"

He bent down and kissed her on the forehead. "Better not. I'll just keep you awake. I'll see you tomorrow."

CHAPTER 6

The next day, Erin's mind was not any calmer, but was buzzing with questions about the person who had died in that cave. Who he had been and what had happened. How much did the police know? She knew that she couldn't find out the details from Terry; he was far too careful of what he said to her. There were other ways to find out more information about the investigation. Mostly, she just had to wait, and it would come to her.

Vic was definitely looking worse for wear. She was dressed and ready for work when it was time to go—Terry was still up and said he would drop them off—but Vic was definitely looking a little wilted.

"Are you sure you're okay to work today?"

"I'm fine, boss. Got a few hours in."

"We don't want you chopping any fingers off."

"I'll be sure to stay away from the bread knife. You know how it is; once we get going, I won't be tired anymore."

"Until you get home after the shift and crash. Why don't you see if someone else can come in to cover the afternoon? You can just do the morning and then catch a nap."

"I really am fine," Vic insisted.

Erin shrugged. "Okay," she finally conceded. She'd done everything she could to ensure that Vic had a way out if she needed it. She turned her attention to Terry.

"And you're okay to drop us off? You know all of the warnings about driving tired."

"I can manage to Auntie Clem's and back." It was only a few blocks. "I've driven after much longer shifts."

"That doesn't necessarily mean it was a good idea. Driving tired is driving impaired."

"Are you going to administer a field test?" Terry teased good-naturedly. He closed his eyes and brought both index fingers to his nose. "Okay?"

Erin laughed. "Okay, okay. You pass."

"I'll sleep when I get back," he promised. "I'll get a good long chunk in by the time you're back."

Erin didn't think she would have been able to survive shiftwork, going to sleep during the day like that.

They got their things together and headed out to the bakery.

Erin enjoyed the cool air before the bakery heated up from the baking. It could get pretty hot in the kitchen during the summer, but it was only spring and it didn't get unbearable. Vic and Erin worked together through their well-established routine, getting the morning's goods baked and arranged in the display case.

"You think the body was someone who was from out of town?" Erin asked Vic as they were arranging the display case.

Vic looked at her, brows raised. She nodded. "Yes, I expect so. We would have heard if someone from Bald Eagle Falls was missing."

Erin nodded.

"Why?"

"It's just that Terry... I kind of thought that he thinks it was someone from around here."

"Did he say that?"

"Not exactly. But he said that I don't know everyone in and around Bald Eagle Falls."

"Huh." Vic thought about it. "Well, I mean... it could have been someone I know. He wasn't exactly recognizable in that state. I just figured that since I hadn't heard about a missing person, it must be someone from the city or out of state."

Erin shuddered. "Wouldn't it be awful if it was someone that you knew."

"Yeah." Vic paused in writing the pricing labels, staring in the direction of the front door. Erin doubted she actually saw the door or what was on the other side. "That would be pretty disturbing, actually."

Erin instantly regretted having suggested it. She knew how hard it could be to deal with a scene like that and, instead of reassuring and supporting Vic, she was making it worse by suggesting that maybe it was someone she knew.

"Oh, I'm sorry… that was so stupid."

Vic shrugged. "Well, if it is someone I know, then it would have come up sooner or later anyway. Might as well think about it now and not be so shocked when they identify him."

The Fosters arrived early in the day, before the worst of the gossips came by. Mrs. Foster had been blindsided before by people discussing a murder in front of her children, so Erin was glad that she arrived when it was quiet and the discovery was not yet the main topic of conversation.

"Miss Erin!" The children ran excitedly up to the display case to pick out their kid's club cookies. It had been a long time since they had been there, between Erin falling out with Mrs. Foster and the birth of the latest little Foster.

"It's a boy!" Peter called out to Erin, gesturing to the baby Mrs. Foster wore in a sling. "I can't believe we finally got another boy!"

"I know," Erin agreed. "It's very exciting. Are you helping your mom out with everything? You're a big boy, and taking care of a baby and your sisters is a big job."

He nodded seriously, watching his three sisters crowding around the display case pointing at the day's offerings.

"Yeah, that's what Dad said, too. I try and help."

"Good. Don't leave everything for her to do."

Peter agreed. He took charge of the little girls, asking them what cookies they wanted and trying to talk them into ordering the ones that he wanted them to. Mrs. Foster sighed and listed off for Erin the things that she needed for the week. The baby fussed, and she readjusted the sling, rocking her body back and forth to soothe him. He settled back down. Erin stood on her tiptoes to look over the counter and the edge of the sling to catch a glimpse of his cherubic cheeks.

"Aw. So sweet."

Mrs. Foster nodded, rubbing the dark little curls at the top of his head. "It's always such an amazing experience when they are this new," she said. "Fresh from heaven."

Erin started to collect the bread and other items that the Fosters needed, giving a half-shrug. She didn't believe in heaven or God, and mentions of them always made her feel awkward. She didn't want to challenge people's beliefs, but she didn't want to pretend to agree when she didn't, either. Silence was the best she could come up with.

Vic spoke with the children, using tongs to get each child the cookie he or she wanted. Traci squealed and jumped up and down when she got hers. Peter looked down at his cookie and asked Mrs. Foster if she wanted a bite.

"No, you go ahead and have it," Mrs. Foster told him, giving his arm a pat. "It's yours."

"You didn't get anything."

"I don't need anything, I'm the mom. And I have baby weight to lose."

"You don't need to lose weight."

She smiled and pulled him in close for a hug around his shoulders. "I'm glad you don't think so. But I don't want to have to carry all of these extra pounds around. It's hard enough carrying Allan."

"He's not heavy." Peter stood as tall as he could, grasping the edge of the sling to pull the side down and look at the baby.

"No, but he's going to keep growing. And until he's big enough to walk around, I'll be carrying him."

"You could use a stroller."

"I use a stroller when we go into the city," Mrs. Foster said. "I don't like to use one around town. It just encourages kids to be lazy."

Erin wasn't sure how using a stroller encouraged a child to be lazy but using a sling did not. But she smiled at Mrs. Foster and handed her the order.

CHAPTER 7

*E*ventually, word started to get around about Vic's discovery in the cave. Erin was happy to see that the most common reaction was the same as hers—horror at what Vic had discovered and shudders at the thought of exploring caves deep underground, dark and damp and full of unearthly critters. There were few women who, like Vic or Gema, a woman who had lived in Bald Eagle Falls when Erin had first arrived there, appreciated the adventure and challenge of spelunking.

"Why on earth would anyone want to crawl into a hole in the ground?" Lottie Sturm demanded. "I can't imagine any good reason for tunneling like a worm inside the earth!"

"I understand your viewpoint," Vic assured her. "There are a lot of people who would agree with you. But I really enjoy exploring. Stepping into a place that… few if any human eyes have ever seen before. And you've seen some of the pictures, right? Some caves can be absolutely beautiful. Full of stalactites and stalagmites, or beautiful underground waterfalls and pools. Even gold or other mineral deposits. You never know what you're going to find."

Lottie made a disgusted noise and shuddered dramatically. "You'd never catch me going into such a place. And this just proves it."

"What…?" Vic asked, her eyebrows coming down.

"Finding a skeleton. Anyplace you find a dead skeleton is a place I don't

24

want to be."

"Oh. Yes, you're right, of course. Dead skeletons," Vic agreed. "I can see how you wouldn't want to come across any of them."

"You're acting like it wasn't any big deal," Cindy Prost, mother of Bella, one of Erin's part-time employees, pointed out. "There's something wrong with you if that doesn't bother you."

Cindy flashed a look at Lottie, which Erin interpreted as a confirmation of what they had long believed—that there was something terribly wrong with Vic. As if being transgender weren't proof enough that she was a deviant.

Erin rolled her eyes, directing a mental apology at Vic. At least the customers knew not to run Vic down in front of her. Anyone who did was not welcomed back into the bakery until they had expressed a sincere apology. Cindy was definitely treading a thin line. Erin wasn't going to put up with much more from her.

"I've got a pretty strong stomach," Vic said. "I wouldn't say that it didn't give me a turn, but as far as it keeping me from spelunking anymore... well, it would take a lot more than a pile of bones to keep me out of the caves."

"It just ain't natural," Cindy affirmed.

"Do they know who it was yet?" Lottie asked.

"It's probably some ancient, prehistoric skeleton," Cindy said. "Been down there for a thousand years."

"Not unless they had blue jeans a thousand years ago." Vic leaned forward slightly to deliver this news and to assess the ladies' reaction to it.

"Blue jeans?"

Vic nodded. "Either that or someone dressed up the cave man later. And with the state he was in, that would have been pretty hard."

"Shocking," Cindy huffed. "I can't believe something like that happening right here in—right outside of Bald Eagle Falls. This isn't the kind of place where that happens."

Who did she think she was kidding? Erin had been stumbling over dead bodies and other criminal enterprises since she had moved to Bald Eagle Falls. Rather than not being the kind of place bodies showed up like that, the universe seemed to be funneling them toward Bald Eagle Falls and the nearby Tennessee towns.

"I'm shore he didn't do it on purpose," Vic drawled. She gave Erin an amused look, clearly in agreement that with all that had happened in the time they had both been in Bald Eagle Falls, it wasn't unlikely that she would discover a skeleton in an underground lake.

"Do you think he had a heart attack?" Lottie mused. "Did he look like he had a heart attack? Or like he drowned?"

"I'm sure the medical examiner will look into that... it's not up to me to say."

The women made shocked noises and placed their orders for baking that they probably didn't actually need.

~

After they were gone, Vic looked sideways at Erin. The bakery was empty for the moment, and she had something she wanted to say without others overhearing. Erin read all of this in a glance.

"What?"

"I don't think he had a heart attack or drowned."

"Oh." Erin thought about that. She wasn't sure she really wanted to know the details. But Vic wanted to talk to someone about it, and she didn't want to spread rumors all over Bald Eagle Falls. For one thing, Officer Terry Piper would not appreciate that. "You think that... you could tell what it was? From the bones?"

"Yeah." Vic's voice was low and husky. "The skull was pretty smashed up."

Erin mumbled a response, her stomach lurching. She tried again not to picture what Vic had seen, but her imagination was too good. She couldn't help forming a mental image.

"I don't think it was natural," Vic said. "I mean, yeah, maybe he hit his head... on an overhang, or fell into that pool, but I don't think so. And I don't get the feeling that Terry thought so."

"It could have been an accident."

"If it was... then where was his gear? He went into the cave without any? I didn't even see a headlamp. I'm sure they'll drain the pool and look for one, but... no one would go in there without a headlamp. Not on purpose."

"So, you think it's murder."

"The questions that the police were asking us last night... they didn't act like *they* thought it was an accident."

CHAPTER 8

*T*erry had said that he would go to sleep after dropping Erin off and would probably sleep most of the time that Erin was working. That would get him back on track so that he wasn't in as much of a danger of coming down with a migraine or relapsing in other areas.

When she got home, he was awake. He didn't look like she had woken him up, or like he had just recently gotten himself up and was still groggy. That was good. He must have gotten the sleep that he had needed.

He got up from the couch when she arrived and gave her a hug and a soft kiss. "How was your day?" he murmured.

"Well, you know what it gets like at Auntie Clem's when people are chasing down rumors." Erin bent down to pick up Orange Blossom, who was yowling for her attention. She held him like a baby while she spoke to Terry.

"I suppose there's nothing we can do about it when Vic was one of the witnesses. You can't exactly ground her."

Erin laughed. "No. I don't think that would work very well." She walked into the kitchen with her armful of yowling cat. Marshmallow pricked up his long ears and followed her in to make sure he didn't miss out on any treats. "What do you want today?"

"I can make something. You've been working all day, I've just been sleeping and lazing about."

"You've been sleeping because you were up all night. At least I got a few hours of sleep."

"I've had more than you by this time. How much did you get? Two hours? Three?"

Erin shrugged. She didn't really want to stop to calculate. Less than she needed, that was for sure. But she would sleep better tonight. "We'll make something together, then. Some pasta?"

Terry nodded his agreement. Erin put down the cat and washed her hands. They moved around the kitchen together, coordinating the preparation of pasta, a green salad, and rolls from the bakery with butter. Marshmallow hung around Erin's feet while she chopped vegetables for the salad, so she cut a few chunks for him.

Of course, that set Orange Blossom off again because the bunny was getting a treat and he wasn't. So Erin had to get him something. And she didn't want K9 to feel left out, so she got a doggie biscuit out of the jar for him. She thought about Nilla over in Vic's apartment, but it seemed a little silly to make sure that he got a treat. Vic would see to it that he had what he needed. Hopefully, he hadn't torn things up again while Vic had been at work and he had been in the apartment by himself. At least, Erin assumed that he had been alone, and Willie had been out checking out one of his mines or another venture.

"You didn't hear Nilla during the day, did you?" she asked Terry.

"Nilla? I wouldn't hear him from here, unless he was howling."

Which meant that he hadn't. Erin nodded. "Good. I hope he's settling into the routine."

They worked a little longer in silence.

"Have you heard from the sheriff?" Erin ventured.

"Heard what from the sheriff?"

"Any update on the case. Have they been able to identify the body?"

"Preliminary steps are being taken. Can't really say more than that. There are particular procedures to follow, channels to go through."

"I know. I just wondered if you'd heard an update from him."

Terry nodded, but didn't give any further information to Erin.

"Vic said she thought that it was a murder investigation. Not an accident investigation."

He turned around from the sauce he was stirring and looked at her.

"Well, that was very astute of her," he said. "Or did you hear something from Melissa?"

"She didn't come to the bakery today." Melissa worked part time at the police department with administrative work. And she was a little too eager to spread information on matters that should have remained confidential.

"Well, that's good news. The longer we can keep that woman out of the bakery, the better."

Erin smiled, scooping irregularly-cut vegetables into the salad bowl. "You know that if she didn't come into the bakery, she would just take the news somewhere else, don't you?"

He grunted. "Let's take this one step at a time."

"She didn't come by. So I guess your investigation is still safe."

He nodded and stirred the sauce. He poked a fork into the pot of pasta and teased a piece out to test for doneness.

"So, Vic was right?" Erin asked. "It was murder?"

"That hasn't been determined."

"But you're investigating it as murder? You think it was?"

"We're not making assumptions either way."

"Vic said he wasn't even wearing a headlamp."

"Vic was there. I can't comment on witness testimony."

"If he wasn't wearing a headlamp, or there wasn't one with him, that would mean that there was someone else down there with him. Or he was dragged down there and put in the pond after he was dead."

Terry was silent. He turned off the burner that the pasta was on and picked up the pot of pasta to pour into the colander already positioned in the sink.

"You aren't investigating this, Erin."

"I didn't say I was investigating it. I'm just curious… about what happened. If you think that it was murder like Vic does, or something else."

"We're investigating. A determination has not yet been made."

"Okay." Erin sighed. She placed the salad bowl on the table and circulated through the kitchen, getting out plates, glasses, and cutlery. "And you think… it might be someone local to Bald Eagle Falls?"

"I didn't say that."

"Someone local to Bald Eagle Falls… killed in a cave underground or dragged in there… I guess that means that if it is murder, then the murderer is local too."

"All the more reason to stay out of it. I don't want you to walk into anything."

"Is this cave... who does it belong to? Is it on private land or public land?"

"Why?"

"I can ask Vic... I just wondered if it was on someone's private property. If there was some kind of fight over who the cave belonged to or something like that."

"Leave that to us."

"It wasn't one of Willie's mines?"

Terry finished draining the pasta and transferred it into the saucepan, where he stirred it to coat it with tomato sauce.

"You'd have to ask him that."

"They weren't trespassing on someone else's property, were they?" Erin considered. That could be a problem. She didn't want Willie and Vic to get in trouble for trespassing. They had called the police and cooperated with the questioning, so the police wouldn't lay any charges against them for trespassing, would they?

"Let's eat," Terry diverted. "This smells really good."

Erin got a couple of bottles of salad dressing out of the door of the fridge, thinking through the possibilities.

CHAPTER 9

*A*dele stopped by later in the evening. Usually, she didn't come in when she knew that Officer Piper was there. Not because she had ever run afoul of the law—other than the unfortunate incident when her ex-husband had shown up in town—she just liked to keep things quiet. She lived alone in the summer cottage in the woods on Erin's land, running trespassers off, performing whatever rites and rituals she did late at night where she would not be observed by anyone in town. But she did occasionally come over when Terry was there, or to participate in Thanksgiving or Christmas observances. She was obviously not comfortable doing so and preferred to be by herself.

Erin swung the door open to invite her in. "Adele! How are you doing?"

Adele nodded. "I'm just fine, Erin. And yourself?"

"Can't complain."

"Good."

Adele looked around. She lowered herself into one of the easy chairs. She nodded in Terry's direction but didn't address him. But she didn't ask if she could talk to Erin alone, either.

"I hear there was some excitement," Adele said obliquely.

Erin nodded. She looked at Terry to see if he would contribute anything, but he didn't.

"Yes... I don't know a lot yet. I mean, *I'm* not involved in the investigation, but sometimes I hear things."

Adele smiled wryly and nodded.

"Vic is the one to ask. She's the one who found the body—the remains."

Adele wasn't as comfortable with Vic as with Erin. There was that small matter of a kidnapping that got in the way of things. Vic understood that Adele hadn't known anything about it, but Adele found it difficult to get past.

"I know. But I figured she would have told you all about it. The police can't disclose anything, obviously," Adele looked at Terry, and then back at Erin. "I just wondered... about some of the details. Not that it's any of my business, of course."

"There's not a lot to tell. She found a skeleton in an underground pool. The police are trying to identify the victim and whether it was murder or not."

Adele nodded. "You don't know who it was, then?"

Erin raised an eyebrow at Terry. "I don't know. I guess they have some leads. But they don't release it to the public before they're sure and then they have to talk to the next of kin first. Right, Terry?"

"That's about right."

Adele nodded. She looked out the window into the darkness of the night.

"Do you know something about it?" Terry asked.

"No. Just curious. Like any of the old gossips around here, I suppose."

Erin doubted that. Adele had always been different from the ladies who came to Auntie Clem's. She wasn't just interested in hearing the latest gossip. She had a reason for asking. Erin glanced at Terry briefly and saw that he too was wondering where Adele's inquiry was going.

"It's kind of disturbing," Erin prompted. "You know me, I hate the idea of going underground. I can't imagine what it would be like to go into one of those caves and to find... bones or any other kind of human remains."

"Wouldn't be my first choice," Adele agreed. "I prefer the fresh air aboveground. It may be interesting to search through underground tunnels where so few have visited... but it's not my cup of tea."

"You were just wondering whether the remains had been identified?" Terry asked.

"I suppose so. I wouldn't want to be wondering about a family member… waiting for them to return home, not knowing they never would…"

"You don't have any family in town, do you?"

"I'm not speaking of myself. Just hypothetically. It would be very difficult, not knowing what had happened and whether you would ever see them again."

"We'll do our best to make sure that doesn't happen. We will inform the next of kin as soon as we are able."

Adele nodded.

They all sat there in silence for a few minutes, thinking about it. Erin wasn't sure why Adele was there. Adele knew that Terry wouldn't tell her anything and that Erin didn't have the scoop on what had happened this time. Erin hadn't been involved in even a minor way. It was all Vic.

"Do you know what they were doing in that cave?" Adele asked eventually.

"I have no idea," Terry said firmly. "I have no way of knowing why he was in the cave or what he might have been doing there. Exploring, prospecting, meeting someone? That may become clearer during the investigation, or it may always remain a mystery. We don't have a time-travel machine."

Adele nodded. She slid her hands to the seat as she prepared to rise. "Well, you folks have a good evening. I'll be on my way."

Erin walked her to the door, said her goodbyes, and returned to sit with Terry once Adele was gone. She looked at him.

"Do you have any idea what that was about?"

He shook his head slowly. "It sounds like she knows something… but I don't know what it is."

Erin tried to put the whole investigation behind her. It would probably be some time before the police had confirmed the identity of the body absolutely. Then they would be talking to the next of kin about it. Maybe they would release a name to the public and maybe they wouldn't. How the man had died might always remain a mystery.

"Do you remember when you were attacked in that mine?" Erin asked

Willie as he drove them to Auntie Clem's again later in the week. "When you hit your head and ended up in the hospital?"

Willie looked sideways at her. "No, actually."

He'd had amnesia at the time, of course. But Erin thought he might remember more of it now. And he at least remembered that it had happened, even if he didn't have any recollection of the event.

"I was just thinking about that. I don't know. I was thinking about how you were hit on the head when you were in the mine, and when you came out, you were disoriented and you couldn't remember anything."

"So I've been told."

"And you don't remember any of it happening."

"No. And I doubt I ever will. The doctors figured that it would all start to come back, but they were wrong. I've never been able to remember what happened that day. And maybe that's a good thing, because I'm not sure I really want to."

"So with this guy, it could be the same thing. He might have hit his head—either he hit it himself on an overhang or took a fall, or someone hit him—and then he was disoriented and didn't know what to do. He might not have been able to find his way out again. Or maybe he bent down to take a drink from the pool and then tumbled into it. We don't really know."

"No." Willie shook his head. "I can't imagine anyone drinking from the pool without at least filtering the water first, but people do things without thinking. If he had hurt himself or was disoriented, I could see that happening. But where does that get us?"

"I don't know." Erin sighed. "I just keep trying to construct it in my mind. What happened. How he got there. Why he was in the pool. I guess... trying to figure out how it might just be innocent. An accident."

Willie and Vic exchanged looks. Erin wondered if there was more to it that they had not told her about. Maybe because they were trying to protect her from the extent of what they had seen. Vic had edited herself when she had told Erin about it.

"What is it, then?" she asked. "What aren't you telling me?"

"It just didn't look like an accident, Erin," Vic said eventually. "I don't think it was."

CHAPTER 10

During a lull at Auntie Clem's Bakery, Erin found herself watching a woman through the door and front window. A skinny, tattered looking woman with several children in tow, all looking similarly worn and thin.

"What's up?" Vic asked, noticing her distraction.

"Oh… I was just watching that woman…" Erin nodded toward the window. "Do you know her? I don't think I've seen her before."

Vic squinted toward the window. She nodded. "Yeah, I think I've seen her around. Not in here, but… around town."

"She looks like she needs some help."

"People are proud. She probably wouldn't accept anything."

The woman shouldered a pack and, as she readjusted it, Erin realized she had a baby in her arms as well. A baby, a backpack, and the other children around her feet that she had to keep nudging forward and then grabbing if they got too far off track.

Making a quick decision, Erin bent down to the display case and grabbed several different varieties of granola bars. She hurried across the street toward the little group, Vic calling something after her.

"Hi," Erin greeted brightly. "I'm the owner of the bakery over there, and I thought your children might like some granola bars."

"We're not coming in there," the woman said, her expression pinched.

Her eyes darted in the direction of Auntie Clem's Bakery and then back to Erin.

"No, I brought some with me." Erin displayed them. "We made too many today, so I'm giving out some free samples. Wouldn't you like some?"

The children immediately started to clamor for the granola bars. Erin grimaced, realizing that she might have made a mistake in offering them in front of the children before the woman could make a decision. What woman wanted to tell her children that they couldn't have free treats?

"Maybe I could get you something else instead," she suggested. "Maybe... a loaf of bread? Some sandwich rolls?"

"We don't need your charity."

"No, it's not charity." Erin had never figured out why sometimes charity was good and sometimes it was bad. It seemed to her that if someone had a need and someone else was offering to fill it, that was a good thing. "Won't you take anything?"

Scowling, the woman finally gestured to the children. "Fine. Give them the granola bars, then." As Erin passed them out, the woman spoke to them. "And don't think this is a regular thing. You're not going to get granola bars every time we come into town or see the bakery. Got it? This is the only time."

"Thank you, Mama," one of the oldest of the children said politely. The rest took theirs without any thanks, snatching them out of Erin's hands as if they were afraid she might change her mind and withdraw them.

Erin tried to keep the smile pasted onto her face, to look friendly and non-threatening and not bothered by their behavior.

"They're good kids," the mother said in a tight, clipped tone.

Erin nodded reassuringly. "I'm sure they are. You certainly look like you have your hands full! I'm Erin." She put her hand out, uncertain whether the woman would respond.

The tired-looking woman nodded, but didn't take Erin's hand or respond with her own name.

That, apparently, was all that Erin could do. The encounter was finished. She nodded, wiggled her fingers at the children as a goodbye, and retreated to Auntie Clem's.

A couple of the children said 'bye,' but mostly, their mouths were full.

"What was all that about?" Vic asked when Erin returned. "Did you know them?"

"No. I just thought... they looked like they could use a little pick-me-up."

"But they didn't appreciate it," Vic guessed.

"No. I guess like you said, they're too proud. I thought that just a few granola bars... it would be a way to break the ice. Find out who they were and start a friendship... then maybe I could help her with something else."

"You've got a soft heart," Vic said, smiling. "I remember when you said you were going to help me out. I couldn't believe it. You didn't know me from Adam, but you helped me with the police and gave me a job, and even invited me into your home." Vic shook her head. "That could have turned out very badly, you know. I could have been a serial killer."

"But you weren't."

"How do you know that? Maybe I'm just very good at hiding the bodies."

"Well then, at least you've decided not to kill me."

Vic grinned. "Not yet!"

They got back to work.

~

Sitting in the living room that evening, Erin couldn't help noticing Terry looking through the kitchen at the back window much more frequently than he normally did.

"Is something wrong? Did you see something out there?"

"Uh... no." Terry pulled his attention away from the kitchen window and looked at Erin, focusing on her. Acting like he hadn't been looking out the window to begin with.

"What is it, then?"

Erin's brain started working a mile a minute, thinking about all of the things Terry might be worrying about. Had he heard something about someone he had arrested in the past? Or heard that Crazy Theresa was in town, looking for Erin or Vic? Or was it something else? A danger that she hadn't even thought about yet?

The world could be a dangerous place, and if something was making Terry nervous, then that made Erin nervous.

"Nothing."

"There's something. Why do you keep looking out there?"

"Was I? No. Just thinking about something. Staring off into space."

But she knew that wasn't true. She looked back down at the Bald Eagle Falls newspaper, pretending to be reading again. It was only a few seconds before Terry was looking out the back window again.

This time, though, Erin saw Willie's headlights as his truck pulled onto the gravel pad.

Terry had just been distracted by the lights.

Terry got up. "I need to talk to Willie about something."

Erin wanted to follow. She leaned forward in her seat, trying to decide whether to get up and act like whatever Terry wanted to talk to Willie about was her business. Or to pretend to be getting something from the kitchen and to see if she could overhear them. Or just to stay where she was, with the cat on her lap, and mind her own business.

Eavesdropping won out.

She didn't want to be obvious about it, but she did want to see if it were anything that impacted her or Vic. The men might just be arranging another fishing date. Terry was busy with the investigation of the remains found in the cave, but maybe he had reached the end of the trail of clues and needed to wait until the lab got back to him with the results of some of their forensic testing. Or maybe he'd decided to listen to everyone who told him that he needed to take it easy and not work every day.

But she doubted that.

Erin shifted Orange Blossom to the couch beside her, but Blossom wasn't too happy about this action and yowled in protest. He didn't lie down where she put him and go back to sleep, but blinked owlishly at her, wanting to know why she was disturbing his nap time.

"I just need to get up for a minute," Erin told him. She went to the kitchen and ran water into the tea kettle. Orange Blossom followed her, nudging at his dish and looking at her significantly.

"Are you hungry? It's not time for bed yet."

He meowed loudly a couple of times, expressing his displeasure. First, she woke him up, and then she wasn't even going to feed him?

"Okay, fine," Erin said. "I'll get you a couple of treats, okay?"

At the word 'treats,' the other animals put in an appearance. Marshmallow and K9 were much quieter and better-behaved than Orange Blossom, but they wanted their treats too. Erin got them all their snacks, straining her ears to hear what Terry was discussing with Willie. She couldn't hear anything. She opened the window a crack, which helped, but she was still having a hard time hearing what was going on.

"I've told you everything I know," Willie said gruffly, raising his voice so that Erin could suddenly hear him clearly. "It isn't like there is that much to tell. We found the skeleton. We left the cave and called the police. We weren't involved in anything we shouldn't have been. Just doing some spelunking."

"On land that isn't yours."

"Public land."

"That remains to be seen."

"If a survey shows that it wasn't public land, I'll apologize to the landowner, if there still is an owner. According to my map, it's on public land, and that means I have as much right as anyone to explore there."

"How many times have you been there before?"

"How is that your business?"

"Are you being obstructive?"

"Is this part of your official investigation?" Willie challenged.

Terry didn't say anything for a moment. "I'm just making friendly inquiries at this point."

"Then I'm not required to answer them and I'm not being obstructive. If you have something else you want to know, I can refer you to my lawyer."

"Have you mined in that cave?"

"Talk to my lawyer."

"It's not that hard a question to answer. I'm just trying to get a clear picture."

"I'm not required to answer you, Officer Piper. I'm exercising my civil rights. You can't do anything about that, official investigation or friendly questions."

"And you don't have any idea who the man was."

Willie said nothing.

"Had you ever run into anyone else on that property before?"

Willie still didn't answer, standing there by his truck, waiting for Terry to return to the house.

Eventually, Terry made an exasperated noise and turned back toward the house. Willie nodded and headed up the stairs to Vic's apartment.

The kettle started to sing as Terry returned to the kitchen, so Terry would know that she had been in the kitchen long enough to overhear most of the conversation.

He looked at her for a minute without saying anything. He sat down at the table and snapped his fingers to call K9, who was gnawing on his doggie biscuit, to come to him. K9 looked at Terry's snapping fingers, picked up his biscuit, and walked over to Terry's side, where he lay down and continued to eat the biscuit. Terry scratched his ears.

Erin took a couple of cups over to the table and filled them each with hot water. Terry helped himself to a teabag from the basket on the table and dangled it into his cup.

"You think Willie knows something he's not telling you?" Erin asked tentatively.

"I'm sure Willie knows plenty of things that he's not telling me. Finding out whether any of them are related to this case, that's the tricky thing."

"I suppose." Erin sat down with him and started to prepare her tea. "But he's not a suspect, right?"

Terry stirred his teabag around.

"Willie wouldn't hurt anyone," Erin asserted. "And if he did, why would he put the body in the pool and then take Vic out there to find it? And call you in to investigate? I'm sure he knows plenty of hiding places that are better than that, even in that one cave."

Terry raised his cup to his lips and sipped the too-hot tea. "You're probably right about that."

"It wasn't anything to do with Willie."

"Unfortunately, you're not a police investigator. I can't go by your gut instinct. I need to actually follow the evidence. And you know as well as I do that Willie was in the Dixon clan for five years. He is still involved with them, from what I can tell."

"But just doing things like computer consulting. Not... you know... mob stuff."

"You don't know that. Even if it's true, that's still working for organized crime. It's still a problem. And it means we have a trust problem."

"*You* have a trust problem," Erin corrected, not wanting him to include her in the statement. She did trust Willie. He'd proven to her in the past that he had her welfare and Vic's at heart. Whatever else he might be doing, she was sure that he wouldn't intentionally do anything that might endanger them. And that included taking Vic somewhere he'd disposed of a body or putting her in the middle of a murder investigation.

There was no way that Willie had had anything to do with the death of the man in the cave.

"Yes. I have a trust problem. The police department has a trust problem. Willie Andrews is not someone we can trust to tell the truth or stay on the right side of the law. If he is involved in a case, we have to consider the possibility that he is the perpetrator of a crime. Seriously consider it."

"He hasn't ever been convicted of anything, has he? He's never done prison time."

Terry raised his brows at Erin. She realized that she didn't know that for sure. She knew that he had been part of the Dixon clan because his family had been part of the clan, and that he'd done things that he had come to regret. He had gotten out when he could, but that meant putting in five years of service first. Who knew what he had done during that time. And Erin couldn't state for a certainty that he had never been convicted of a crime or done time. He might well have wanted to keep something like that under wraps.

Willie lived away from Bald Eagle Falls for an extended time, so the gossips in town might not know if he'd had to do prison time. Or maybe they did, and that was why they looked down on him so much and acted like he was lazy and shiftless when Erin knew him to be a very self-motivated, hardworking man.

Terry didn't answer one way or the other. Maybe he didn't want to admit that Willie hadn't ever been convicted or done time. Or maybe he was protecting Willie's right to privacy.

CHAPTER 11

There were a few quiet days. Days when Erin almost forgot about the man in the cave. The image of the skeleton or a decaying corpse started to fade from her dreams. Vic didn't say anything about Willie being questioned by the police and Erin didn't ask or mention the conversation she had overheard in the back yard. Everything was going back to normal and, pretty soon, everyone would forget all about what had happened.

Then on a warm afternoon, Melissa walked into the bakery with a bounce in her step. She pretended to be examining the sale prices on the products in the display case. But Melissa was there often enough to know what she liked and what the regular prices were. Unless she were interested in one of Erin's latest experiments, she really didn't even have to look in the case at all.

Instead, she was there to trade in information. She had something to tell.

"Afternoon, Melissa," Erin greeted. "What can we do for you today?"

"The sheriff wanted me to pick up some sticky buns for the department," Melissa said with a smile. "And he's actually covering the cost this time. He apologized for sending me over to do the legwork, but I actually don't mind that part."

"Sticky buns it is." Erin agreed. "A dozen?"

"That will be more than enough."

"I have some still in the tray in the kitchen. I'll just be a minute."

Erin retreated to the warm kitchen and breathed in the smell of the cinnamon and yeast. It was one of her favorite scents. She could practically taste the particles that hung in the air.

She assembled a box for the cinnamon buns, loosened the buns from the baking tray, and then slid them in. Everything came out without a problem, no ripped buns sticking to the tray. Erin slathered the tops with extra frosting and put a small tub of it into a condiment container so the police officers and staff could add more of their own if they wanted to go into sugar shock.

She closed up the box and carried it out to Melissa. "Still warm from the oven."

"Oh, those smell so good," Melissa enthused.

"They are! They're so good... it's almost criminal."

Melissa groaned at the joke. "Okay, that's enough of that! No bad jokes allowed."

She counted out the money to pay for the buns and passed it across to Vic at the till.

"Did you hear that they have identified the bones you found in the cave?" She asked in a dramatically lowered voice.

Vic raised her brows. "Did they? I'd almost forgotten about that."

Melissa's mouth dropped open and she began to protest, before realizing that Vic was just teasing her.

"Just for that, maybe I won't tell you."

Vic shrugged. "Well, my loss, I suppose."

She knew that Melissa couldn't bear to keep a secret.

"No, no," Melissa protested. She leaned closer to Vic, looking at Erin to make sure that she was included in the conversation. "His name was Darryl Ryder. He was a... a drifter around here."

"A drifter?" Erin repeated. "What exactly is the definition of a drifter? Do you mean he's new in town? Or that he's... some kind of scammer? Or what?"

"I don't know exactly where he lives. You know how it is with these guys. They float around and never do settle down anywhere. No one ever knows where to find them."

"So... he's homeless?" Erin suggested. She hadn't seen a lot of homeless people around Bald Eagle Falls. She saw them when she went into the city. It could be profitable to beg or busk in the city, where there was a large enough audience to make some good money. And there were proper shelters and soup kitchens. It was different in Bald Eagle Falls. There were no shelters, no food pantries, no services to help homeless people to get jobs. Consequently, the homeless people didn't come to Bald Eagle Falls.

At least, not that she had seen.

Their streets were clean of both trash and homeless folks sitting and begging, setting out their caps or holding up their homemade signs. Erin did what she could to help with the situation in the city, donating baked goods that didn't sell quickly enough. She froze them, and once she had as much as she could fit in her freezer, she made a run into the city and donated them to one of the kitchens or shelters. Or to a school breakfast program or whatever else she could find. Erin liked to be part of the solution. She had been on the edge of homelessness enough times herself. She wanted to help others. Make sure that they knew that they were valued and worthwhile people.

"We don't have homeless people here," Melissa argued, wrinkling her nose. "We don't have to deal with problems like that. Big city problems. But… that doesn't mean we don't have our poor people, and people who… would rather get a free ride from a friend or family member than take care of themselves or their own families. What kind of a person won't work and makes other people support his family instead?"

"So you knew him?" Erin asked. "This Darryl? He was out of work?"

"I don't know if you can say out of work, exactly. If you're not looking for a job, are you really out of work?"

"Darryl Ryder," Vic said thoughtfully. Her brows were drawn down like she was trying to think of whether she'd ever heard that name before. "I don't think I've ever run into him."

"Well, except that one time," Melissa pointed out, breaking into giggles at the inappropriate comment.

Vic made a noise of disgust. "Melissa!"

"I'm sorry. I know you meant you never saw him while he was alive."

"Yes."

"Well, I guess we'll see about that. Now that the police have verified his identity, they can investigate the case more deeply. It's pretty hard when you just have a John Doe and you're trying to figure out who might have had motive to kill the guy."

Erin adjusted the positioning of some of the baking in the display case. "Does that mean that it's been determined it was murder? Not an accident?"

Melissa nodded meaningfully. "That's what it looks like," she agreed. "They're still waiting for tests back from the lab and medical examiner, but it looks like the guy was smashed over the head. Not an accident."

"He could have hit it on something in the cave," Erin suggested. "An overhang. He could have slipped and fallen."

"This was no slip and fall," Melissa said. She looked at Vic. "Was it? You know it wasn't."

Vic took a deep breath in and let it out. "No, I don't think it was an accident," she admitted.

Melissa was off, headed back to the police department to make everyone fat on sticky buns.

Erin wasn't sure she wanted to know any more about the man in the cave. She preferred to let the nightmares fade away again.

Vic kept looking at her sideways, waiting for Erin to start asking her questions.

Erin didn't ask Vic any more about the condition of the remains.

"You don't know this Darryl Ryder?" she asked Vic eventually. "I don't think I've ever heard the name before."

"No, can't think of it. It sounds familiar, like I might have heard of him before, but I'm pretty sure it isn't someone I ever met. Pretty sure he never came in here as a customer!"

"No. Doesn't sound like the kind of person who usually comes into Auntie Clem's."

How would she have reacted if he had? If he were poor and possibly homeless, Erin hoped that she wouldn't have turned him out, but that she would have found some way to help him. It was difficult to know what to do or say sometimes. She didn't want to enable someone with an addiction or to end up with someone stalking her because she had been nice to him. But people with addictions still had to eat too. If the man were hungry, she hoped that someone would have reached out to feed him. Even if he hadn't gone into Auntie Clem's.

"I'm glad we don't have a big homeless population here," she commented. "That's at least one thing we avoid by living in a small town instead of in the city."

"I think there are a lot of positive things about being in a small town. I wouldn't want to live in the big city." Vic gave a mock shudder. "I'm a country girl at heart. I think I'd waste away to nothing if I had to live in the city, surrounded by nothing but concrete all the time. I need my green spaces. Trees and sky, things that feed the soul."

Erin nodded. "Yes... though you can get some of that in the city, too. Living in the city doesn't mean that you never see the outdoors again. There are parks and sky. Cities are trying to cut down on light pollution so that you can see the stars again."

"Still not for me," Vic asserted, shaking her head.

Terry seemed to be in a good mood when he picked Erin up. He suggested that they go out for a dinner date, which was a nice change from having to make supper. It was still nice to get out sometimes. She liked the idea of letting someone else wait on her for one meal.

"That sounds good," she agreed. "What do you want? Barbecue?"

"Yes," Terry agreed quickly. "Barbecue would be amazing."

Erin smiled at his enthusiasm. "Barbecue it is. I'm surprised that you're hungry."

He raised his brows. "Why?"

"Melissa bought sticky buns today. I figured with one or two of those under your belt..."

"Oh, that." Terry gave a little laugh. "I'd already decided that I wanted to go out tonight, so I didn't overindulge. I didn't even have a full one. Gave the rest to Stayner."

Stayner was a younger man with a faster metabolism, and he probably didn't mind too much having a sticky bun for dinner. He probably went to the restaurant all the time. That, or ate a lot of macaroni and cheese.

She felt a little guilty at assuming he ate like a bachelor. What did she know about his diet? She knew from experience that the man knew how to clean up a kitchen properly. If he knew how to clean up and where to put things away, chances were he'd done a fair amount of cooking himself. He might be a gourmet, she wouldn't have any idea.

They got settled at the restaurant and placed their orders. Erin sipped a soft drink while they waited for their food. "So, I guess you got the identity of the man in the cave confirmed today."

Terry nodded. "The Bald Eagle Falls grapevine is alive and well, I see. Yes. Darryl Ryder. It helps with the investigation. Pretty hard to figure out motives and timelines before you know who you're dealing with."

"That's good, then, I'm glad you have the information you need. So... is he someone known to the police? Melissa said that—the grapevine said—he was a drifter. So does that mean you didn't know him? Or you did?"

"A drifter. Well, that's not the way that I would classify him. I think people around here use the term to describe anyone they see as less desirable. They don't belong in Bald Eagle Falls. So even if they've been here ten years, they're 'drifters.'"

"Had he been here a long time, then?"

"We will need to gather more information about that. But he wasn't just passing through town."

"Did he live in town? Or on a farm?"

"We'll sort that out."

"You don't know?" Erin was surprised.

"With some people, where they live is not as clear."

"He was homeless?"

"We don't have homeless people in Bald Eagle Falls." Terry swirled his drink and reconsidered his answer. "Not permanently homeless, out on the streets."

"Right. But without a legal address?"

He shrugged. "People living with friends or family until they can get on their feet, squatting on land in a shack or an RV, moving from one place to another. I suppose we have a few who are... less adequately homed."

Erin looked at him, her brows drawn down. She shook her head. "Less adequately homed?" she repeated.

Terry looked away, chuckling. "Okay. You got me. I guess we do have our share of homeless. But... it doesn't look the same as it does in the city."

"Even in the city, homeless doesn't always mean begging on the street or living out of your car or a shelter. Sometimes it's couch surfing, or a whole family squeezed into someone's back room, a mom and her kids moving from one relative to another because she doesn't have a place of her own and no one can take her long term."

Terry shrugged. "I suppose. You just don't see those ones. You see the beggars and buskers on the street."

"Yeah. So your Darryl Ryder, did he have a 'less adequate' address?"

"Trying to sort that out. He and his family apparently moved around. They were looking for somewhere more permanent, but hadn't found it yet."

"He had a family?" Erin's heart sank. Those poor people. No home, and now they had lost the head of the family. How were they going to fend for themselves?

"A wife and young children," Terry confirmed, the corners of his mouth turning down. "We are trying to find them."

"You don't know where they are?"

"That's one of the problems with homelessness. It isn't always easy to find people when you are looking for them."

"So where do you go? How do you find out?"

Terry sighed. "Just keep asking questions. Find everybody you can who knows them. Ask if they've heard anything. Ask who else might know. Hopefully, people cooperate enough that you're able to narrow it down over time."

"But people don't exactly trust the police."

"That would seem to be the case," he agreed dryly.

Erin felt herself flush. She knew that she didn't tell him everything. And he knew that too. There were parts of her life that she didn't feel comfortable sharing, even with all that they were to each other.

Their meals arrived, and Erin did her best to forget about poor Darryl Ryder and his young family and to focus on her time with Terry.

CHAPTER 12

*E*rin worked on her tai chi before bed, enjoying the warm weather outside and the feeling of the grass between her toes. She watched carefully to make sure there were no surprises in the grass. K9 was good about using the dog run, but Nilla wasn't very disciplined in his habits. Even though they tried to monitor him carefully when he was in the yard, he did manage to sneak past them every so often.

Vic was sitting on the steps watching Erin go through her forms. Nilla was calm for once, sitting while Vic slowly fed him kibble one tiny piece at a time.

"So they don't even know where Darryl lived?" Vic asked.

"No. Doesn't sound like it. Terry is asking around, trying to nail it down. They have to inform his wife and talk to her about when she last saw him. If there was anyone he'd had a disagreement with. Stuff like that. They have to sort out all of those things before they can figure out who—how he was killed."

"Yeah. But if he was a drifter, then it wasn't likely anyone in town, right? Maybe he had a business partner who came to see him. Or an estranged family member. Some enemy that followed him here."

Erin let her mind assess these possibilities. She could see that it was possible. Ryder's death might not have anything to do with anyone in Bald

Eagle Falls. And that would be good. She'd be happy if that were what the police determined. She didn't want to think about anyone in her Bald Eagle Falls family being involved with Ryder, even peripherally.

"Maybe. I guess I can't figure out why anyone would want to kill a drifter or homeless person. I mean, it doesn't make sense that it would be for some kind of gain, because he wouldn't have anything. And as far as jealousy, he has a wife and kids. Married men can fool around, but if they weren't from around here, who would he be involved with? Wouldn't he be too busy trying to find a job and get his family settled?"

"Some men are never too busy."

Erin nodded at the truth of this.

"Or maybe he just got in someone's way," Vic suggested. "Started a fight or got in an argument over something stupid."

"In a cave?" Erin paused in her movements to look over her shoulder at Vic.

"Well… maybe."

Erin shook her head. "I still think it must have been an accident. Sometimes an accident scene can look like homicide."

Vic gave her a long look, then went back to feeding Nilla the bits of kibble.

Vic and Erin were working together again the next afternoon. Bella had been scheduled to take the afternoon shift, but something had come up and she called in to cancel with profuse apologies. Vic shrugged and said that she could stay on, so they were covered. Everything was fine until Vic got the call from Willie.

"Hi hon'," Vic greeted, tapping her Bluetooth headphone to answer it. She wouldn't have if she had been out in the customer area, but she and Erin were both in the kitchen while things were quiet, prepping some fresh muffins for the after-school rush.

"I'm heading over to the police department." Erin could hear Willie clearly over the headphone, his voice raised in irritation.

"To the police department. For what?"

"More questions about the Ryder case. I was really hoping this was all out of the way!"

"What else do they want to ask about that? We already told them every-thing we know. It isn't like we were trying to cover anything up."

"I guess since they identified Ryder, they want to ask me about him."

"You don't know anything about him, do you? Just tell them you never heard of him before and don't have anything to say."

There was no immediate answer from Willie. Maybe he was getting his truck started or was focused on something else.

"Willie? You still there?"

"Sure. I'm here."

"Just tell them you don't know anything about Ryder."

The suggestion was again met with silence. Vic looked at Erin. She probably knew that Erin could hear the whole conversation. And even if she couldn't hear Willie's part of the conversation, she couldn't help but hear Vic's end, which was interesting enough.

"Willie... you don't know Darryl Ryder, do you?"

"Yes. I do. Or did."

"Oh." Vic processed this. She picked up a pan of muffins and started loosening them from the tin. "Well... I guess they figured that out, then. Someone must have told them that you knew him."

"Yeah. I don't think they're just fishing."

"Okay. So you knew him. But that doesn't mean you know anything about what happened to him. Or that you had anything to do with his death. Good grief. You couldn't have."

"I didn't," Willie agreed.

"You couldn't have. You wouldn't have taken me there if you knew his body was there. How stupid would that be? If you'd had something to do with it, you wouldn't have ever gone back there. Let someone else find the body, and they wouldn't ever be able to draw a connection back to you. Do they think you're an idiot?"

"I don't know what they are thinking. I guess I'll find that out. Maybe they think that I did it and then regretted it later. Wanted to find a way to get him off my conscience."

"That's ridiculous."

But was it? Erin could see the police's way of thinking. Willie didn't want Ryder rotting away in that pool, his family thinking that he had aban-doned them or forever wondering what had happened to him. So if he could find a way to 'stumble across' the body in a natural way... the police would never suspect that he was involved.

Except that they did.

CHAPTER 13

"Okay, well maybe," Vic conceded. "I think that's a pretty far stretch, though. And why would you kill him in the first place? You'd have to have a reason."

"Yeah," Willie agreed. "You're right about that."

"How did you know him? Just because you saw him around town? Or was he involved in mining too?"

He'd been found in a cave; it wasn't hard to believe that he'd had a reason to be there. Something that connected him to Willie.

"I'm just pulling up now," Willie said. "I guess... I'll talk to you later. Let you know how it went tonight."

"You don't have to go in if you don't want to talk to them," Vic pointed out. "You're not required to unless they arrest you, and they haven't done that."

"Not yet. I'm hoping to avoid that."

"They're not going to arrest you. If they want to keep you half the night, just tell them you're going home. I want to see you."

"I'll get there when I can."

He apparently disconnected, because Vic didn't have to. She worked on getting the muffins out of the tin and onto the cooling rack, her brows drawn down. Eventually, she looked over at Erin.

"How much of that did you get?"

"Well… pretty much everything. Sorry."

"It's okay. Then I don't have to explain anything, right?" Vic shook her head. "I can't believe that they are treating him like a suspect. They say they're not biased. But they are. They think that Willie is a criminal. He's the most likely suspect because he doesn't have a regular job like they think he should. They think he's lazy and dirty. He was involved with the Dixon clan *years* ago, so they think that any time he's faced with a decision, he's going to pick the illegal route. But he's not like that. He isn't a criminal."

Erin remembered what Terry had said and that he had refused to confirm that Willie had never served time. But it didn't seem like a good time to bring it up. Asking Vic whether Willie was a convicted criminal after that tirade was not a good idea.

So she just nodded sympathetically. She wouldn't like it if someone were accusing Terry or Vic of having something to do with Ryder's death either. She liked Willie, and she didn't like the idea of their thinking that he had anything to do with it. Vic was closer to Willie, of course, but he was Erin's friend too, and she didn't like the direction the investigation was going.

"They'll figure it out," she assured Vic. "They'll talk to him this afternoon, and he'll answer whatever questions they have, and then it will all be okay. They'll go on to the next person on the list."

"I don't know." Vic shook her head dubiously. "I doubt that he's going to answer all of their questions. And they'll think that means he's guilty of something. So then they'll have more questions and suspicions. They're not going to go on to the next person or theory unless they feel like he's cleared himself. And I don't think that's going to happen today."

"But if he didn't have anything to do with it, then he shouldn't have any problem answering their questions."

Vic glared at Erin. "And is that how you felt whenever the police wanted to question you about something? That if you just spilled everything to them and told them the truth, they wouldn't suspect you anymore? You wouldn't end up in prison, because they would believe everything you said?"

Erin had to laugh at that. "Well… no. Definitely not. I guess that even after everything that has happened, I still have an idealized view of the police. Blame it on Terry."

"I don't think Terry's given you reason to think that."

"He hasn't arrested anyone without good evidence."

Vic nodded, but didn't look convinced.

Vic was probably right. Erin and Terry rarely saw eye-to-eye on investigations. Erin jumped to conclusions. She jumped into things with both feet without looking first, sometimes getting herself into some pretty dicey situations. How many times had Terry told her to stay out of things and she hadn't listened to him?

If she trusted that the police would eventually arrest the right person, then why was she always putting herself into the middle of police investigations?

When Erin and Vic got home, both Terry and Willie were still at the police department. Probably on opposite sides of the table. Usually, Erin would invite Vic to join her at the house for supper, but Vic was worried about Nilla having already been left alone too long, and wanted to keep him company.

"Why don't you come over to the loft? You never spend any time over there, and you should be as comfortable there as I am in your kitchen."

"Are you sure? I would think you would want your privacy..."

"Some days, yeah. But not all the time. And it isn't like I have a bunch of contraband or questionable literature lying around the place. No secrets."

No secrets?

Beaver had said that Vic had secrets.

Of course, she had said that Erin had secrets too.

Which was true.

Nothing terribly shocking, no dead bodies buried in her wake, but still things that she didn't feel like revealing to her friends and loved ones. Old associations, embarrassing stories, guilty feelings still lingering after years.

One of Vic's secrets had been Theresa. Not because they had been seeing each other behind Willie's back—which would have delighted Theresa—but because Vic was embarrassed about some of her old associations too, and didn't want to have to explain Theresa and their shared past. It was over and done, something best left alone. Until it had flared to life and they had found themselves in a situation that had nearly gotten them killed. Terry and Detective Jack Ward could easily have both died that night if the others hadn't managed to overcome Theresa and to find them when they did.

Odds were Vic still had secrets. But who didn't?

"Okay. I'm just going to feed the animals and shower off, and then I'll be over."

"Perfect. I'll see you soon."

It was funny that after spending almost all of their time together, the two of them were still perfectly willing to spend the evening together too. But they were. It seemed like the most natural thing in the world. Like Erin had always thought that having a sister would be. She and Vic were as close as sisters. Closer than Erin had ever been with any of her foster sisters. And certainly closer than Erin ever expected to be with Charley, who really was her sister.

Nilla appeared to be the perfect gentleman when Erin let herself into Vic's loft apartment. There was no sign that he had torn around the apartment trying to destroy everything he could sink his teeth into. Everything looked remarkably tidy and untouched. She could still see a few areas that he had attacked in earlier days, leaving teeth marks or scratches on various furniture, the wall, and the doors.

Instead, he sat on a dog bed on the couch, regal as a king. Erin sat down on the other end of the couch. Not too close to Nilla, worried that he might get overly excited and either attack her or run away.

Vic came out of the bathroom. "I thought I heard you. Long time, no see!"

"Yes, such a long time," Erin agreed with a smile. She nodded at Nilla. "Isn't he behaving himself well."

Vic gave Nilla a long look, seeing if he would stay still like he was supposed to. Then she stepped closer to him and petted him on the head. "Good boy. You want some treats? Haven't you been good!"

He panted at her happily, waiting for his reward. Vic got out a few pieces of food and fed them to him slowly by hand.

"I think he's finally starting to settle down. I don't know whether he was just really anxious after Beryl died because everything changed, or…"

"I think she just didn't know how to train him. Or hadn't bothered to. It looks like you're doing a really good job with him now."

"I hope so! As long as he doesn't turn into demon dog the minute I start to relax…"

The white, fluffy dog just sat there panting and smiling at her, waiting expectantly for the next piece of food. Like he'd never been anything but an angel. Erin would have believed it if she hadn't seen some of the chaos he had caused.

"What can I help you with? What were you planning for supper?"

"I don't know. Just warm up whatever is around or open a can of something. You sit for a few minutes while I figure out what it's going to be. It won't be anything fancy."

"I don't need fancy. A lot of what Terry and I are doing lately is soup and salad. Better than too many rolls with honey or jam at the end of the day!"

"Well, more nutritious. Maybe not better tasting…"

Erin conceded this point. She wasn't a salad eater. She really didn't appreciate a wide variety of vegetables. She was forcing herself to eat better to stay in shape, but most nights all she could say about her supper was that it was satisfying. Not that she had really enjoyed it.

"Seems like there aren't a lot of things that are both delicious and low calorie," she sighed.

"We'll have to figure a few out. Heaven knows, I don't want to end up all plump and rolls of fat either."

Vic at least had extra height on Erin. She could weigh more without looking heavy.

Vic stuck her head in the fridge to look through the various leftovers and ingredients she had on hand, glanced in the freezer, and opened up a cupboard full of canned goods. "How about tacos?"

"Sure, tacos sound good."

"All right. We'll do them super simple. You can open a can of beans and I'll get some vegetables chopped. We've got salsa, avocado, taco shells, and cheese. That should be all we need."

They got to work. They were only halfway finished eating—and Erin was enjoying the tacos much more than soup and salad—when they heard Willie's truck roar into the parking space beside the garage.

Erin looked down at her plate. She should really go and give Vic and Willie a little privacy, but she couldn't exactly walk out gracefully with her plate still half full of food.

"It's fine," Vic assured her. "We've got all night."

"I'll try not to be too long…"

Willie's heavy boots were clomping up the steps outside the garage and, in a moment, he was opening the door.

"I swear, there are days that I would like to just pick everything up and move—" He saw Erin at the table. "Oh. Hello, Erin."

"Sorry, I'm just finishing up. I'll leave the two of you alone in just a minute…"

"No rush. You'll give yourself indigestion. I'll just save the more choice parts of my conversation until later when I won't burn your ears with my colorful language."

"You can say what you like. I won't be offended. It isn't like I haven't heard bad language before." Erin laughed. "I did grow up in foster care, you know. The language that some of those kids used…"

He chuckled. "I can imagine."

"No… I don't think you could."

Willie sat down on the couch and bent over to unlace and remove his boots. Nilla yipped at him and growled deep in his throat. Willie looked over and stared him down. "You don't growl at me, you little rat."

"Don't tease him," Vic objected. "He's been behaving himself really well, and I don't want him to regress."

"I'm not teasing him. I'm telling him not to push his luck with me."

"He doesn't understand that. Just leave him alone and don't get him excited."

Willie rolled his eyes and continued to take off his boots, ignoring the dog.

"So…?" Vic ventured. "How did things go over at the police department?"

She didn't ask whether everything was all right and cleared up with the police. Erin had a suspicion that things were not all sunshine and rainbows. The interview that must have lasted several hours for Willie to be arriving home so late.

"Well, no blood was shed. There are no more bodies to be cleaned up."

"Oh, well that's good, then." Vic's tone was dry. "I'm certainly glad to hear that. I don't think you would likely be sitting here in my apartment if there had been bloodshed."

"That might depend on who it was."

Erin wouldn't want to hear that anything had happened to Sheriff

Wilmot or any of the other regular staff. Officer Stayner, on the other hand…

She tried to push the thought away and think about him charitably. He did have his good points. He was, apparently, a good investigator. He'd gotten good marks and reports in his training. And the man knew how to clean a kitchen. She would try to focus on those things rather than on all of the things that she didn't like about him.

"Did Terry come home too?" she asked Willie. If Willie was finished, then hopefully Terry was too and would be home soon, if he weren't already waiting for her back at the house. She stole a glance at her phone screen to make sure that he hadn't messaged her. The screen was blank.

"He didn't come back with me. I imagine he has a bunch of paperwork to fill out. You know how much red tape and bureaucracy there is in a police department. One reason you would never find me in that job."

Erin expected Vic to make some quip about other reasons Willie wouldn't want to be a cop, but Vic bit into her taco and didn't say anything. It would, perhaps, be a little too close to home after spending hours being interrogated about his relationship with Darryl Ryder.

"So how well did you know Ryder?" Vic asked after a few more bites.

Willie threw his boots toward the door. Nilla yipped and jumped after them, growling and menacing them.

"Nilla!" Vic snapped. "Stop. Leave the shoes alone."

Nilla ignored her, stalking the shoes. Willie didn't get up to retrieve his shoes or to chase the dog away from them. He stretched his legs out in front of him and watched Nilla indifferently.

"Nilla!" Vic put her taco down. She licked her fingers and wiped them on a napkin, then went after the dog, clapping her hands in warning. "Nilla, no! Leave them alone!"

The dog darted out of Vic's way, circling around to the other side of the boots, nose still down, sniffing to investigate how much of a threat they were. Vic picked up the shoes and set them upright, together at the side of the entry mat.

"Leave them," she warned. "They're just Willie's shoes. And if you chew on them, you're going to be in big trouble!"

Nilla sat back on his haunches, considering Vic.

"Go sit back on your bed. Go to bed." Vic pointed at the bed. "Go on. Go to bed."

Nilla didn't go to his bed, but he didn't hunt down the boots, either. Erin considered that progress. Vic approached Nilla slowly, then picked him up and took him back to the dog bed. She put him down gently and murmured to him to stay put. He lay down, putting his chin between his paws, and watched her.

"Good," Vic told him. She went back over to her chair and tried to pick up the taco she had put down without making a big mess. "There's food if you want it," she told Willie. "Come have something. You must be famished."

"No. I grabbed a burger and a beer on the way home."

"Oh." Vic raised her eyebrows.

"I didn't know what you were making, if anything. And I knew you wouldn't want me drinking on an empty stomach." He smiled.

"Well, no, that's true."

"Nothing against your cooking."

Vic shrugged. "Fine. There is beer in the fridge here."

"I needed time to decompress. Didn't want to bring all of my troubles home to you."

Erin thought about the way that Willie had pulled his truck into the parking spot and burst in the door, expressing his displeasure. That was after he had decompressed and had a drink? She would not have wanted to see him immediately after his interview with the police.

And even with a meal and drink, he had still beaten Terry home. She hoped Terry wasn't putting in too many hours.

"So..." Vic returned to the earlier conversation. "Ryder? You knew him?"

Willie considered the question. He rubbed his forehead, just over his eyebrows. A fatigue headache. Tired after so many hours spent in the interrogation.

"I knew him," he agreed.

"I didn't know that. He hasn't lived in Bald Eagle Falls for long?"

"He's been here a while."

"Was he... a friend?" Vic asked tentatively.

Willie grunted. "No. Wouldn't call him that."

"Did you work with him on something? How did you know him?"

"He was... interested in the mines and caves around here. Had it in his head that if he could find a good claim, he could make it rich. Young folk these days," Willie shook his head. "Think that they can get the money without putting the work into it. All they have to do is show up and people will hand it to them on a silver platter."

"He was interested in mining."

Willie nodded.

"And you guys talked about that? Like, over drinks, or…?"

"No. Not over drinks." Willie scratched the back of his neck. "Maybe over the barrel of a shotgun, but not over drinks."

CHAPTER 14

*E*rin was mid-bite, and had to suppress a gasp and an exclamation of surprise, or she probably would have choked on her taco, or at least inhaled some of the dripping juices.

"Over the barrel of a shotgun?" she repeated.

Willie looked at her as if he had forgotten that there was another witness. Eventually, he decided that what was said was said. He couldn't take it back. He shrugged.

"The guy figured he could squat on my claim. Thought that everything around here was up for grabs, he just had to decide what he wanted."

"So you ran him off," Vic said.

Willie nodded. "I did. What else would I do? Invite him over to tea?"

Vic and Erin both shook their heads. Of course not. But it wouldn't play well with the police. No wonder they had been so insistent about interviewing Willie and had kept him for so long. He threatened a man at gunpoint who later was murdered. Willie looked as guilty as the day was long.

"I didn't kill him," Willie asserted to Vic. "You and the police know that he wasn't killed with a shotgun. Whatever happened to him, it was nothing to do with me. But I can't say I blame whoever did it. If the guy was planning to jump my claim, how many other people did he bother?"

Probably Willie wasn't the only one. Erin didn't know a lot of people

62

who were still mining in the hills. It wasn't like it had been in the early days in Tennessee, when mining was the main industry in the area. The mining was mostly done by big corporations now, and not in the small caves and tunnels around Bald Eagle Falls. Most of the mines around Bald Eagle Falls were abandoned, as far as she knew. And abandoned because they were not producing enough to support a person or a family. Willie was one of the few Erin knew of who still made a living, or part of his living, from mining and processing minerals.

"Melissa said that he had a young family," she said to Willie.

He nodded, scowling. "Yes, he did. Thin, washed-out looking wife and a passel of kids."

"What's going to happen to them?"

"Not my responsibility. Especially since I had nothing to do with the death of her husband. I don't feel responsible for her. She can go back to her own kinfolk and they can look after her. I'm sure she probably has family in these parts. I doubt if either of them ever traveled out of the state in their lives."

Terry had said that a lot of people lived with family or friends. Erin supposed that was probably exactly what Mrs. Ryder would do. She would go to stay with an aunt or a sister until she could find some way to support the family herself. Someone would put a roof over their heads. Although if there were a lot of kids, as Willie suggested, it made it more difficult to find someone who would take them in.

"Have the police been able to inform her that… about what happened to him?"

"Sounds like they're still trying to find them. They asked me a few times where he was living and where they would find his family."

"Where did he live?" Vic asked.

"They live out there." Willie nodded toward the window. "I had to kick them out of a mine they had taken up residence in. Like I said, squatters. They think they can stay wherever they want. If they stay there long enough, it becomes theirs."

"They were living in a mine?"

"Yeah. Had all of their junk stored in there. Kids everywhere. Camp stove in a clearing to cook on. Imagine they were hunting to try to keep food on the table." Willie shifted his position, crossing one leg over the other, stretched out in front of him. He slid his hands into his pockets, considering. "You have to admire them for at least trying to live off the land instead of relying on government or family to feed and shelter them. They were trying to make their own way. I can admire that."

"Those poor people."

"Literally," Willie agreed. "But there's no excuse for trying to take what isn't yours. If he wanted to live off of the land, he should have built a place of his own. Buy or rent a piece of property, put up a house, and live that way. Putting up in a mine or somebody's fishing shack or trailer, that's not making do by yourself. That's theft."

Maybe Willie didn't realize that not everyone would be able to do that. As far as he was concerned, all that was needed was the desire and two good hands. But building a house required materials, tools, and know-how. Not everyone had that. Or the physical ability for the hard work needed to build a shelter.

She couldn't shake the mental picture of the thin woman and her passel of kids, living in some abandoned shack or cave out in the sticks, waiting for her husband to come home. She had thought that kind of thing didn't happen in Bald Eagle Falls. Many people struggled to make ends meet, but she thought that the townspeople took care of each other. That they wouldn't put a family out on the street. There were no beggars on street corners, so she had thought that there weren't any homeless.

"Police will find them and let them know what's going on," Willie told Erin, voice gruff. "They can go back to live with her people."

"Maybe. Not everyone has family or gets along with them. Or if they are abusive, you wouldn't want to take children there. Some people are alone."

"Then some friends can help her out. Or she can go to the city to a shelter or apply for welfare programs. She's on her own now, she'll qualify for help."

She was surprised he would suggest this after saying that he admired them for trying to make it on their own.

"Do you have to deal with that very much?" Vic asked curiously. "Is there a problem with squatters, or was it just a one-time thing?"

"Ryder I've had to deal with more than once. Most people... you confront them once, and they make themselves scarce. They don't want to have to deal with angry owners. They want to stay unnoticed. Invisible."

"I didn't even know that. You never mentioned him."

Willie considered before answering. "I think I did, actually. Rip Ryder."

"Rip? I thought the police said it was Darryl?"

"People go by other names. He took on the name Rip. That's what I knew him by. Didn't even know his last name. Didn't know who the police were talking about until they brought up the picture on his driver's license."

"Rip Ryder. Should have been in Hollywood with a name like that," Vic laughed.

"Yep. Maybe he and his family would have done better out there. There isn't much around here for people looking for the easy way to strike it rich. Not putting his own labor into it, but looking for something that would be a shortcut. The big score."

"You don't know that," Erin said. "He might have been working hard, he just wasn't able to do what you could have."

"I know that some people make it, and some people never do. And he never did. And with another fifty years on this planet, he still wouldn't have. People who are always trying to find the shortcuts never finish what they start. Because it's too hard. If you're not willing to put in the hard work—like you have, Erin—you don't ever make it to the finish line. They'll always have excuses. Why other people could do it but they couldn't."

Erin pressed her lips together and didn't argue. She hadn't, after all, known Rip Ryder. She had never even heard of him until he was dead. But she hadn't lived a sheltered life. She had seen a lot of different people trying a lot of different things. It was true that some of them never made it, and some people never seemed motivated to try hard enough, but she wasn't convinced that it was always their fault. Nor had she been able to start up Auntie Clem's Bakery and make it a success on her own.

She took a couple more bites of her taco and set the rest down. "I'm stuffed. That was really good. I should probably head home, see if Terry is back yet."

Vic took her plate from the table, smiling. "Be sure not to get lost on the way."

"I'll try," Erin agreed.

She said goodbye to them both, gave Nilla a careful pet, and went back to the main house.

CHAPTER 15

*I*t was a while before Terry made it back. Erin had guessed that he wasn't home yet when she had left Vic's, but she thought Willie and Vic needed some time to talk in private, and Willie didn't need her challenging him about Rip Ryder.

She was sitting on the couch with Orange Blossom, reading one of Clementine's journals, and saw Terry's headlights as he pulled up to the house. She didn't get up to open the door for him, which would involve upsetting the cat from her lap. He let himself in and gave a deep sigh as he stepped into the house.

"Long day?"

"Very," he agreed. "I'm fine, mind you. Just fine. But bone tired."

"I don't imagine it's easy to interrogate a friend."

He looked at her for a minute, then shook his head. "An interrogation is never easy. And it is harder when it is an… acquaintance, and they might think they should be given the benefit of the doubt just because you know them."

"Well… I guess I can see that. You expect your friends to believe what you say."

Terry nodded. He stooped to give her a kiss, then went into the kitchen for a beer. He returned and sat on the couch next to her.

"Have you had something to eat?"

"Yes, we ate at the police department. Got some delivery. Everyone was tired and hungry."

Erin nodded and relaxed beside him, happy that she wasn't going to have to jump up and make him a sandwich or warm up something from the fridge.

"So you believe Willie now? About not having had anything to do with Rip Ryder's death?"

"I see you've already gotten his side of the story."

"Not in any detail, but I was over there having dinner with Vic, so we did talk."

"There isn't anything to stop him from telling you whatever he wants to, but I can't respond from the department's viewpoint. I'm not allowed to talk about any of the details of an active investigation."

"I know. I just figured… now that you've heard his side of the story, he's off the hook, and you can go on and investigate other possibilities. There must be other possibilities. Other… suspects."

"There are other avenues for us to investigate, yes. And talking to Willie doesn't stop us from investigating those other avenues. No one is railroading him. We are looking at all of the possibilities."

"And you still think that he's a viable suspect? You know he wouldn't do something like that. It doesn't make sense, any of it."

"People do stupid, impulsive things. That's how they get caught. If everyone was as thoughtful and careful as you think they would be, we would never be able to catch anyone. Someone getting killed in the midst of an argument or altercation—that's not a reasoned decision. It's an instinctual, animal impulse. And even after the deed is done, the perpetrator is not thinking straight. They make mistakes at the scene and they continue to make mistakes."

Erin still couldn't imagine Willie causing someone's death. Or being so stupid as to put the body in a cave where he was later going to go hiking with Vic. Erin knew Willie to be calm under pressure and in an emergency situation.

"I feel very sorry for his family. Did you have to make the notifications?"

"We are… trying to track his wife down."

"Oh. I guess it's harder if they don't live in Bald Eagle Falls." Erin fished for more information.

"People can be very difficult to track down if they aren't living in... traditional situations."

"So they are homeless?"

"I don't know if they are homeless or not... we won't know that until we find them. I am aware that they have been squatting, using land close to the cave, off and on. But whether his wife and kids are still out there somewhere, or if they have moved somewhere else... it's going to take some time to find out."

"What about a phone? Does she have one?"

"Doesn't look like it. Or if she does, it might just be a prepaid phone, which could be in anyone's name. Sometimes family buys phones, so that their loved one will be able to reach them in case of an emergency. It would be helpful if we had Ryder's phone, but we don't."

Erin nodded, thinking about it. "Did he have one? For sure?"

"Nothing in this case is for sure. Circumstances can change from one day to the next. There's really no telling. He did have a phone up until a few days ago. But again, no way to tell who it was registered to. We would have to find out who he'd talked to, so that we could find out what number he was at, and then trace that number to see who else he was talking to and when was the last time and location that the phone was used. All of that takes time. And a starting point. Right now, we don't even have a starting point."

"You can't find his wife or his phone. One would probably give you the other."

"Yes. But neither... gets us anywhere. Just asking more questions from more people, trying to find out where he has been and what he has been doing. It's a lot harder to track people when they operate below the radar like this."

"Maybe if you sleep on it, you'll come up with something."

He took a long swallow of his beer. K9 went out to the kitchen, and Erin could hear him slurping up water from his bowl. He'd had a long day too. Though he probably didn't find his as frustrating as Terry's.

Unless he wanted to go outside and do foot patrol, which was what he liked to do best. If he had been cooped up in an interrogation room all afternoon and evening, then maybe he was just as frustrated.

"I saw a woman in town recently. Thin. With several kids with her. I wonder if it could have been Mrs. Ryder."

Terry raised one eyebrow. "Where did you see this woman?"

"Across the street from the bakery. I just saw them walking along the street... I didn't recognize her or the children, and I thought they looked like they could use some help. I took some granola bars across to the kids. She wouldn't take bread or anything else."

"Could have been her. Fairly young woman? Dark blond?"

Erin tried to picture the woman. "That sounds right, yes. I introduced myself, but she didn't shake hands or tell me her name. She looked tired and... like she'd been living rough for a while. And I'm not sure how many kids she had. Maybe four? Three little ones and a baby?"

"Do you think she was living here in town? Did you see where she came from or where she was going?"

"I didn't watch her for that long. I never thought I would need to know, or I would have. I just thought it would be rude to be watching her and prying into her business. It really wasn't any of my business where she came from or where she was going."

"Did she say anything? About what her situation was or where her husband was? Was she looking for him? Supposed to meet him somewhere?"

"No. There was really no conversation. I felt bad enough for offering the granola bars in front of the kids, because then she didn't really have the opportunity to say no, after they had heard. I just wanted to help out, but she acted offended. You know how people are when they say they don't need any charity."

"Oh, yes." Terry nodded. "I've heard that line enough times."

"Sometimes people do need help. I don't understand why charity is a bad thing. It doesn't mean people are thinking badly about her. Just that they recognize she could use some help."

"I guess you have to be in that position to understand it."

"I have been, though. I mean, not in exactly her situation, not flat out without anywhere to go, but close enough. And I was always grateful when people offered to help. Especially if it was a job. But anything, even a bit of pocket change, at least it was something. I appreciated it."

"Then I guess it is a fundamental difference between you. Maybe the way she was raised. Maybe something happened in her past and she was taken advantage of. Someone made fun of her for accepting charity or thought that she owed them something when she took it. There are plenty of people out there who are not nearly as nice as you are, Erin."

Erin stroked Orange Blossom's head and back and he purred his loud, rumbling purr. "Yeah. There are a lot of people out there who are not very nice. I hate to have them ruining things for those who are good, decent people. There are lot of people who won't help you out without a lecture or religious sermon first." Erin shrugged. "But I figure, what does it hurt? Let them blow off some steam. If it makes them feel like they're doing some good, why not?"

Terry put his arm around Erin's shoulders, squeezing lightly, and rested his head momentarily against hers.

"I don't like to hear about you being that bad off. I didn't know that things had been that rough."

"Not all the time. Usually, it only took me a few days to be back on my feet. I would find work and a place to stay. That's what was so good about being a carer, a lot of times you could get a job and food and place to stay all at once."

"But they didn't always work out."

"No. Someone didn't like you for some reason or another, or the person you were caring for, if they have dementia, they lose things and accuse you of stealing. The family doesn't realize it's just the dementia talking, think you are bleeding them dry or selling off the family heirlooms." Erin rested her head against Terry's shoulder. "Or it would all work out really well, but then the person dies, and... you don't get to stay after that. Doesn't matter if it's the middle of the month and you don't have anywhere to go. The person you are taking care of dies, and you're back out on the street."

"That would be a shock. Didn't they know... that it would mean you were homeless?"

"No." Erin shrugged. "I wouldn't tell them that. I'd do everything I could to make it an easy transition for them. So that I could get a reference at the next place. If I caused trouble, insisted that I needed to stay there until I could find a new place... they'd resent me, and they wouldn't give a good report."

Terry nodded. "It must have been a very precarious existence." He rubbed her back and shoulders with one hand.

"That's one way to put it. Coming here to Bald Eagle Falls and starting the bakery... It was terrifying. But at the same time, I was so excited. I never thought I would have an opportunity like that. My own business. Running things the way I wanted to. Hiring employees of my own." She looked fondly around the living room. "I never had a house of my own before. I never had pets." She snuggled against Terry a bit more, even though her movement made Orange Blossom lift his head to glare at her. "I never had someone to share it with."

CHAPTER 16

*E*rin's sleep was restless, interrupted with thoughts of the Ryder family. Had it been them she had seen across the street from the bakery? Where were they staying now? What could she do to help with the homeless—or less adequately homed—population in Bald Eagle Falls? The more she learned about their plight, the more she wanted to get involved. She couldn't just ignore them, pretending they didn't exist. Even if that's what everyone else did.

The next morning, she arose a little drowsy, her lids heavy, wishing that she could sleep in for once. But even when she didn't have a shift at Auntie Clem's Bakery, her body was so used to her baker's schedule, she couldn't sleep in. Even without anything that needed to be done urgently, she couldn't sleep for more than half an hour after her usual waking time.

And she didn't have the day off, so she forced herself to swing her feet out of bed and head to the bathroom. Walking, turning on the light, and a duck into the shower for a few minutes woke her up enough to function and get her through the rest of her morning routine.

The houses outside her windows were still all dark. No one else found it necessary to be up so early. Even Vic didn't get up quite as early as Erin did, able to get ready for work in just a few minutes and not be in a state about getting everything done on time.

Vic's light went on in the loft around the time that Erin put on the kettle. She wasn't in Erin's kitchen by the time the kettle started to whistle, but it wasn't much after that.

"I don't know how you get ready so fast." Erin shook her head.

Vic pulled her hair back into a ponytail and wound it into a bun as she took a chair at the table. "I'm just really motivated to get as much sleep as possible. So I get as much ready as possible before bed… just jump into my clothes and head down the stairs."

"You're crazy. And you have to wake Willie up if he's driving us. That must take a few minutes too."

"Nah." Vic shook her head. "As soon as I move, he's awake. He's a very light sleeper."

Erin found that reassuring, somehow. Willie didn't sleep over with Vic every night, but when he did, it was nice to know that she had another watchdog nearby who would be out of bed in an instant if he heard something untoward.

Erin poured hot water into their cups, and they both set about making their morning tea. As soon as Willie was down the steps and in his truck, they would pile in and head over to the bakery for their usual early start.

Erin stared at the blackness of the kitchen window, still hours before sunrise, thinking about the Ryder family. Did they have beds to sleep in? Were they in a safe shelter? Or were they out on the street somewhere? Or in sleeping bags in another cave? All of those little children and the thin woman with her baby. Erin's hips ached just thinking of her sleeping on the ground or on the floor.

"What is it?" Vic inquired.

"Oh. Sorry. Just thinking."

"Long thoughts. About what?"

"Rip Ryder's family. Where they are and if they were sleeping somewhere safe tonight."

"Yeah. I guess. It would be a tough way for a family to live."

"Uh-huh."

Erin sipped her tea. "Did you and Willie talk about it more last night? I mean… don't tell me anything confidential. Just wondering if… he said anything else about the family. Where they might be squatting now. The police are going to be looking for them; they haven't even been able to do the death notification yet. That poor family doesn't even know that he's never going to be coming back."

"They probably have a pretty good idea by now. I mean… just the fact that he left and didn't get back when they expected him to. Wouldn't you figure after a few days that that was it?"

"Not necessarily. We don't know if they even saw each other every day. Sometimes when someone has to go away to work… we don't know whether they would normally see each other once a week, or once a month, or if he was going back to her every day."

"But if they were squatting out in the wilderness…" Vic frowned. "I mean, he wouldn't just leave them all out there to fend for themselves. Would he?"

"If he didn't have any other choice."

Vic shook her head. "Well, I hope they're back here in town by now. I wondered about that family that you fed the other day. That could have been them, couldn't it?"

"Yeah. I told Terry about that. She fits the general description. I'll watch for them while we're working today. If she's still in the area, I might see her again. I can ask if she is Mrs. Ryder, or if she knows where the Ryder family is. The homeless usually have a 'bush telegraph,' ways that they keep informed on what is happening in the neighborhood. So maybe if it isn't Mrs. Ryder, she'll still be able to give us a lead."

"Sounds like a plan." Vic looked toward the other window and saw Willie descending the steps. "That's our cue."

Erin picked up her purse and slung it over her shoulder. She had finished enough tea that she didn't want to be bothered taking it with her, so she dumped the rest in the sink and set the cup down to wash later.

Vic cocked her head as she looked at Erin's purse. Erin touched it protectively. "What?"

"That doesn't look as heavy and deadly as usual. You got your planner?"

Erin squeezed her purse and realized she did not. "Hang on a sec! I was writing in it before bed last night…" She hurried back to the bedroom and tried to retrieve it as silently as possible so that she wouldn't disturb Terry. "Good thing you reminded me! I wouldn't want to be without my lists."

"None of us would want that," Vic agreed with a laugh.

~

There was plenty to do before opening, and if Erin did see Mrs. Ryder, she was sure it wouldn't be until later in the day like the last time, so she tried to put her worries about the little family to the side while she and Vic baked the day's goods and prepared to open the store.

She still found herself inventorying everything that she was working on, weighing whether she should put something aside for the Ryders. A couple of loaves of bread. Some muffins. Maybe some cookies.

But Mrs. Ryder hadn't wanted any charity. So even if Erin put things aside for her, she would probably refuse to take them.

Could she? If she were hungry, if they couldn't afford anything to eat, then they would take the food, wouldn't they? It wasn't like there were soup kitchens and homeless shelters in Bald Eagle Falls. If they weren't able to fend for themselves, they would have to depend on the charity of strangers, like it or not.

"I hate to think of anyone out there on the street," she told Vic.

"You've got a good heart. But you can't help everyone."

"I can try. If there are people who need food here in Bald Eagle Falls, then I should donate to them before taking baking into the city. Don't you think? I'm giving it away either way, but I should serve my own community before going farther afield. Especially since they already have services in the city. They really don't have anything here, do they?"

Vic shook her head. "Maybe someone could go to one of the churches to ask for help. I'm sure they could get taken care of that way. But not everybody is religious or wants to go to a church for help. Would you?"

"I'd go wherever I had to, if I was hungry. I've gone to missions and churches before."

"I guess you can't be choosy."

CHAPTER 17

*E*rin asked a few of the customers who came into the bakery whether they had heard of the Ryders, or whether they knew who might be willing to help the homeless—or less permanently homed—in Bald Eagle Falls.

Most disclaimed any knowledge of the Ryders or of any homeless in or around Bald Eagle Falls. Erin only asked the women that she thought might be willing to help, yet even some of those she selected gave her a disapproving look for suggesting that there might be people *like that* around Bald Eagle Falls. The townspeople might be poor, but they looked after their own. No one was turned out onto the street.

She watched for the family, but didn't see them again. Apparently, it wasn't a regular routine. They had just happened to be by when Erin had seen them the last time. Maybe they had been in town to buy groceries for the week, which they would cook on their camp stove wherever they were currently squatting.

She was tired at the end of the day, but not ready to go home. Not ready to give up on helping the family or at least some of the people in Bald Eagle Falls who didn't have enough to support themselves. She could be part of the solution instead of the problem. *Seeing* the people who were in trouble. Not letting them be invisible.

It was Terry who picked Erin up, and she was not eager to ask him for help. He had probably been looking for the family for half of his shift anyway.

"Do you mind if we drive around a little? I'd like to see if I could see that family that I gave the granola bars to before. Make sure that they're okay."

Terry looked at her. "Where are you going to look?"

"Well... it isn't like it's the big city. We can check out the most likely places in a few minutes. If we don't see them, then I'll go home. But I'd like to at least try."

"Where?"

"The churches. The library. Maybe check around the grocery store. The dumpsters behind the grocery and the restaurants. Places that they might go for shelter or food."

"We don't have a homeless problem in Bald Eagle Falls. I would know if people were loitering around here, going through dumpsters. That's not legal."

"People need to eat. They need a place to sleep. It's warm enough now that they can sleep outside, but still, somewhere that's sheltered, safer..."

"We can drive around a bit." Terry turned his head to check in with Vic in the back seat. "Do you want to be dropped off or to join Erin on her quest?"

"I'll come along. I'm curious to see what she finds."

Terry nodded. He pulled out into the street. "Library first?"

"Yes."

They cruised over to the library. Some children were playing outside, and a few cars were in the parking lot. Certainly, nothing that looked out of the ordinary. But now that Erin knew what she was looking for, she looked more carefully. Were they children that she knew? Were they dressed like the rest of the kids in the town, or were they wearing dirty or worn clothing? Did any of the cars in the parking lot look like they were being lived in?

"I'm going to pop inside," she told Terry. "You can just wait here."

Terry looked at Vic. "I guess I've been told."

"It might be something to do with the fact that you're a cop. People who are living on the street or have something to do with a murdered man might not want to have any contact with the police."

"True enough," he agreed. He didn't get out of the truck.

"Should I come with you?" Vic asked Erin.

"If you want, but I will probably only be a second."

Vic sat back. "I'll let you have the first run at it. It isn't like you're going to run into anyone dangerous in the library."

Erin went in by herself. She didn't expect to find anything in the first place she looked, but libraries were a good place for homeless people to hang out. They had climate control and a person could stay there for hours without anyone kicking them out for not buying anything. There was built-in entertainment, with both books and computers available for public consumption.

She walked into the tiny library and looked around. It was pretty quiet. At the counter, the librarian was scanning books from a bin of returns and placing them on a cart. She looked at Erin as she came in and smiled. Erin didn't go up to the desk to talk to her. It wasn't like she needed help finding a book. And she suspected that if she asked too many questions, the Ryders and others in the homeless community would avoid her. She had to be more discreet than that.

She wandered over to the children's books but didn't recognize any of the children looking at books or playing on the computers. None of them reminded her of the children she had seen with the thin woman.

Erin made a quick circuit around the library. The woman and her family were not there. There was a man in a baseball cap sitting in one of the chairs with a book open in his lap. He was wearing a baseball cap and watching Erin. She drifted closer to him.

"Hi."

He looked away from her and didn't say anything.

"I'm looking for someone," Erin said, not trying to meet his eyes. She let her gaze wander over the interior of the library and the other people there. "The Ryders. Have you seen Mrs. Ryder and her children around here?"

"What makes you think I know them?"

"Maybe you don't. I was just wondering."

"There isn't any Mrs. Ryder."

"Rip Ryder's wife?" Erin prompted. What did that mean, there was no Mrs. Ryder?

"They ain't married."

"Oh. I'm sorry. What does she go by, then?"

"Dunno her last name. First name is Genevieve."

"Genevieve. Has she been around today? I wanted to get a message to her."

"Nope. Haven't seen her."

He didn't offer any other way to get in touch with Genevieve or the best place to look for her.

"Do you know where she's staying? Where I might be able to track her down?"

"Seems to me you don't really know her. Not if'n you don't even know her name."

"No. I ran into her the other day. I don't really know her. But I wanted to tell her something."

He shrugged.

"Do you know where I might be able to find her? Or how I could get a message to her?"

"Nope."

Erin suspected that he could have given her a lot more. But he didn't know her and might suspect her motives. A stranger poking her nose into a homeless person's business wasn't necessarily helpful or welcome.

Pushing him any harder wasn't going to get her the answers she wanted. So Erin just nodded graciously as if he had told her everything she wanted to know. "Thank you for your time."

He grunted and dropped his gaze to the book in his lap. But his eyes didn't move back and forth like he was reading. He would watch her all the way to the door. Make sure that she wasn't going to cause any kind of trouble.

And maybe if he saw Genevieve, he would tell her that someone was looking for her.

CHAPTER 18

*E*rin got back into the truck. "No luck there. Apparently, her name is Genevieve and she was not actually married to Rip Ryder."

Terry nodded at this. Something that he had already known, but not been at liberty to share? Or was he mentally filing the information safely away for later?

"Do you know her last name?" she asked Terry.

He shrugged with one shoulder, not looking at her. Erin wasn't sure whether that meant he didn't know, or that he wasn't going to tell her. It came out to the same thing either way.

"Where to next?"

Erin looked out the window. "The grocery, I guess. Just… check around it. Maybe stop in the parking lot and I'll check back behind."

"I don't think you should be wandering down deserted alleys or confronting someone back there that you don't know."

"You don't think the alleys are safe? I thought you said there weren't any homeless people here."

"I don't think you're going to find who you're looking for, but you never know who you might run into back there, out of sight. It isn't like we've been completely crime-free in the time you've lived here."

"You'll just scare anybody hanging around here away. Would you feel better about it if I took Vic with me?"

Terry considered. He looked over his shoulder at Vic, then nodded grudgingly. "Better than you being alone. At least one of you can run for help if the other runs into trouble. Are you carrying, Miss Victoria?"

Vic hesitated, unsure what answer to give him. Which clearly meant that she was, but wasn't willing to tell him so.

"Fine, go," Terry said.

Erin and Vic got out of the truck. Erin glanced over at Vic. "At least he didn't insist on frisking you."

Vic laughed. "I'd give it up before that. But I think he wanted me to be armed."

"I think so. And it wouldn't normally be a problem, except…"

"No, I still don't have my replacement carry permit card. But that doesn't mean I'm not licensed, just that I don't have proof of it on me. Technically, the sheriff did tell me to leave it at home until I had my card."

Erin shrugged. Terry hadn't objected to Vic carrying her handgun. He probably would have preferred it if Erin, too, were armed. So far, she hadn't been able to bring herself to buy a gun, even though she had been in several situations where it might have been helpful. She was more worried about it provoking a violent reaction from someone who would not have hurt her had she been unarmed.

They circled around the grocery store, watching through the big windows in the front for the thin blond woman and her little family. Erin didn't see anyone who wasn't at least familiar to her. They went around the side and then the back. Erin looked up and down the alley. It was deserted. After Terry's anxiety over her safety, it was a bit of a letdown. No one lurking in the shadows.

"Let's just go down there and check the dumpsters." Erin motioned.

Vic walked with her. "Check the dumpsters for what?"

"Just see if there is anyone in there."

"Why would they be *in* the dumpster?"

Erin rolled her eyes. "To get food. Have you ever tried to feed a family with no money?"

Vic seemed to think it unlikely that anyone in Bald Eagle Falls would resort to dumpster diving for food, but she walked with Erin and checked each dumpster. Plenty of cardboard and rotting produce, but no sign of anyone going through them. Erin looked farther down the alley toward the restaurant dumpsters but still couldn't see any sign of life. She hadn't really expected to stumble across Genevieve and her family immediately. Still, she had thought that she would see other people there. She could ask them about Genevieve like she had at the library. But not if there were no one around.

"Okay, let's go back to the truck," Vic suggested.

Erin nodded and they returned. Erin racked her brain for where to look next for the mother and children. If they weren't whiling away their time at the library or foraging for food, where were they? Staying with friends or family? All crammed into someone's guest room or basement?

"Is that it?" Terry asked. "Ready to go home?"

"No… what about the park?"

"What park?"

"The playground over by the school."

Terry nodded. He put the truck back in gear and drove a couple of blocks to the elementary school. Erin could see before they rolled up to it that there were children on the playground equipment. She watched the children. By the time they reached the playground, she could see that it was the family that she had met on the street. She was out of the truck, feet hitting the ground, almost before Terry had pulled to a stop.

She tried to make herself walk slowly. She didn't want to frighten them. They would think she was some predator or crazy lady if she jumped out of a truck and ran at them. She looked around for the mother and found her sitting on a bench nearby, watching the children and nursing her infant. Erin approached her, trying to look casual and non-threatening.

The woman's eyes narrowed as she watched Erin's approach. She looked around for an escape, but there was no way for her to disappear quickly with the children. Erin knew what it was like to try to get children out of a playground. They would complain and negotiate. Even if they had been trained to leave when they were told to, it would still take time for them to finish what they were doing and pull themselves away from the fun.

The woman didn't call them to her. Erin sat down on the bench next to her.

"Why are you here?" the woman demanded. "Just because you gave my children granola bars once, that doesn't make you my best friend. You don't get some special status for that."

"No. I was just… I'm looking for someone, and I thought…" She didn't know whether to say she was looking for the woman herself. Should she pretend she didn't know? That she was just making initial inquiries? "I wondered if you might know where I could find her."

"Who?" The question was clipped.

"Genevieve. Rip Ryder's wife. Or… partner."

"Why do you want her? What business do you have with her?"

"I just wanted to talk to her."

The woman shrugged. "I don't know where she is."

"I thought… you might be her."

"Why? You think we all look alike? Everyone who is… fallen on hard times?"

"No. You match her description. That's all. You have a young family. I didn't know either one of you. I hoped…"

"I'm not Jenny." The woman looked down at her nursing infant, then adjusted her position.

Erin looked down at the baby's face. A tiny thing, probably not more than a couple of weeks old. It was hard to believe that the woman's thin frame could have supported a baby. She must have looked ungainly, with a basketball belly and her stick-thin arms and legs.

The baby rooted around, unsatisfied. His face had been resting peacefully, but he grew agitated. He didn't have the chubby round cheeks that the Foster baby had. Erin wondered whether the woman had enough milk, and whether she was able to supplement if not. Would she have the money to buy formula? Would she be able to qualify for any government benefit programs if she didn't have a fixed address?

"He's cute. What's his name? Or hers?"

"Sarah."

"How old?"

"Three months."

Erin thought Sarah very small for three months. Maybe she had been premature.

"I'm Erin," she introduced herself again.

She knew the baby's name, the woman knew Erin's name, it was only right that the woman would give her own name. It wasn't the first time that they had met. They were sitting together.

The woman looked at her for a long few moments. "Adrienne," she said finally, sighing. "But don't go spreading that around. You don't *know* me."

Erin nodded. "I know. It's just nice to be able to call you something."

She watched the children playing on the climbers. Terry and Vic were waiting for her; she couldn't sit there visiting for too long. She had so many questions that she wanted to ask Adrienne. If she were on her own or was married. If she had been in Bald Eagle Falls for long. Where she was living. But none of that was her business, and she didn't want Adrienne to push her away when they had just started to get to know one another.

And what she was really there for was to find Genevieve. Jenny, Adrienne had called her.

"Jenny has a baby too?"

Adrienne hesitated, then nodded. "Younger."

"What about your other kids? Do you both have kids the same age?"

Adrienne looked at her, then away again. She switched Sarah to the other breast and tried to convince her to latch on, but the baby just fussed. Adrienne eventually did her shirt back up and put the baby to her shoulder, patting her back and trying to get her to settle.

"Why do you want Jenny?"

"I have something I need to tell her. I really can't talk to anybody else about it."

"Something about that no-good husband of hers?"

"Someone said they weren't actually married."

"What does it matter? The only difference is a piece of paper. Having to pay a fee to the judge."

Erin shrugged. She didn't know enough about the legal implications to answer the question. She knew that a lot of people had religious compunctions, but that wasn't an issue that bothered Erin.

"It *is* about Rip," she said finally.

"I hope the guy stays away and never comes back."

"Was he... not good to her?"

"Any guy who abandons his wife and children like that doesn't deserve to have them. He's off on a drunk or a gambling binge, and he won't be back until he's blown every last cent. If I was her, I wouldn't be taking him back!"

Erin nodded. But Jenny wouldn't have that choice. "You don't think... he could be off on a job? Something good for the family?"

"If he was, he would be calling her to tell her about it. No man hides his accomplishments. Just his failings."

"Do you know where I could find her?"

"No. I don't know where she went."

Erin sighed. "Okay. Do you think… you could call me if you hear anything about her?"

"I don't have a phone."

"Not even—" Erin bit back her response. If Adrienne said she didn't have a phone, she didn't have a phone. Erin had no idea what kind of life she was leading. If Erin had to choose between buying a phone and feeding her kids, which would she choose? A phone was a luxury, something children could survive without. Or could they?

"Well… you know where to find me if you hear something."

"The bakery."

"Yes. Auntie Clem's Bakery." Erin looked over at Sarah, falling asleep on Adrienne's shoulder. "And look, I always have leftovers at the end of the day. I have to bake enough that we won't run out, and if I do that, it means that there's always something left over at the end. I put stuff into the freezer and then when there's enough, I take it into the city for the shelters there. I'd rather help people in Bald Eagle Falls if I can."

"I told you I'm not taking charity."

"If you're ever trying to pull dinner together at the end of the afternoon and need some bread or rolls, or even something sweet for dessert, then come by and see me. I can't stand to throw it out, and taking it to the city is a waste of gas and time if there are people in Bald Eagle Falls who could use it."

Adrienne was silent, thinking about that.

Erin wanted to say, "It's not charity," but she didn't want to push her luck. It probably was charity. She didn't really know. But she wanted to help the little family and others in Bald Eagle Falls who were in need. She hated to think of them going hungry while she tried to figure out what to do with her overage at the end of the day.

"I guess… I'll be going. You know where to find me if you hear something about Jenny."

Adrienne gave a brief nod. Did that mean she would tell Erin if she heard something? Or just that it was time for Erin to leave and she didn't want to hear about it again?

Erin got up and headed back toward the truck. A couple of the children peeled away from the climbers and ran toward her, laughing and shrieking.

A tousle-haired little girl grabbed her by the arm, hiding half-behind her, like Erin was the 'safe' place in a game of tag. "I know you!" she declared. "You're the lady with the food!"

"Yes, that's right." Erin smiled down at her. "Good memory. But I'm afraid I don't have any today."

"That's okay," the little girl declared cheerfully. "We've had something to eat today."

Erin patted her on the head, choking back an answer. She forced another smile for the little girl and shooed them both back toward the playground.

There was a lump in her throat as she climbed into the truck.

CHAPTER 19

*T*erry seemed to sense Erin's mood when they got home and didn't engage her in conversation, letting her just work things through on her own.

As much as Erin wanted to help, she couldn't do that unless people were willing to be helped. And if Adrienne was a representative sample, not everyone was going to accept help.

She could invite Adrienne to work at the bakery and help her that way, only what would she do with the children while she was working? Especially Sarah? She wasn't in any position to take on a job.

She must have a husband or some way to make a little money. The children had eaten, so she found some way to feed them. And they were living somewhere, even if it was just a tent or a car. What more could Erin do for them?

"Where are you going to look next?" she asked Terry.

"Me? You're the one who seems to have taken on this search for the Ryders."

"I just thought… if it was the family that I had seen once before in Bald Eagle Falls, I would be able to find them again. But I don't have any idea where to go next."

He nodded as if saying that had been his point in the first place.

"But you have to do the death notification. How are you going to find her to do that?"

"Hopefully, we'll be able to find a way. If she's in the area, she'll turn up sooner or later. Even the people who live in the bush have to come into town at some point, even if it is only every few months. So she'll surface again at some point. With kids depending on her, it's even less likely that she'd be able to stay away from town for any significant amount of time. Kids need food, visits to the doctor, all of that."

"So you're just going to wait? You're not going to look for her?"

"Of course we'll look for her. We'll keep chasing down the leads that we have. But if she's like your Adrienne and doesn't have a phone, or has one but only turns it on in case of an emergency, then we can't use that to track her. And if she has no fixed address and lives out in the bush somewhere, there are too many square miles of land for us to search. Others in the community are probably in touch with her now and then and, hopefully, word will get back to her that we're looking for her. But whether she'll want to contact us or not is another story."

"Yeah."

"She'll know that either she's in trouble for something, or we have bad news for her. There isn't really any other reason that we would be trying to reach her. If she doesn't want to hear the bad news... she just quietly moves away and never comes back again."

"But wouldn't it be better to know? Wouldn't you rather know? And especially if she thinks that he's just taken off on her. Wouldn't it be better to know that something has happened to him than that he just abandoned her?"

"For you, maybe. Not everyone's brain works the same way. Some people would rather not know and be able to make up their own reasons and excuses, and leave open the possibility that one day, maybe he'll return."

"But he won't."

"You and I know that, but if you didn't know he was dead, you could always believe that he might come back someday."

Erin had lived a lot of years fantasizing about her parents returning, even though she had known they were dead. It was sometimes easier to deal with a fantasy world than the stark reality.

"There aren't any homeless encampments? Tent cities? Where everyone bands together so that they are more protected?"

"Not out here. People here are choosing to live somewhere isolated. If they want to live in a large homeless community of some kind, they can find their way to the city. Walk, hitch-hike, get arrested, there are plenty of ways to get to the city, if that's what they want to do."

Erin wasn't sure what Willie had told Terry about his interactions with Rip Ryder, so she asked her next question carefully.

"Do you think Rip got into some kind of argument? About land he was squatting on or something someone thought he had stolen or taken that wasn't his?"

"He clearly upset someone pretty significantly."

"You don't think it could have been an accident?"

"It wasn't an accident, Erin. You can put that out of your head."

"There's no chance?"

He shook his head. "No."

"Has the medical examiner made a determination?"

"Not yet, but I can tell you that it wasn't an accident. After seeing the scene, no. It wasn't an accidental death."

"Sometimes an accident can look like homicide."

He raised his brows. "You're telling me?"

"I just meant... I know you're the professional, but sometimes... you bring your own biases to the scene. You think there is no way someone could have done this to themselves, either intentionally or accidentally, so you see the scene through that lens."

"That can happen," he agreed. "But you're going to have to trust me on this one."

Erin went into the kitchen to get herself a drink. She sipped the cold water from the fridge dispenser. She was teetering between wanting to know more and being afraid that it would be too much for her and give her nightmares or flashbacks. Things were improving and she didn't want to set herself back to where she had been a few months back.

She returned to the living room and set her glass on the coffee table. She moved around the room, tidying up and thinking.

"Can you tell me a bit more?" she asked finally. "Was it... was the murder weapon at the scene?"

"Yes."

"And... was he shot?" Erin vaguely remembered Vic saying something about the state of the skull. She didn't think it was a gunshot.

"No." Terry looked at her. "You know there isn't very much I can tell you. You can read what's in the paper."

"If it's in the paper, then you can tell me. Was he shot?"

"No. He wasn't."

Erin thought about that. She had seen the brutality of stabbings and bludgeoning. She didn't really want to picture either one. But if she just followed the idea to its conclusion… if it wasn't a gunshot, then it was probably a close-quarters killing. Hand to hand. Within reach of each other. If it was something less violent, like poison, Terry probably wouldn't be as sure about it not being an accident. They wouldn't have toxicology reports back yet. An allergic reaction could be an accident.

If the murder weapon was at the scene, then it was something obvious.

Erin tidied away some papers that she had left scattered when she was reading through Clementine's papers the previous day. She liked to have everything put neatly away. If she left papers out, they might get damaged or lost, and she wouldn't be able to put her hands on them when she needed them.

Eventually, she sat down on the couch next to Terry. He looked away from the TV and at her to see if she wanted to talk, his hand raising the remote.

Erin shook her head and bent over to take her planner out of her purse. She had a sip of her cold water and put her planner across her knees to look at the week ahead and what was on her task list.

"You okay?" Terry asked.

Erin nodded. She turned to her project pages to see what she and Charley and Vic had last discussed about themes, promos, and upcoming events. She had almost forgotten about the next book club meeting at the book store across the street from Auntie Clem's. Naomi loved it when they made her a themed treat for the book club meeting. Erin wasn't required to, and sometimes she just sent over a few bites of whatever they had in the display case and freezer. But she liked it when she could match up with a theme. She made a note on her task list.

"I'm really impressed with how you've taken to the planner," Terry commented. "I didn't think we were ever going to wean you off your random bits of paper."

Erin dropped her gaze to her purse. "It makes it so much easier to find things and keep it all tidy."

He nodded. "Of course, if we could get you into the digital world, you could have it all on your phone and you wouldn't need that bulky book."

Erin gripped her planner tightly. They would have to pry it from her cold dead hands.

Terry laughed. "Nobody is going to take your book away from you. I'm just glad it's working out for you. Ingrained habits are hard to change."

Erin smoothed the corner of the page she was reviewing. "We'll see how it goes when my life is really disrupted by something. That's the real test."

He made a noise of agreement. "Do you drop it and go back to random papers or neglect your lists altogether? Or do you use it to pull yourself through the crisis?"

"Yeah. I want to say that I'll use the planner and keep up my good habits, but I know how disrupting stress can be. Who knows how I'll react."

"What are you working on now?"

Erin wrote a few headings on a set of fresh, blank pages. "Uh… nothing… just some planning…"

His eyes were on the TV, and he didn't persist. He was just being polite. It didn't really matter what she was working on. He was making conversation.

Erin wrote down what she knew or had deduced about the murder. She started a column of names, marking them as witnesses, suspects, or persons of interest. She wrote down what she could think of as clues that might point in a particular direction. Of course, she should get the details such as how long Rip had been dead and what the medical examiner had ruled about the cause of death.

She started a list of questions she would ask if it were her investigation. She doodled in the corners of the page, thinking about it, wondering if she knew more than she had noted. Motives. What she knew about Rip's background, which was next to nothing. Was he a native Tennessean? Or had he brought his family there for some reason? Did he have friends and relatives —or enemies—in the area?

Adrienne said that he was out drinking or gambling, so Erin assumed those were known vices. Willie had fought with him because he figured he could get possession of Willie's property by squatting on it. Willie said they had argued more than once, and Willie had managed to send him on his way, but who knew where he had gone. They might have crossed paths again.

Erin shook her head slowly. She was not going to fall into the trap of suspecting Willie. No matter what anyone said, Erin didn't believe that he could have had anything to do with Rip's murder.

CHAPTER 20

"What's all this?" Mary Lou inquired, looking at the new sign on the display case. Her brows came down, and she shook her head. Her short gray hair stayed perfectly coiffed. She smoothed her tunic shirt over her hips. "Families in need? We already take care of the families in Bald Eagle Falls. You know we had that big collection for needy children at Christmas. And there are other programs in place. There's a hot lunch program at the school for anyone who needs it."

"There may be people who can't access that. And what if the family needs more than children's lunches? What about breakfast and dinner? What about the adults? And weekends and holidays?"

"Bald Eagle families are proud and self-sufficient. You don't want to start giving handouts, people will just come to expect it and get lazy. We don't want to end up with the same problems as they have in the cities."

"Making sure people have enough to eat isn't spoiling them. I just think that we should take care of our own first. I have been taking my extra baking into the city for the shelters or soup kitchens, but if people here in Bald Eagle Falls need it, I would rather get it to them first."

"No one is starving in Bald Eagle Falls."

Erin thought about Adrienne's fussy baby. How her cheeks were narrow instead of round and fat. The children had been happy to get one meal. Had

93

that been from the hot lunch program at school? What was Adrienne eating? She was so thin.

Nobody was hungry in Bald Eagle Falls?

"I have food for people who need it," Erin said. She nodded toward the sign. "Nobody has to show ID or prove their income level, and I won't be sharing their names with anyone else. If they need food, they can come to me and I will make sure they get what they need."

"That's very generous. But I'm not sure it is well-advised. People need to work for their bread. That's what God said to Adam in the Garden of Eden. By the sweat of your brow. That's how he intended things to be in this world."

"So if I feed hungry people, I'm breaking God's law?"

Mary Lou waffled. "I would not say that. But the people who choose not to work, who just take and take, they are not following God's plan for mankind."

Erin avoided rolling her eyes. "I thought that Jesus was the one who said feed the hungry and love thy neighbor and all of that."

"We can still love our neighbor without making them dependent on us. We are supposed to judge wisely, not to just fall for every sob story people give us."

"I don't think anyone is going to ask for free food if they don't need it pretty badly. Like you said, people in Bald Eagle Falls are proud and independent. But if they are in a hard spot and can't feed their families, I think someone should be willing to help."

Mary Lou gave a shrug and spread her hands apart dramatically. "Of course it is up to you. I would just think that you might ask some of us who have been in Bald Eagle Falls for generations what we think about it before rushing in and trying to change the social order all by yourself."

Ignoring the sign, she peered into the display case and pointed out the items she wanted.

"How is Josh?" Erin asked, as she began to put Mary Lou's purchases into bags.

"Well, he's eating, I'll say that for him. He's regained the weight that he lost when he was being held captive. Most of it, anyway. I wonder whether he's going to stop or if he's just going to keep eating! But he's a teenage boy, and you know what their metabolisms are like. They can eat just about anything."

"I'm glad he's getting healthy again. And how about his... outlook? Is he feeling safe? Comfortable with going back out into the world and carrying on with his life?"

Mary Lou didn't say anything. Erin passed the bags over to Bella, who was running the till. Bella quickly entered everything and rang up the total.

"Trust you to ask that question," Mary Lou said, giving a nod of understanding. "I think... that will take longer. He's going to take the rest of the semester off of school. Not what I would have recommended, but he's nearly an adult and I can't make all of his decisions. I could insist that he stay enrolled, but he wouldn't go, and then he would fail. I'm hoping that he'll get bored and feel like he can go back out into the world where it is safe." She looked at Erin. "Because it is safe. Nothing like that is ever going to happen to him again."

"No," Erin agreed. "That would be really unlikely. But I can understand him feeling afraid."

"Certainly. But like the rest of us when we face opposition... he will need to pick himself up, dust himself off, and move forward."

Erin hoped that he could. She made a mental note to visit Joshua soon. She couldn't write it down in her planner right away, so she would have to remember to do it once she was able.

CHAPTER 21

When Erin got home, she found Vic and Terry in the yard talking. From their body language, it wasn't a casual conversation. She hung back, unsure what to say or do, listening to find out what was going on. The smell of barbecue hung in the air, one of her neighbors obviously cooking.

"You can't convict someone based on what family they come from," Vic snapped.

"No one is convicting you of anything. But I would be remiss if I didn't talk to you, considering the fact that you come from the Jackson clan."

"I'm not part of the Jackson clan. You know I don't have anything to do with them anymore. I can't help the fact that I was born into the family. I never worked for the clan. I left home. You've seen my family, you know I'm not welcome there."

"Things change. People change their minds. I don't know if you have reconciled with your family or have contact with anyone else in the clan. You were corresponding with Theresa without anyone knowing about it."

"That wasn't because she was clan. It was because we had a previous relationship. It wasn't anything to do with criminal enterprises."

"But you can't say that you haven't had contact with anyone in the clan. And I don't know how many other people you might have personal relationships with. That's why I would like to talk about it. Go through the details. Make sure there are no connections."

"This wasn't a clan killing."

"It could have been. Ryder may have stepped on some toes. He may have been trying to horn in on someone's business, the same way he was trying to push his way onto claims that were not his. People don't always realize when they are in dangerous territory. If he was trying to make a buck selling drugs or doing something else that the clan felt was interfering with their business…"

"Then you'll have to talk to someone in the clan about that," Vic said icily. "I wouldn't know anything about it, because I'm not in the clan."

"You're refusing an interview?"

"Yes, I am. And Willie should have too. I don't know what made him go ahead with it."

Terry shook his head, his expression darkening at Willie's name. "Willie might not have killed him for the Dixon clan, but I can tell you, there are other reasons to suspect that he is still doing work for the clan. He isn't as pure and innocent as you think."

"You don't know what I think," Vic snapped. "That's none of your business. Willie and I found the body, that's the only involvement we had in it. I didn't kill him. Willie didn't kill him. We didn't have business dealings with him. We don't have any business dealings with either of the clans. Do you think that we could be together if either of us was still part of our clans?"

"People have been known to defect."

"Oh, so now I'm a traitor? Is that it? I didn't like the Jackson clan and I wanted to date Willie, so I decided to join the Dixon clan instead? That way, we wouldn't have any trouble with clashing clans."

"I didn't say that." Terry sighed and rubbed the bridge of his nose. "Look, Vic, I didn't come over here for a confrontation. I wasn't trying to start a fight. I was just hoping that the two of us could talk things through like two adults so that I could come to a conclusion about your involvement. So that I could go back to the sheriff and say that I was pretty sure you weren't involved in any way."

"Pretty sure. Well, thanks for that."

"I'm not sure how I'm supposed to get to more than pretty sure. Do you have an alibi for the period of time in which Ryder was killed?"

"Which is?"

"One to two weeks before you found the body."

Vic stared at him. "How could I give you an alibi for a full week? Unless I was in a coma for that entire time, I don't know how I'm supposed to prove that I never went out to that cave and killed Ryder."

"That's exactly my point. That's why I could never be one hundred percent sure that you could not have killed him. But I can be pretty sure. If you can convince me."

Vic crossed her arms over her chest. "I don't have to convince you."

"No, you don't. But it complicates my investigation if you won't. I don't want to have to spend my time chasing down rabbit trails instead of the actual killer."

"Then lay off of me. Because you already have a pretty good idea I didn't have anything to do with it."

"Now *you're* saying pretty good."

Vic glared and didn't say anything.

"Fine," Terry said. "Be advised that you may be asked to come in for questioning, Miss Victoria. If you refuse an official invitation, we will have reason to believe that it's because you were involved in Ryder's death."

She raised one eyebrow and still didn't say anything.

Terry turned around to go back to the house. He saw Erin standing in the doorway, and his face tightened. He hadn't expected her to witness their conversation. He tried to smile as he approached her.

"Erin. I didn't realize it was that late."

Erin nodded. She stepped back and did not accept a kiss from him as he reached the doorway. He walked past her into the house. Vic was looking across the yard at Erin. She didn't smile or wave, she just turned around and went the other way, up the steps into her apartment. Erin stepped back into her house and shut the door.

"I'm sorry," Terry said immediately. "It's my job. I had to talk to her about it."

"You know Vicky isn't in the clan."

"I know she says she isn't. That's not quite the same thing."

"I don't understand what you could be thinking. She's baking by day and off murdering people by night? That's not happening."

"No, I don't think that. But it doesn't mean she couldn't have had an altercation with someone. And it doesn't mean that Ryder's death didn't have anything to do with the Jackson clan. We have to consider it. Just like in New York they have to consider whether any drug-related killing is cartel related."

"But if Ryder's death was related to the Jackson clan, that doesn't mean it has anything to do with Vic. They're two separate things."

"They are two intertwined things."

"She's estranged from her family."

"She's estranged from her parents. Or her father. And even that could have changed. You and I wouldn't necessarily know anything about it."

"That's semantics."

"She is still in touch with Jeremy, and you don't know what his clan involvement may be. And either one of them might still be in contact with the two older boys. And she could secretly be in touch with her mother or have made up with her father."

"I don't see how somebody getting killed in a cave out in the sticks could have anything to do with the clan."

He opened and closed his mouth a couple of times before answering. "And you know I can't tell you. But I would think you could trust me to the point that you know I wouldn't be asking Vic about the clan if there wasn't a possible connection."

"Do you know there was a connection? Or you just think there could be one?"

"It's a point to check."

"Fine. So you checked, and there's no reason to believe that Vic or the clan are involved. So you can mark that off of your to-do list."

Mentioning a to-do list made Erin suddenly think of her planner and that she needed to add a few items to her lists. And maybe she would look again at the pages she had composed about the murder. Maybe she could make a connection that Terry and the police department hadn't.

She got her planner out of her purse.

"Does that mean the conversation is over?" Terry asked.

"Yes."

He stood there for a moment. Erin headed to the bedroom to change and spend a few minutes with her planner. She looked at Terry, who still hadn't moved.

"But I don't know who won," Terry protested, the dimple appearing in his cheek as he let out a breath and laughed.

"Obviously, I did."

"Okay, then."

CHAPTER 22

*E*rin and Vic had been texting most of the morning. As soon as Terry headed out for his shift, Erin let Vic know that he was gone, and she came over to the house.

"Sometimes that boyfriend of yours drives me mad," Vic renewed the complaint she had already texted to Erin.

"I know. He's just trying to do his job, though. A man died, leaving a young family behind. He's trying to figure out what happened."

"He should know that Willie and I didn't have anything to do with it. If we had, we wouldn't have bothered to call the police. We would have just left him out there. The bones would have gotten covered over by silt. No one would ever have known he was there."

Erin shrugged. She wasn't going to argue the point. She hadn't appreciated Terry interrogating Vic about it, and she wasn't about to defend him.

"Let's go."

Vic had permission to borrow Willie's truck. "We really should get another car."

"We?"

"Well, I meant you. Just that when you and I go somewhere, it would be nice not to have to borrow one of the men's vehicles."

Erin conceded. "Yes."

"You were talking about getting Clementine's Volkswagen fixed up. Are you going to do that?"

"I don't know. I guess at some point. I don't really want to get something else. I might as well use what's available. No point in locking it up like the good company china."

They climbed up into the truck. Erin did up her buckle. "You know the way? Do you need me to set it up on the GPS?"

"I know where it is."

Erin sat back and tried to be cool and relaxed as Vic drove them out of town and out onto the highway. She watched out the window, wondering how many families and others who did not have the money to cover rent or a mortgage squatted and tried to eke out a living from the land. Getting rid of the one major expense would help, but they would still need to eat. Hunting and gardening would provide some, but not everything. And there were clothes and bedding and other supplies. They would need a way to make some money. Some cash was necessary to survive in the modern world.

Vic turned from the highway onto a secondary road, and from that road to a gravel road. Vic's gaze and posture were alert as she watched for whatever landmarks she knew along the way.

They pulled into a clearing and Vic shut off the engine. Erin looked around. They weren't far from Bald Eagle Falls, and yet they were in the middle of nowhere. She looked at Vic.

"Here?"

Vic nodded. She walked around the clearing, looking down at the ground. She kicked at something in the grass.

"This is where their cookstove would have been. You see where they cleared the grass and put down some rocks?"

Erin nodded. "Okay, yes." They had been careful to avoid setting the grass on fire. They weren't inexperienced in camping.

"There are some clods of dirt that were pulled up by tent stakes." Vic pointed several out. "The underbrush has been cleared here. There is probably a path to their latrine."

"So this was a permanent camp? They intended to stay here?"

"Semi-permanent. They were probably here for a few weeks. But when you squat on someone else's land, you take the risk of getting run off. Especially if you're trying to jump someone's mineral claim."

"Where is the cave? Is it a mine or a cave?"

"A lot of the caves around here are both. If there are mineral deposits visible in the cave, it's worth trying to follow the veins. Get whatever you can that's close to the surface before you put in the effort to dig deeper."

"So... what kind of minerals are there?"

Vic led Erin into the trees. Erin couldn't see any cave. They didn't go too far, though, before encountering a rock face. Erin looked at Vic and then looked around for the entrance to the cave. But it all seemed to be overgrown and the foliage undisturbed.

Vic led her around the rock face and, eventually, they reached a crack. Erin followed it as it widened, and finally she reached what she assumed was the entrance to the cave. She had seen and been inside a few caves, and knew that the entrance was not necessarily an indicator of how big it was inside. A wide hole could lead to a small, shallow cave, and a small cave could open up into a wide cave and multiple branches leading to a whole network of tunnels. She bent down and looked into the hole. It was wide enough to allow a man Willie's size or larger. She couldn't see the inside beyond the entrance.

"Will you go in?" Vic questioned.

"No."

"Just for a second? See what it's like inside?"

"Without a gun to my head—no."

She could see Vic considering this comment, but then deciding that she wasn't going to encourage Erin at gunpoint.

"Do you mind if I go in for a minute?" Vic asked. "Just to refresh my memory."

"Yeah, go ahead. Just don't get lost or hurt in there, because I don't plan to come in after you."

"I won't be long. Do you want to wait here, or back in the clearing?"

"I'll wait here."

Vic nodded. She turned on her phone's flashlight app and disappeared into the cave.

Erin looked around. The cave wasn't easy to find, but it wasn't hard either. If someone knew about its existence, it wouldn't be hard for them to discover. And if someone didn't know about it, they could still find it while scouting for water or a latrine location, hunting, or berry picking.

Erin put her face close to the hole, turned on her own flashlight app, and looked around at the interior. There were a couple of branching tunnels. The walls glittered with water or crystals. But Erin wasn't going to go any farther than that.

Where had the Ryder family gone? Were they still somewhere close? Or had they gone back to Bald Eagle Falls, or to another, more distant point? Maybe to Jenny's parents? Did she have a family? Adrienne hadn't said. Maybe it was just that simple. When she realized her husband wasn't coming back, Jenny just pulled up stakes—literally—and went back to her own people.

CHAPTER 23

*V*ic was longer than Erin had expected her to be. Erin hung around the entrance to the cave, anxious. She didn't want to entertain the idea that Vic might be hurt or in trouble. She did not want to have to crawl into the cave to check. She didn't want to crawl in there for anything.

When Vic and the others had been caught in a mine collapse, it had been Erin who had heard the rumbling thunder of the explosion and falling rock, and who had called it in so that they could get search and rescue in to do their thing. She remembered standing there just inside the mine entrance, facing a wall of loose rock. She had tried to shift it at first, but it soon became apparent that it was a much bigger job than she could ever hope to accomplish. Even with the number of townspeople who had come out to try to move it, they had not been able to dig the trapped explorers out. Search and rescue had needed to drill into the tunnel from an adjoining tunnel to get them out.

She looked in again and shone her light around. "Vic? Everything okay?"

At first, there was no answer, just her own voice echoing off of the rocky walls. Then Vic answered, sounding very far away. "I'll be out in a minute. Everything is fine."

"Okay," Erin said softly, and sat down in the dirt to wait. It was longer than a minute before Vic came out, and Erin was relieved to hear her approaching footsteps and finally see Vic's face. She let out a sigh of relief.

"I'm fine," Vic assured her. "Nothing happened. Here, I took some pictures. Figured if you won't go into the cave, the cave will come to you."

Erin hesitated. "Is it okay, do you think? There isn't anything... gory?"

"No. The remains were taken out the day that we found them, so it's just an empty pool now. You can see... a little bit of dried blood in some of the pictures. If it's too much for you, just give the word. You don't have to look at anything you don't want to."

"Okay."

Vic met her eyes, not turning her phone around yet. "Okay? You're sure? You want to see?"

Erin nodded.

She and Vic sat down on the ground, leaning against the rock wall, and Vic brought up the pictures on her screen. They were not too bad, the phone's flash doing a pretty good job lighting the scene up well enough to take in the details. Erin saw a large underground cave. Vic had taken several shots to give her a feel for the size of the cave and what it looked like from each side. Then they moved on to the pool where the remains had been found. Even though Vic had said that there was nothing left there, Erin still found herself tensing before examining the pictures more closely.

There were no bones, no body parts; everything looked quite clean. Like it was a man-made fountain built there just for them to look at. Erin could see the silt in the bottom. She didn't know how deep or shallow it was. Maybe there was enough that it could have completely covered the remains, and maybe there was only an inch or two. Erin didn't think that mattered at all.

"If it only happened a week or two ago, then how could he be a skeleton already?" Erin asked. "I thought bodies took a lot longer than that to... skeletonize?"

"It depends on the condition. This may look like a still pool, but there's actually a good amount of water draining through here. So it helps to... wash stuff away as it decomposes."

Erin nodded.

"And there was... you know, there are fish, and they're not picky about the source of food." Vic grimaced apologetically.

"Okay. Yeah. So in those conditions, the process was pretty quick."

"Right. That's what I understand anyway, from what has been released so far."

"What else have they released?" Erin thought about Jenny reading the paper or coming across a story on the internet. She would know that the cave was close to where she had camped with Rip and the children. Would she guess that the remains were her husband's? Or maybe she already knew that from gossip, and that was why she wasn't around for anyone to talk to. If Rip had been a gambler or an addict, Jenny might have lost it, furious with him for losing their hard-earned money once again, leaving her with no way to feed the children. Even though they didn't have much money, that didn't eliminate money as a motive.

She wished she had brought her planner with her to write these new insights down. If she could capture all of her thoughts, she would have everything sorted out all that much faster.

"Okay to look at some more?" Vic offered.

"Yeah."

"So everything has been taken out, but there were a few bits of personal property in the cave." Vic showed her some ground shots with nothing very interesting in them. "Like, a backpack, some water, that kind of thing. Not very much and, like I said, he had no spelunking gear to speak of. No headlamp."

"He could have used his phone like you did. Just for a quick look around."

"He'd have to know where he was going, to know that his phone light wasn't going to die before he turned around again. And... there was no phone recovered there."

"Oh, yeah. They dragged the pool? So they know it wasn't in there, just buried in the muck?"

"I guess so. We didn't get to see that whole process, but they did bring a pump truck down here to drain the pool and run everything through a mesh to catch anything small. I don't know how much they would have been able to go through the silt. It's pretty thick. Maybe they used radar."

"No phone. He must have had a phone. You can't survive in today's world without one, can you?"

"I know I couldn't," Vic agreed fervently. "And I would think that if you were trying to get a job, find land to live on, maybe find a mine that could help to keep you on your feet, you would need a phone for those things. Assuming he didn't have a laptop and Wi-Fi connection."

Erin looked around her. "I think that's a fair bet."

"Wait, let me check," Vic said, minimizing the photo app and switching over to her settings. "See... no Wi-Fi signal, and barely any cell signal. We had to walk out to the road to get a strong enough signal to call the police."

"So, maybe he didn't have a phone because there wasn't any point. He couldn't make it work out here."

"I don't know. I still think you would have to have something, even if it was just an ancient flip or a sat phone. What if... a kid fell and hit his head? Or there was a wildfire? Or someone... had a confrontation and wanted to reach the police?"

"Yeah. I don't think there are too many people these days who don't have a cell phone."

Vic went back to her photo app. "So, this is one that might bother you."

Erin took a deep breath to steel herself. She had seen plenty of scary things. She had seen dead people. Cases that weren't just accidents. And Vic didn't have any remains to show her. Just whatever things were left in the cave.

"Yeah. I'm fine," she said in a strong voice.

"Good. Here." Vic swiped to the next picture and showed it to Erin. There still wasn't very much to see. Just a place on the cave floor that was darker than the rest.

"What is that?"

"That's blood. And they took the murder weapon, but it was right here too."

Erin looked at the bloody cave floor. She tried to measure the distance to the pool with her eyes. Everything was distorted because she didn't have anything to show scale.

"So... that's where he was killed, you think. And how far to the pool?"

"All the way on the other side of the cave. Maybe... twenty feet."

"And he didn't crawl in there himself? Hit his head on an overhang and just got disoriented..."

"No. It wasn't an accident. He didn't crawl over there under his own power. The injury was... very traumatic... if not instantaneous, then close to it."

Erin could see better now why they were so sure it was murder. If the death was close to instantaneous, and he had lost that much blood and hadn't been able to crawl across to the pool where he was found, there was clearly someone else involved. Someone who had, at the very least, dragged the body to the water to hide it there. And at the most... who had stalked Rip Ryder, followed him into the cave, and intentionally killed him. And then dragged him to the pool.

"How big a guy was he?"

Vic raised her eyebrows at the segue. "Hmm. I'd have to ask Willie. I couldn't really tell you from what I saw. Willie knew him before he died and would be better at answering that. If there are no pictures of him online and Terry won't tell you that."

"He might tell me that. What the man looked like can't be confidential."

"Why are you asking?"

"I'm just wondering... how big or strong the person who moved him to the pool would have to be."

"Oh." Vic nodded. "Makes sense."

"Is that all you had to show me?"

Vic looked through additional pictures on her phone and nodded. "Yeah, that's everything that seems like it could be important."

"Let's go back to the clearing."

Vic led the way back through the trees. Erin looked back a couple of times to see the cave entrance or the path leading up to it. Someone wandering around could stumble across it. Someone who had maps, pictures, or even just a description would not have a hard time finding what they were looking for.

Which had it been? Had someone come across Rip in the cave by accident and taken advantage of an opportunity? Or had he been looking for his victim? Or meeting Rip to discuss something or make some kind of deal, and then had turned on him? Had they had an argument and it was done in the heat of the moment or was it an ambush? Could he have planned to meet someone there?

Willie had said that Rip had been trying to jump his claim. He'd been hoping to make it rich off of the minerals he would find in the cave. So where had he heard about it? Had he just happened to find it and didn't realize that someone else had a claim to it? Or had he known about it and went there with the intent of taking what was not his?

They reached the clearing; Erin looked around once more, noting all of the things they had previously spoken of, and then looked for more. She kept her ears pricked for anything out of the ordinary, not wanting to take the chance of anyone sneaking up on them and catching them unaware. Erin had had enough of caves and kidnapping to last her a lifetime.

CHAPTER 24

"*W*here would they go?" Vic asked. She had been scanning the trees, perhaps as anxious about intruders as Erin was.

"If Rip's family was forced to move away from here, where do you think they went?" Erin prompted.

"I would think… they'd probably move a few miles down the road. Find out where Willie's property ended so that they wouldn't have to deal with him again, and move to the other side of that line."

"Do you think they had another cave or mine in mind already, or would they just… go in a random direction?"

"If they knew about this cave, then I would think they'd know of others in the area."

"Do *you*?"

"Know of any other caves?" Vic considered. "I think I've got some maps in the truck."

They returned to the cab and Vic pulled maps out of the side pocket of the door. She shuffled through them slowly, looking at the labels on them carefully. They were not highway maps, but surveys like Erin had found at Clementine's when she and Vic had first met. Green to show vegetation and blue for water, irregular curves showing slope, close together where it was steep and farther apart where it was gradual. There were various locations marked with codes, some kind of letter and number designation. Vic glanced over at Erin.

"I probably shouldn't even be looking at these. Willie is pretty private about his mines."

"But he takes you to them."

"Mmm. Some of them. Places he doesn't mind showing me. But if it's an active mine, he might have other ideas."

"Oh. Well, I don't want to make trouble, but this is for the greater good… We need to find Rip's family and make sure they're okay, and so the police can make the notification, if they haven't already heard about what happened to Rip."

Vic rolled her eyes and continued to study the maps. "Okay, so I think we're here." Her finger jabbed the page, indicating one string of letters and numbers. "So the road is here." She traced a faint brown line. "The property line seems to be just over here." Vic indicated a straight line on the map, and then gestured to the trees ahead and to their left.

"So they could have camped anywhere over there, and they wouldn't be on this property. Willie couldn't complain."

"Right."

"Let's go over and check. And if… they were not just interested in a place to camp, but in mining particularly, are there any mines or caves close by that they might be interested in?"

Vic stared down at the map. "These hills are like Swiss cheese. There are caves everywhere, and probably a few that haven't been discovered or put on any map, too. There are a few marked locations. Maybe ones that he's interested in investigating or in buying, if the opportunity arises."

Erin nodded.

Vic slid the map onto the seat next to her. "Okay, so let's see if we can find them."

They drove back out to the dirt road. Vic turned carefully, and they traveled along it, watching for any sign of an encampment. People, a vehicle, smoke rising from a fire, anything that might show them that there were people nearby. It was wild. Erin felt like there wasn't anyone around for miles. Maybe all the way back to Bald Eagle Falls. But she knew that wasn't true. There were plenty of little places outside of Bald Eagle Falls. Farms and homesteads. Many people didn't want to live right in town; they wanted space or lived on old family property or farmed.

Way back in her however-many-times-great-grandparents' time, it had been a different world. People moved there with nothing but what they could fit in a wagon, looking for cheap land, full of hope at being able to make a living for their families. Was that the way that it had been for Rip and the other families like his? They were trying to grasp the American dream, to get land of their own and make something of it. Starting with nothing and hoping to end up with comfort or wealth.

"We should be close to the turn-off," Vic said, scanning the trees on the right for a break.

"There... I think it's there..."

"Yeah."

They followed the new path. Trees scraped the top of the truck and Erin found herself ducking, even though she knew they were outside and couldn't reach her.

"Is there enough space?"

"There's no space to turn around," Vic said, keeping the truck rolling slowly forward. "And there has been a vehicle through here."

Sitting up tall to look out the windshield and down at the ground in front of the truck, she could see places where the vegetation was mashed down. She knew that most of it would spring up again quickly, so it must have been driven over more than once to stay crushed down. She settled back down in her seat.

"Maybe we'll find them. Could it be that easy?"

Vic raised her brows. "I'd be surprised. Nothing is that easy."

They both strained to see through the trees. It was a few minutes driving down the long drive before they finally made it through the trees. Erin saw several tents set up. Her heart sped up. Had they found the Ryders?

Vic drove to where there were a couple of vehicles parked rather than right up to the tents. They waited for a moment before getting out of the truck, watching for any dogs or guards with shotguns.

They opened the doors and Erin climbed down. A couple of people came out of the tents to see who was there. A man came out of one, a woman out of another. But she didn't match the description of Jenny Ryder. Or whatever her last name was.

Erin walked toward the woman anyway. She would rather talk to the woman than the man. Vic stayed back, close to the truck. Available if Erin needed her, but out of the way so they weren't intimidating. As if either of them could be intimidating.

"Hi there."

"Who are you?" the woman asked warily.

"My name is Erin. I own the bakery in Bald Eagle Falls."

She scowled. "What are you doing here? What do you want with us?"

"I'm looking for Jenny... Ryder. I don't know her right last name, someone said she wasn't married to Rip. But that's who I'm looking for."

"What do you want with her? You don't think she's got enough problems? If that no-good Rip ripped you off or dumped you, don't go crying to Jenny about it."

"I'm not. I didn't know him. I was just trying to find her. Make sure she's okay."

"Why wouldn't she be okay?"

"I know that Rip disappeared..."

"Good riddance. Best thing that could have happened to her. In fact, if you have any idea of getting them back together again, forget about it. She don't want nothing more to do with him."

Was that what Jenny would say for herself? Or was the brunette just hoping that was what Jenny would say? Some women kept going back to the same abusive or irresponsible men over and over again. Erin couldn't understand why.

"Do you know where Jenny is?"

"It's none of your business. Just leave the woman alone."

"Is she close to here? I know that they were camped just over there," Erin motioned in the direction they had come. "But Willie Andrews ran them off."

"What a jerk. He doesn't live on the property. So what does it matter to him if someone else uses the land? It's better for him if it's occupied, isn't it? Make sure that no one is there to do any harm. It's empty land that brings trouble."

Having Rip and his family squatting outside or inside the cave had not helped Willie. In fact, it had put him right in the middle of a murder investigation.

"I'm not going to cause Jenny any trouble. Could you tell me where she is?"

The brunette's gaze wavered. Not over to Vic or to one of the other tents, but the other direction, farther away from the cave. Then her gaze refocused on Erin's face, the woman trying to correct the 'tell.'

"How about you get off of our property?" The man had come closer to Erin and the woman, and his voice was sudden and harsh in Erin's ear, too close to her.

Erin immediately reacted, stepping backward and turning to face him full on, prepared for an attack. Whether she was expecting a verbal attack or a physical one, she wasn't sure. Her body reacted before her brain had had a chance to process anything.

"Your property?" she repeated. She doubted it was theirs, any more than the land that Jenny had camped on was hers.

"You see our settlement here. We've claimed this land, and you have no right to be here."

"Okay... I'll head out. I guess... you folks don't care much for Jenny, then."

Both of them reared back at this accusation. "Don't care about her?" the man demanded. "What makes you say we don't care about her?"

"I'm trying to help her out, but all you're doing is being obstructive. I guess you only care about yourselves." She looked at the tents. "Your settlement. Jenny is... an outsider and she can take care of herself. Without Rip. Without any help."

"She has help," the woman disagreed. She stepped toward Erin, putting her hands on her hips. "We're a community. We help each other. Whatever we need. We take care of each other."

"She's got a new baby and no husband. And a passel of kids. Every woman's dream."

"It's not our fault what she's got," the man said. "But we do our best to take care of our own. We don't need... whatever it is you think you're going to do to help her. Who exactly are you? Some social worker?"

"She's the baker," the woman told him. "The one from in town. Bald Eagle Falls."

The man looked at her with a frown of consternation. Erin didn't know anything about him, but he looked like he had heard of her. And he knew she was out of place coming to talk to them or to Jenny Ryder. What good reason did she have to talk to any of them?

"The baker." He appeared to be fishing for some memory, eyes screwed up while he tried to retrieve it. "Erin?"

Erin nodded. She put out her hand to shake. "Yes. That's me. And the woman over by the truck, the one who drove me in, that's my assistant, Vic."

What had he heard? That she was a busybody? Always interfering with everyone else's business? She hoped it was something more positive than that.

"Wiseman," he said automatically on taking her hand. "What do you want Jenny for?"

"I just want to talk to her." Erin let out a sigh. "Really. I'm not here to hassle her. I want to help."

"I don't see what you can do to help her."

"I don't either. But I'd like to do what I can. If I can just find Jenny and talk to her, then she can make that decision. I don't see why you should make it for her."

"I'm not making it for her. We're just protective of our own community. No one else is looking out for us, you know."

Erin had to admit that was probably true.

"Is she over there?" Erin nodded in the direction the woman's eyes had betrayed. "If we go over another road or two, we'll find her?"

Wiseman and the brunette just looked at Erin for a moment, not sure how to respond. Erin could hear children playing nearby, their voices carrying through the trees as they laughed and shrieked.

There was a baby or young child's cry from within the nearest tent. "Mama!"

The woman looked toward it. She looked tired, the sun spotlighting the fine wrinkles around her eyes and the deeper ones around her mouth as she frowned. She had lived a hard life, and she wasn't that old.

Her eyes flicked back toward the man, and she shrugged. She gathered herself and turned away from them, going into the tent.

Erin looked at the man to see whether he was going to answer the question. He gave Erin a long, measuring look. She could almost see the gears turning in his head as he thought things through.

"Fine," he said, shrugging. "Yeah, if you go farther east, you'll find her. You would anyway, so it doesn't matter whether I tell you that or not."

Erin nodded her agreement. "Thank you. Is she doing okay?"

He shrugged. "How would you expect her to be doing with a new baby and a bum of a husband who couldn't be bothered to stick around?"

"Not good," Erin agreed. "Well… thank you for your help." She hesitated, not sure whether to say anything further or not. "If you know anyone who is in need of some baking, I'm trying to get rid of the day-old stuff at the bakery. Bread, muffins, whatever. I've been taking it to homeless shelters in the city, but I'd rather help the community around here."

He looked at her, scowling again.

"I know." Erin held up her hands in a 'stop' motion. "Nobody wants to take charity. But it's better than me throwing it in the garbage and little tummies going empty. If you know someone who needs it, send them over. It's confidential. I promise."

His expression softened a bit but still remained stony. He gave a brief nod.

Erin went back to the truck.

CHAPTER 25

She climbed into the cab and melted into the seat, closing her eyes and letting out a long sigh. Vic climbed up into the driver's seat, and Erin could feel Vic looking at her.

"So… you at least had a conversation. How did that go?"

"Try the next road over. We might get lucky."

"We might, or we will?"

"I don't know if it's the next one or not, but we're going in the right direction. We'll get to them sooner or later."

Vic put the truck into gear, turned it around in the little clearing, and headed back out on the road that was too narrow for even the truck by itself. Erin hated to think of what would happen if they encountered a vehicle coming the other direction. There wasn't exactly room for either one to pull off to the side. One of them would have to drive in reverse until they reached a point where one could pull over or pass.

Luckily, they didn't meet any other vehicles coming the other direction. They drove on, found the next access road, and tried it. They came to the end of the road pretty quickly. Erin looked around, searching the trees for any sign of the family or a tent or a vehicle, but didn't see anything. "Not this one, I guess."

Vic turned around and again headed back out to the road. Erin caught her looking at the fuel gauge.

"Just checking," Vic said lightly. "Gotta make sure we have the gas to get back home again."

"Yes. I wouldn't want to break down around here."

"Who knows how long it would take to get a tow truck or someone with a gas can out here. And to direct them to the right place..."

"Maybe we should have brought Terry's truck. At least it has a GPS locator."

Vic laughed. "Yeah. Somehow, I think we might have gotten another call from him..."

Erin had to chuckle too. Terry had not been happy when she had taken his truck out of town previously without his permission. They hadn't gotten a call from Willie complaining about them going out of town, but Vic had probably told him where they would be going. Erin wouldn't put it past him to have a locator on his truck too.

Trucks were expensive. It was an appropriate anti-theft measure. Not to mention, it could help them out if there were ever a day when he didn't come home from checking out a claim.

Erin shuddered, remembering the last time that had happened. It had not been fun for any of them. At least he had recovered.

They got luckier with the next road. It snaked farther through the trees and, with each mile, Erin was sure that they were getting closer to Jenny and her children. But she hated the idea of their being out there, so isolated if something were to happen to any of them. What did a person do when they lived so far out in the sticks and a child got sick or injured? A trip to the hospital in the city would take a couple of hours. That kind of delay could be critical.

"Something up ahead," Vic said, her voice quivering a little with suppressed excitement.

"Is it her?"

Erin didn't even know why she asked. How would Vic know if it were her? Neither of them had ever seen her before.

They reached the next clearing, and Vic pulled in near a beaten-up Ford truck that looked like it had seen better days. In the sixties.

Maybe it was a classic. Maybe fixed up, it would be worth thousands. But with more rust than fenders, Erin suspected not.

Erin was glad to get out again. She hoped that this was the end of her journey. She would find Jenny Ryder. Connect with her and let her know that the police were trying to reach her. Make sure that she and her children were all well and safe. It might not be any of her business, but she couldn't help taking an interest in a woman out in the bush all on her own with a baby and young children.

Of course, it wasn't Rip's fault that he had gotten killed, but Erin was angry with him all the same. Why hadn't he been more careful? Why hadn't he done whatever it took to keep himself safe so that he would be around to see his little family grow up?

Children were playing around the tent, not hidden away in the trees like the children at the last settlement. All blond and skinny. Minimal clothing. By all appearances, having the best time of their lives, wild and free. Erin smiled a little. She couldn't help it. As much as she knew what Jenny and the family must have been going through, seeing the children playing with wild abandon made her smile.

"I guess this is it," she said to Vic.

They walked toward the grouping of tents. Not just one tent for everyone to sleep in. Maybe a few tents for everyone to sleep in, the older children on their own and the little ones with Jenny. One that was set up as a kitchen, not fully covered, with a collapsible table, a cookstove, and a closed cooler, as well as dishes and boxes of tools.

Back in the trees somewhere, there would be a latrine set up. A hole or trench in the ground, a toilet paper roll stuck onto a branch, a shovel to cover up solid waste.

The children shrieked with laughter. Living rough obviously wasn't hurting them.

One of them went into the bigger sleeping tent when the children noticed they had company. The rest continued to play as if they were used to people coming and going. If they were a part of the larger homeless community, then maybe they were used to visitors.

In a few moments, Jenny Ryder pushed her way out of the zippered front of the tent. She turned around and zipped it tightly shut behind her to keep the bugs out. She dusted off her hands and walked toward Erin and Vic.

"This is my property," she asserted. "You don't have any business here."

"Jenny?" Erin said.

Jenny stopped, looking at her with a frown. Obviously, she was caught off-guard by someone knowing her name.

"Who are you?"

"I'm Erin Price. The owner of Auntie Clem's Bakery."

"What are you doing here? And how do you know my name?"

"When I heard that you were on your own, with all of these children, I needed to check and make sure that you are okay. With Rip not having come back…"

"How do you know Rip?" Jenny's voice was suspicious. Jealous, even.

"I don't know him. Just heard about him. I'm sorry to bother you, but I didn't know if anyone was looking out for you, and wanted to make sure…"

"And you can see that we're fine. So you can just go back to Bald Eagle Falls to the bakery and bake your bread. We don't need any of your kind looking out for us."

"I'm glad that you have a community out here where everyone looks after each other. That's great."

Jenny nodded. She stood with her arms crossed over her chest, staring at Erin and Vic. The children stopped and watched, whispering to each other.

"I don't know if you're aware… that the police department in Bald Eagle Falls is trying to reach you."

"Why would they be trying to reach me?"

"They want to talk to you about Rip."

"What kind of trouble has he gotten himself into now? I'm not responsible for the man. I'm not paying bail if he's gotten himself in jail."

"You should call them. Do you have a phone or access to a phone? It's so remote out here."

"I can get a phone," she snapped.

"Then… you should call the police department. They can fill you in."

Jenny shrugged. But Erin could see that she was curious. She wouldn't beg details from Erin, and Erin was just fine with that, because she didn't want to be the one to have to break the news to Jenny that her husband—or partner—was never coming back. Ever.

"So. You've delivered your message. You can get on your way now."

"Okay. We will. Do you need anything? I can bring you out some supplies. I know that you have a new baby, and it can't be easy to take care of… him…? Her…? Out here, with all of the other kids to worry about. I'd be tired with just one…"

"What do you know about raising kids? You got any?" Jenny looked Erin over critically. Erin was embarrassed to think that Jenny was examining her pelvis to see whether she'd borne any children, or her breasts to see if she'd nursed them. But it wasn't like she was giving Jenny advice or critiquing her parenting skills. Just saying that it was a hard job.

"No. I don't have any of my own. But I've lived in big families… and had caregiving jobs. I know it can be exhausting."

"Well, until you have a family of your own, I'll ask you not to be sticking your nose into my business."

"I'm just asking if you need anything." Erin was getting just a bit put out that everyone was making a federal case out of her wanting to look after people who needed help. What was she supposed to do? Ignore them? Then people would be upset about how everyone always ignored them.

"I don't need anyone's help."

"Okay. Good to hear it. I'm glad you're making things work out here."

Erin took a deep breath, and then repeated her spiel about the bakery needing to get rid of its excess product, and wanting to help the local community if there were any need.

"You see any soup kitchens around here?" Jenny demanded. "We take care of our own here, we don't need charity."

"I want to help take care of my community too. I don't think that anyone should have to go hungry while I throw out bread or take it into the city. And I've seen a lot of people in the last few days who look like they spend a lot of time hungry. That's not right. No one should have to go hungry."

The children whispered more. One of them ventured to speak to Jenny.

"I'm hungry, Mama."

"Then go make yourself something in the kitchen," Jenny snapped, motioning toward it. "There's plenty to eat."

The children looked at each other, but none of them stepped toward the kitchen. It was probably against the rules. They were probably not allowed to take anything that their mother hadn't divided up between them. Kids could eat a lot. One child being greedy could throw off the carefully planned meals that a trip to the grocery store was supposed to supply, leaving them without key ingredients. Or calories.

"Are we going to get bread?" one of the little tykes asked.

Jenny clenched her jaw. "We'll get bread when I make bread. Or when I buy it. Not because some do-gooder thinks that I can't provide for my own kids."

The children were silent.

How *could* she provide, now that Rip was gone? How could she make money to support a family with so much responsibility already on her hands? She might not need much, squatting and getting as much as she could from the wilds, but she would still need a little bit of money to buy the supplies they needed. Or medicine if a child fell ill.

Maybe the woman in the other settlement traded off babysitting with Jenny so she could go into the city to work. Or so that she could crochet washcloths or blankets or whatever she did to earn a little bit of money to survive.

"Will you call the police department?" Erin ventured.

"We'll see."

Erin looked at Vic and shrugged. It was time for them to go. She didn't know if she could call what they had done that day progress. They had found Jenny Ryder and her children. But they might be gone again by the time the police department got out there. Erin suspected Jenny had no intention of calling the police department to get news of her no-good husband. She thought that he'd been out cheating or gambling and she wasn't going to help him out.

CHAPTER 26

$\mathcal{T}$he ride back to town was quiet. Vic fiddled with the radio, eventually managing to find a station that would keep playing instead of going in and out every time they went down a hill or through the dense trees.

Erin listened to the scratchy songs the station played, sounding like they were records from a bygone era, even though Erin knew them to be modern popular songs. She watched the trees out her window. How many other people were hidden away in the trees, trying to subsist like Jenny and the rest?

Were they ever counted?

Did the government even know they existed?

Erin couldn't imagine that anyone spent much time trying to track them down or count them.

"Well, you did it," Vic said finally. "I didn't know whether we had any hope of finding her, but you did."

Erin nodded. "Yeah."

"Something good will come of it. You care about people, and that's not a bad thing, even if they don't accept any help. At least they know that someone cared. Someone *saw* them."

Erin didn't say anything for a minute, then looked at Vic.

She remembered Vic the first day they had met. Grubby, homeless, spending her nights sleeping in the bakery before Erin had discovered her. She had been one of them. Invisible. Unacknowledged. And she had accepted help. Erin had made a difference to Vic, even if she couldn't help Jenny Ryder.

~

Erin knew that Terry would be happy to hear that she had found Jenny Ryder and the children. But not happy that it had been Erin who had done it. She and Vic had gone off on their own to do what was really the police department's job. He always told her to stay out of police matters. Erin knew better. And yet, she couldn't seem to keep away from them. There was always something that drew her back.

Solving the puzzle. Keeping friends out of trouble. Righting a wrong.

She could say all she liked that she wasn't an investigator or a 'sleuth.' And yet, what was she doing? Over and over, she got involved in a police investigation or family matter, following a compulsion to find out just a little more. Maybe it was some kind of illness. Something that could have been explained away if they saw the way her brain worked. Some kind of deficit in regulating her curiosity...

"I guess... maybe you should drop me at the police department," she told Vic.

"Why don't you just wait until he comes home?"

"I don't want him to say that I didn't tell him right away. I'm not holding information back, I'm telling them right away."

Vic gave her a sideways glance, then nodded. "If you're sure that's what you want."

Erin didn't exactly *want* it, but she thought it was the right thing to do. So when they reached the town limits, she steeled herself, trying to talk herself into being confident and strong, rather than coming across as tentative or weak. Vic pulled Willie's truck up to the town center. Erin opened the door. "I'll see you later. Be home... whenever I'm done here."

Vic nodded. "See you tonight, then. Or for work tomorrow."

~

At the police department offices, Erin presented herself to Clara, the receptionist. Clara was wearing big brassy moon earrings that dangled in front of her red hair. She looked disapprovingly at Erin through her narrow-framed glasses.

"What can we do for you today, Miss Price?"

"I need to talk to Terry, if he is around."

Clara considered this. "Is it a personal matter or police business?"

"Police business. Is he in?"

"I'll see whether he is busy. Please have a seat."

Erin sat down in one of the uncomfortable waiting room chairs. Clara picked up the phone handset to make a call. Erin waited. After Clara hung up, she nodded at Erin. "He'll be by in a bit."

So he was out, not just closeted in his office. Erin supposed that was better. He always preferred being out in the fresh air and on patrol to sitting in a stuffy office doing paperwork. He would be in a better mood when he got home at the end of the day. Except that he wouldn't necessarily be in a good mood about her coming by the police department to talk to him. Maybe she should just have waited until he was home to give him her news.

Erin took her planner out of her purse and began to go through it, checking items off that she had completed, adding notes and tasks to her projects and lists. It kept her mind occupied so that it didn't seem like it had been more than a few minutes since Clara had called for Terry.

She heard K9's panting before Terry walked in. Terry looked at Erin, sitting there, and forced a smile. Not the kind that reached his eyes and brought out his dimple.

"Erin. Good to see you. What's up?"

"I have some information for you."

He looked at her for another moment, then nodded. He motioned to his office. Erin closed her planner and tucked it back into her purse. Terry shared an office with Stayner now, but Stayner was apparently out. Maybe not on shift that afternoon. Erin was relieved, because she didn't really want to have the conversation in front of him. Erin sat down in one of the chairs, and Terry sat down behind the desk. K9 lay down behind the desk, out of Erin's sight. But she heard him sigh loudly, something he did when he was bored and wanted to be outside working instead of inside waiting.

"I found Jenny Ryder," Erin explained. "Or... whatever her legal name is. I guess she and Rip weren't actually married, but I didn't ask her what it really is. Genevieve, but I don't know her last name."

"You found her. Where did you find her?"

"Out near where Rip was killed. A few roads over. She's still camping out that way with her children. Squatting. Is it camping when it's a permanent location? Or only when you're on vacation?"

"Where exactly?"

Erin did her best to describe it, beginning at the clearing near the cave and counting off the roads to get to Jenny's encampment.

"So you just thought you would go looking for her."

"I was worried about her. Especially with a new baby. I thought someone should find her."

"Yes, and that someone should be from the police department."

"I didn't know whether you were going to be able to find them. You did have a head start."

"We were trying to track her down through her extended family. But apparently, none of them knew where she was. And she didn't have a cell phone, or we could have used that."

"I told her to call you. I asked if she had access to a phone, and she said she did. But I don't think she meant she had her own, just that she could borrow one from someone else or use a payphone. Are there any payphones in Bald Eagle Falls?"

"There are a couple if you know where to look."

"I guess she would. If that's the only way for them to make contact."

Terry fiddled with a pen on his desk, the corners of his mouth turned down. "So exactly what did you tell her?"

"Just that she should call here. I didn't say what it was about or that Rip was dead. I think she figured he was under arrest. She said she wasn't going to bail him out."

Terry did smile at that. "Well, at least she has some sense. Do you think she had any inclination to call and find out what it was about? Or I guess the more important point... is she going to run, because someone knows where she is camped out now?"

"She could, I guess. But it would take time for her to get everything packed up and ready to go, and I just left. I don't think... she could go somewhere else, but she was all settled there. Everything set up. She's part of a little community. They help each other out. I don't think she'd want to leave all of that behind. But maybe she knows where there are other places she could go... or she could retreat deeper into the woods, hoping you wouldn't look any farther."

"How long ago did you leave her?"

Erin looked at her watch and tried to calculate it out. "An hour and a half, maybe? I really don't think she could pick everything up and be gone in that length of time."

He nodded. "But she also has however long it takes me to get out there to see her. I'm just going to have to cross my fingers that she doesn't run, or doesn't get out of there as fast as she would like to."

CHAPTER 27

$\mathcal{E}$rin knew that she wasn't going to get to see much of Terry that evening. Even if all he did was drive out to Jenny's, inform her that her husband was dead, and drive back, he wouldn't be back until after supper, and Erin had to retire to bed early to be up for the bakery.

And she suspected he would spend more than a few minutes talking to Jenny, unless she chased him off with a shotgun. He would comfort her, question her, try to fill in all of the blanks about who might have had a grudge against Rip and what day he had failed to come home. He would probably ask her about her own movements, and about phones, and what things might be missing from Rip's possessions. It would take a lot of time, so Erin wasn't expecting to see Terry much before bed.

She sat with the newspaper and her planner and thought about upcoming promotional opportunities and themes, what new ingredients were becoming popular in the trendy food shows, and anything else that might dictate the direction of her marketing efforts. If she wanted to keep Auntie Clem's interesting and fresh, she had to keep changing and adapting.

There was a knock at the door. Erin blinked, wondering whether she had drifted off to sleep. She looked toward the window, but it was the wrong angle to see if there were anyone at the door, and she didn't see a vehicle parked on the street in front of the house. Despite the fact that Bald Eagle Falls was a small town, Erin found that people often drove from place to place. It wasn't very good for the environment. But she was as guilty of doing it as anyone else. Part of that was Terry's fault, since he didn't want her walking to the bakery in the dark. So it wasn't all by choice.

Erin went to the door and looked out the peephole. It was dark out, but she got a good view of the woman's silhouette, and it was one that she recognized. She let Adele in.

"Hi, come on in."

Adele stepped in and took a quick glance at the room. The tall, slim redhead would know from the lack of Terry's truck in front of the house that he was out, but Vic was also a frequent visitor and Adele wouldn't be able to tell if Vic were there unless she saw her through the window or there were some other clue. While Vic didn't harbor any bad feelings toward Adele for what her ex-husband had done in the past, Adele was still uncomfortable spending time with her.

"Just you and me," Erin confirmed.

"We haven't talked for a while, so I thought I would stop in for a visit, since Officer Piper is out."

"Do you want some tea?" Erin didn't wait for an answer. She and Adele always had tea together. She went into the kitchen to start the kettle boiling. Adele followed her, more comfortable in the kitchen than anywhere else in the house. Her own little cottage in the woods behind Erin's house was a tiny one-room affair, where the stove, table, and bed all shared the same space. It was a warm, homey place, and Erin didn't get there as often as she probably should. But she wanted to give Adele her space and a sense of privacy, even though the cottage was part of the property left to Erin by Clementine.

She puttered around in the kitchen. Adele arranged the rest of the tea things and sat down at the table.

"Anything new?" she asked.

Erin wondered how much Adele had heard about Rip. Adele was a solitary person, yet she often knew about things going on in Bald Eagle Falls before Erin did.

"I guess... you know about Rip Ryder...?"

Adele nodded her head once. "Yes. Are you... involved in that case?"

"Well, no..." Erin laughed. "It's nothing to do with me. But..."

"But you like solving puzzles."

"I guess so, yes," Erin admitted.

Erin poured the boiling water into their cups.

"So what is it about this case that interests you so much?" Adele asked. "Just because it was Vic who found him?"

"Partly, yes. I feel like if it's something to do with my family here in Bald Eagle Falls, that... I should do what I can to sort it out, make sure that the wrong people don't get saddled with the blame."

"Why would they blame Vic?"

"Well... with her being the one to find the body, and her family being in the clan, it's just where they go. What if she did it and... I don't know, returned to the scene of the crime. Same with Willie, except it's worse for him, since he had a fight with Mr. Ryder."

Adele look at Erin blankly for a moment. Then she nodded, and amended, "Or two or three."

Erin dipped and lifted her tea bag a few times and looked at Adele. "Two or three? How do you know that?"

"I hear things."

"Who did you hear that from? I didn't think it was common knowledge."

Adele just smiled and didn't answer.

Erin was again left wondering how Adele came by her information. She imagined Skye, Adele's crow, flying back and forth over Bald Eagle Falls and bringing back all of the juicy tidbits he'd heard back to his mistress. She smiled at the thought.

Adele knew people who knew things, that was all. She was quiet and discreet, so Erin didn't know all of the people that she knew or was friends with. But she clearly knew people who heard the gossip around Bald Eagle Falls. Not just the Baptist women who came to the bakery to share the gossip they had heard, but other, less visible people in Bald Eagle Falls as well.

"Well, I guess you're not the only one who knows that Rip and Willie didn't get along together. So the police know and they think, maybe they got into another fight, and it turned physical, and Willie killed him."

Adele raised her brows.

"And put him in that pool and then came back later with Vic to find him," Erin said, pointing out the obvious flaw in this theory.

"Why would he do that?"

"You would have to ask the police department. I don't know the answer.

If Willie did kill him by accident or in a moment of anger—and I don't believe he ever would—then why would he do that? Leave the body in the cave there, and then go back later to let Vic find it? Or else bring her in on the secret and 'discover' it together? It doesn't make any sense."

Adele sipped her tea. "People don't always make sense."

"I guess. But that doesn't mean you think Willie did it, do you?"

"I don't suspect Willie Andrews or anyone else. I will leave that to the universe—and our esteemed police department—to sort out."

"I hope they do. And soon. And I'm sure it's not Willie. It couldn't be anything to do with Willie or Vic. It wouldn't make any sense, however much people try to force them into the mold. They don't have any motive."

"Other than Mr. Ryder disagreeing with him about the legitimacy of Willie's mineral claim."

Erin frowned. She stirred her tea, then forced herself to set the spoon aside to stop fiddling. "The legitimacy of Willie's claim? What do you mean by that? It's his claim."

"Is it?"

"Well, yes. He said…"

"He said it was his. But have you seen proof of his ownership? Or did he just lay claim to it and hope to keep everybody else off of it?"

"I don't know. He said it was his. I didn't question…"

"And that's exactly what he intended. He told Rip that it was his claim and he had to take himself and his family somewhere else. He didn't want Rip anywhere near that cave and, even after he moved off of the property, Willie still wasn't satisfied. He was still 'too close.'"

"How could they be too close? Either they were on his claim or not, you can't be *too close*."

Adele nodded her agreement. "You see Rip's argument."

"But it is Willie's, right? He might have been out of line in telling Rip that he was still too close and he wanted him to go farther away, but… it was his claim."

"As far as I know, he never showed any deeds to prove it."

Erin shook her head, finding it hard to believe that the claim might not be Willie's. "So he must have thought that the claim was pretty valuable. Potentially."

"I'm sure he wouldn't tell me if it was. Or anyone else, for that matter. He's worked mines and mineral claims around here long enough to know to keep his mouth shut and not attract attention to any one location. He is very discreet and circulates around from one mine to another. You can't tell by looking at the outsides which one is producing and which is not."

Erin had to admit that was true. "He doesn't even tell Vic. He's taken her caving a few different places, but he doesn't take her to his mines, and he doesn't tell her which one he's going to from one day to the next."

"But he did take her to this one."

Erin sipped her tea as it started to cool. The only way to know what Willie had found inside the cave, and whether he was removing anything from it, would be to go inside.

"Has he allowed anyone else in there?" Adele prompted.

"The police, of course. To remove the remains. He couldn't very well keep them out." Erin shrugged, raising her hands up. "That takes us right back to the beginning again. If he wanted to keep something about the cave a secret, why would he hide a body there and then bring Vic back to find it? And not to help him take it out and bury it, but then they call the police to come take a look and get it out of there."

"That's an interesting suggestion."

Orange Blossom had roused himself from his warm nest on the couch and had just realized that there was someone else in the house. He went over to Adele and started rubbing against her and vocalizing.

"Is he bothering you? He can be such a pest."

"No, I think it's nice having a cat around. I'm still thinking about getting one myself, though…"

Though Erin had told her that she would need to keep the cat inside to keep it safe, and Adele wasn't keen in caging any animal. Skye lived outside and could come and go as he pleased. He just seemed to want to be with Adele sometimes.

Erin bent over to scratch Blossom's ears, then sat up again. "What's an interesting suggestion?"

"The idea that Willie might have taken Vic to the cave in order to relocate and bury the body."

"I didn't say that's what happened. It obviously didn't happen."

"But that doesn't mean it isn't what Willie intended. Maybe he figured Vic would help him to dispose of it. Only she had other ideas and said they had to call the police. Either before or after he explained his plan."

"No, Willie wouldn't do that."

"You have a very… generous view of the world. You realize that, don't you? You think the best of everyone."

"Well… I try to, I guess. I want to believe the best of people."

"And not everyone lives up to your expectations, do they?"

"Most people, if you give them a chance, they'll do the right thing…"

"I'm not sure that's true. I think people's natures tend to be the opposite. They act in their own interests before anyone else's. Unless there is sufficient motivation to pursue another direction."

"You're not like that," Erin pointed out. "You're a good, giving person."

"I have found that to serve me well. It is innately selfish to want to treat others in such a way as to make yourself comfortable. To avoid conflict just because it is an easier path."

"You only make good choices because you want the rewards that come from making good choices? Isn't that sort of… twisted?"

"Perhaps it is. And perhaps it is what the majority of the world does."

Erin massaged her temples. She looked at the clock on the wall. She was getting tired, and the conversation was going in the wrong direction. She didn't want to have to evaluate her own motives, or Adele's, or Willie's. It was too much for her already tired brain.

"I guess everyone has their own reasons for doing things," she deflected. Once she said this, she nodded. It was true. It sounded good. And it meant she didn't have to continue the conversation in that direction.

"Yes," Adele agreed. The corners of her mouth curled up slightly as if at some private joke. She took a couple more swallows of her tea and set her cup down. "Well. I should get back to my wanderings. Take care, Miss Erin."

Erin nodded and stood at the same time as Adele. Orange Blossom went back and forth between them, demanding to know which of them was going to feed him.

"You haven't had any trouble, have you?" Erin asked as she walked Adele to the door. Adele was Erin's groundskeeper and, although Erin had first given her the title on the spur of the moment, looking for a way to help Adele out, Adele did actually keep a good watch on things that happened in the woods. People who walked through there and who might be looking to cause harm.

"No trouble," Adele agreed.

"You haven't had any of the squatters come to our woods? They stay far enough out of town…?"

"Why would they come into our woods?"

"I don't know. It would let them live outside, like they seem to want, but still to be close to the amenities. Be able to go to the library during the day or pick something up from the grocery store easily."

"I'll keep my eyes open," Adele promised.

Erin saw her out. When she shut and locked the door and reset the burglar alarm, she stopped to ponder Adele's responses.

She never had actually said that there were no squatters in Erin's woods.

CHAPTER 28

*E*rin was restless going to bed, thinking of Adele and how she had deflected Erin's questions and questioned Vic's and Willie's involvement in Rip's death without actually accusing them. She seemed to know a good amount about the arguments that had gone on between Rip and Willie. More than just someone who had heard about it. How would anyone know that Willie might not actually own the claims he said he did? She would have to be pretty close to the situation.

Adrienne had been in town. She and her children were there a couple of days in a row. Where were they staying? With a friend? In a car? Or in the woods back behind Erin's house, pretending that they lived out of town when they were actually right under her nose?

She was irritated with the thought. She had gone out of her way to help Adrienne, offering help to her and all of those who were indigent or homeless. She had been trying to find Jenny, to be sure that she was okay and that the police would be able to find her to make the official notification of Rip's death. Closure. People needed to know what had happened to their loved ones.

Erin had been doing the right thing, so why were people acting as if she was interfering with them or insulting them? She just wanted to help.

Erin decided to use her Sunday afternoon to do some visiting, something that she didn't have much time for the rest of the week. There were people she wanted to see that she didn't have as much opportunity for the rest of the week.

So she tried Mary Lou first. She knew Mary Lou generally went to the Baptist services, and then to the ladies tea at Auntie Clem's, but after that, she didn't know if Mary Lou worked or ran errands or relaxed.

"Yes, come over, Erin," Mary Lou agreed. "We're not going too far from home these days. We'll be around."

We was Mary Lou and her younger son, Joshua, who was recovering from being kidnapped and held hostage for a week with practically no food or water. They had all worried after the first couple of days that they would not find him alive. Joshua had believed the same, knowing that his time was drawing to an end. But they had been able to find him and to rescue him.

The physical recovery was one thing. Erin could see that his cheeks had filled in and that he looked stronger and more like himself. But he was also different. He was stiff and he watched Erin and the world around him differently from ever before. It wasn't just hypervigilance, which Erin knew was a common reaction to such a traumatic experience. There was more to it than that. He was wary. Not only of strangers, not just jumping at sudden unexpected noises, but seemingly distrustful of even those he knew. Erin felt him examining her, trying to pick her apart and to predict what she was going to do and say. It wasn't enough to know that she was a friend of his mother's, or that she had been instrumental in finding him and bringing him back home. He wanted to disassemble her and see what made her work so that he didn't have to guess.

"How are you feeling?" she asked Joshua. "You're looking better all the time."

"Yeah. I'm fine. Doing good. It's all… everything will be just the way it was before."

Maybe he was repeating what Mary Lou or someone else had said to him. Because he certainly didn't sound like he believed it himself.

"We're all changing all the time," Erin said. "I'm not the same person as I was a year ago. Or ten years ago. That's why they say you can't go back… you can never be the same person as you were before. We're all growing and changing all the time. And something like this… it can really affect you."

"It hasn't changed me," Josh said flatly.

Erin nodded. "Okay." She turned her attention to Mary Lou, hoping that would give Josh a chance to relax. "How about you? And Campbell? I haven't heard how he is. Staying out of trouble?"

"I'm sure I wouldn't know. He's back in the city now. I wish he had stayed around... but on the other hand, it's kind of tense when he's here. His mother expecting him to follow the house rules and him thinking that he's a full-grown man now and doesn't need to listen to what anyone else has to tell him."

"Yeah. Well, he is an adult."

"So I've heard. Multiple times."

Erin smiled. "He's lucky to have you. He might not realize that right now, but someday... he will."

Mary Lou thought about that for a minute. "Maybe. But it isn't as easy for him to see as you. You've lived on the other side. On your own as soon as you were eighteen, without any family resources. It must have taken a lot of hard work to get to where you are today. To be able to pull yourself up all by yourself..."

"It wasn't exactly all by myself, though. Without Clementine... I wouldn't be where I am today. That was an opportunity that I could never have made for myself. I didn't have the money or resources to take a leap and start up my own business without what she had left me."

"I'm glad... she would have been happy to see what you have done with it. How you have taken her legacy and... made it your own. Built on it. Become a self-sufficient small business owner. She would have been very proud." Mary Lou gave an approving nod.

"Thank you... I hope she would be. I hope that the bakery would be something that she would approve of."

"Yes. I'm sure it is."

Erin tried to think of other things to discuss. Joshua and Campbell seemed to be off the table. They had their own difficulties, and Erin didn't want to pry into family business.

"Have you seen the Fosters lately? I'm going to head over there after this, see if they need anything."

"I don't see much of them," Mary Lou admitted. "I know they're just down the way, but I keep to myself too much. I should go see them, but I don't. With a new baby, I'm not sure they want to have visitors over there all the time." She hastened to reassure Erin. "Not that they won't want to see you. That little boy idolizes you. But for me... I'm just the cranky old lady down the street. The children will have to be on their best behavior and that gets very tiresome."

Erin nodded. "I'm amazed at how Mrs. Foster can handle that little brood. So many young ones to keep in order. And she must be exhausted with a new baby."

"There seems to be a whole new crop of little ones popping up," Mary Lou observed. "Like we're having a mini baby boom in Bald Eagle Falls."

Erin thought about the Fosters, Jenny Ryder, and the two other home-less women who had new babies. She nodded her agreement. "Yes, there do seem to be a lot of them around."

"It seems like just yesterday that I had little ones. It's hard to believe they're already older teenagers." Mary Lou shook her head. "You'll be amazed at how fast the time goes, Erin. I know you've probably heard it before. But it really is true. Time just keeps going faster and faster. I remember when I was a child, it seemed like a summer day lasted forever. And the school break over the summer felt like a year off. Now... it seems like I barely get a chance to sleep, and it's a new month. Don't put things off until you are older, because before you know it, you will be older, and it will be too late."

Erin thought about all of the plans she had been writing down in her new paper planner. Writing down her dreams and plans for the future made them seem that much more real. But Mary Lou was right; she couldn't afford to put them off and act like she had as much time as she would need in the future. She needed to be working on them now.

CHAPTER 29

$\mathcal{E}$rin left Mary Lou and Joshua with some cookies and headed over to the Fosters. She had a box of various baked goods for them, although Mrs. Foster was back on her feet and making occasional trips to the bakery now. Erin wanted her to know that someone was looking out for her and doing what she could do ease her burden. It wasn't really much, but Erin did what she could.

The little girls were playing outside. Erin didn't see Peter, which was odd. He was usually helping to supervise the younger children. Jody ran up to her.

"Miss Erin! You come to visit?"

Erin nodded. "I came to visit. How is everybody doing?"

"I hurt my knee." The little girl bent over to pull up the shorts that reached over her kneecaps to show Erin a skinned knee.

Erin winced at the red, raw patch. "Ow! That must have really hurt. Did you fall down?"

"Yes. I was running, playing," Jody turned around and was gesturing, telling Erin all about what she had been doing when she had taken a spill. She spoke quickly, and with her face turned away from Erin. Erin could no longer make out what she was saying.

Erin made attentive noises and, when Jody got to the part where she had fallen down and hurt herself, Erin shook her head. "Ouch. Well, you try to be careful. We don't want you hurting anything else."

"Yeah!" she agreed with feeling.

Grinning, Erin walked up to the house and reached out to ring the doorbell. The door was opened before she reached it. Mrs. Foster stood inside the door and motioned her in.

"Come in, come in."

Erin entered the house. She took the box of baked goods into the kitchen and put it down on the counter. Mrs. Foster could put things away where she wanted them. Or she could have Peter or one of the others help out.

"I'm trying to keep an eye on them," Mrs. Foster said, nodding to the window as they sat down in the living room.

Erin looked out at them. "They are lucky to have somewhere safe to play outside. Burn off some steam."

"I wouldn't want to keep them cooped up all day. Even on a school day, I try to let them have as much outside time as possible. The skillset they develop when they can move around and experiment and do things for themselves is very different from a kid who just sits in front of screens all day. I want my children to be strong and self-sufficient. Not afraid to try things or tied to a box all day."

"Well, you must be doing something right. They are all such good kids. And I know I can't pick favorites, but... Peter is such a bright little guy. I think you've done very well with all of them."

"He should be home in a few minutes. I asked him to pick up a couple of things for me at the store."

Erin looked out the window anxiously. She had thought he might be doing homework in his bedroom. She didn't like the idea of his going out all by himself to the store. Mrs. Foster followed her eyes.

"He's old enough. He walks to school by himself."

"Oh, of course. It's just that... with Joshua being kidnapped, I guess I'm more nervous..."

"We can't let ourselves be ruled by fear. Joshua didn't get snatched off of the street, and it wasn't some random kidnapper. And they caught the person who did it. If he was taken from his room at night... what good will it do us to keep our children inside all the time? Being inside did not help Josh."

"I guess," Erin admitted. "I'm sorry. I'm not saying you're doing anything wrong. It's just a gut reaction. I think Bald Eagle Falls is a pretty safe place for kids."

Mrs. Foster nodded. "It is," she agreed. "And Peter has been drilled over and over again on what he is and isn't allowed to do."

If he chose to obey. Erin knew that he had stopped to talk and visit with her on the way home from school and told her he wasn't supposed to stop to talk to anyone. But then, all kids were like that. They chose what to obey and what they didn't think was worth obeying.

So did adults, for that matter.

They talked about the weather and things going on around town. Erin did not bring up the remains found in the cave. The baby started to cry in another room, and Mrs. Foster sat there for a moment to see if he would stop on his own before getting up to get him.

"Here is Allan," she told Erin, as she brought the snuggling baby back into the room. She tilted him toward Erin so she could get a good view of him.

"Wow, he's already growing. He's definitely bigger than he was last time I saw him."

"Yes, he is." Mrs. Foster stroked the baby's shock of hair. "And already losing his hair, too. It's funny how sometimes they come out looking like they're wearing a toupee, there's so much of it, and then it all falls out."

She sat back down and unbuttoned a few buttons in order to nurse him.

He looked so much healthier than Adrienne's baby. His cheeks were rosy and round. He nursed contently, rather than moving around and pulling at the nipple as if he weren't getting enough. Erin had a pain in her chest, thinking about Adrienne's baby, and Jenny's, and the baby or child she'd heard crying in the tent in the settlement beside Jenny's. So many hungry mouths to feed.

A few minutes later, Erin spotted Peter walking down the street, swinging a grocery bag at his side. "There he is."

Mrs. Foster smiled. "Safe and sound."

"Of course."

Peter stopped to talk to the girls outside for a few minutes, then entered the house. He smiled and held the bag up for his mother. "I got everything. Hi, Miss Erin!"

Erin smiled at him.

"Good," Mrs. Foster said. "Put it away in the kitchen, please?"

He nodded and did as he was asked. Erin thought she heard him rustling through the box of baked goods while he was in there, and he was definitely chewing something when he exited the kitchen.

"Miss Erin brought pizza shells. Can we have pizza for supper?"

"I suppose so. Do you and the girls want to make your own?"

Peter nodded his head vigorously. "And I get a whole one, not a half."

"Yes, you can have a whole one. The girls are too small to eat a full one, so I'll cut theirs in half and they can each put their own toppings on."

Peter nodded his agreement. He paused. "That will make an extra half, though."

"We can put it in the freezer for next time."

"I could eat the extra half," he offered.

"No. You could not."

Peter shrugged and rolled his eyes at Erin, giving her a roguish grin. He might not be a teenager yet, but he was clearly working on a teenage appetite.

"How have you been, Peter? Helping your mom lots with the younger kids?"

"I always do," he told her earnestly. "I'm a good big brother. I help with a lot of stuff, don't I, Mom?"

"Yes, you do. It's good to have you around here."

Peter sat gingerly down on the edge of a chair, looking as if he weren't sure whether he was allowed to join them. Maybe now that he was home, he was supposed to go outside to play with the girls.

"I saw the sign in the bakery window," Peter confided in Erin. "The one about people going there to get food if they don't have enough to eat? I think that's a really good idea."

"Do you? I'm glad." Erin glanced at Mrs. Foster to make sure it was okay to talk about it with Peter. She'd been criticized before for talking with him about things that she shouldn't and for getting him involved in criminal investigations. Not because she intentionally involved him in her mystery-solving, but because he was observant and she had picked up on things he'd said casually. She didn't want to end up in trouble again. "I don't like to think about people in our neighborhood going hungry."

"I don't think you need to worry about that," Mrs. Foster said. "There's a lunch program at the school, so parents don't even need to feed their children three times a day. We don't have unemployed bums around here who don't contribute. And I think anyone willing to put in an honest day's work can buy their family food."

"A lot of jobs don't pay a living wage, though," Erin said. "And if there is only one parent who can work and take care of the kids, how are they supposed to choose between putting money on the table or looking after their children?"

"We don't have those kinds of problems here. There are enough jobs to go around, even during these times. And if there aren't, you can go into the city and find something there. It's not such a terrible commute. You can still live in Bald Eagle Falls, where housing is cheaper."

Erin bit her lip. She didn't want to argue the point, but she knew it wasn't that simple.

"I've run into some families in pretty desperate situations the last few days," she explained. "Not everyone has cars or the money for gas to commute to the city and, even if they do, unemployment is worse there than it is here. And a mom with young children doesn't always have someone she can leave them with while she goes to work. Especially not if she's making minimum wage, which doesn't give her enough to raise a family on, let alone provide for babysitting."

Mrs. Foster raised her eyebrows. "Some people will use any excuse. Those of us who want to can find a way to make things work. It's never been easy for us, but we manage to get along."

Erin nodded. "That's good. I hate to see anyone on the skids."

Mrs. Foster wasn't sure what to say to that.

"I think it's sad when people don't have enough to eat," Peter said. "I saw some kids at the playground. They don't go to school. I don't know if they're too young or maybe homeschooled." He gave a shrug. "They were all real skinny, and their clothes were…" he searched for the right word. "I guess they were hand-me-downs."

"You're lucky to be the oldest, so you don't have to wear hand-me-downs," Mrs. Foster said. "But there's nothing wrong with it. It just makes economic sense when you have more than one child. Get things that the next one in line can wear. Or the next two or three." She laughed.

Peter nodded seriously. "But even the oldest one was wearing hand-me-downs. That's what it looked like."

"Maybe they were from a cousin or a friend. It's nice when families can help each other out."

"Like Miss Erin is doing with the food," Peter said triumphantly. "She is making sure that the people who are hungry can eat hand-me-down food."

Erin smiled. It sounded better than charity.

"I suppose," Mrs. Foster said grudgingly. "If you have leftovers anyway, you might as well use them instead of throwing them out."

"I always have to make more than I need," Erin explained. "I can't be out of food when people come to pick something up at the end of the day. It's okay if one or two things run out, but I always have to have bread and rolls, and some kind of dessert. So I always have something left over at the end of the day."

"You could just sell it the next day," Peter pointed out.

"I can, but I have to mark it as 'day old,' and not everybody wants to buy day old. And I have to mark it down, put it on sale. And if it's any more than that, I really can't keep putting it out for sale, because it will get dry and stale. Then Auntie Clem's would get a reputation for having stale bread, and people would stop coming."

He nodded thoughtfully. "I guess so. So it's good that you can give it to the poor people, like the kids I saw in the playground."

"That's what I'm hoping. I usually freeze as much as I can and then take it into the city, because they have shelters and soup kitchens there that will take it."

"But then what would the kids here eat?" Peter sounded affronted at the idea. "They can't go all the way into the city."

"You're right," Erin agreed. "They can't."

CHAPTER 30

That night, Erin and Terry ate at the Chinese restaurant with Vic and Willie. It felt a little too decadent to Erin after seeing the homeless people around Bald Eagle Falls and worrying whether they were getting enough to eat. The four of them would probably order enough for three families with young children.

She tried to push these thoughts to the side to enjoy her time with her Bald Eagle Falls family.

"So… how did things go when you went out to give the death notification to Mrs. Ryder?" Vic asked as they sipped their drinks and waited for the food to arrive. "Did you manage to find her?"

"I got her," Terry admitted after a moment, apparently deciding that it was not confidential information. Now that the police had notified the next of kin, the paper would be able to publish Rip's name and details. "Kudos to you guys for tracking her down. Even though… you know I would prefer you would leave the sleuthing to the police."

"Well, yeah." Vic shrugged. "But sometimes pure dumb luck overrules."

"I doubt if it was dumb luck," Willie said. "The two of you are pretty bright. It just so happened that you went about it in a different way than the police did."

That was a good way to praise the women without bashing the police for not finding the Ryders.

"I thought she was the woman here in town," Erin confessed. "But that was Adrienne."

"I wouldn't even have known that we had anyone homeless right in town," Vic said. "I wouldn't have thought it."

"I don't know if they actually live in town," Terry said. "They might have just stopped in for a day or two to pick things up or visit a relative."

"I don't think they were taking any pleasure trips," Erin countered, "They wouldn't be able to afford that. I don't know if she's married, she didn't say. But she has a new baby, so hopefully, that means she isn't trying to take care of her family all on her own."

"Then they're probably staying with family," Willie suggested. "Or they have an RV or van they park somewhere."

"Maybe," Erin agreed.

"You don't think so?" Terry asked, sensing her hesitance.

"It crossed my mind that they might be in the woods. Back behind the house."

"Really?" Terry's brows climbed his forehead.

The waitress arrived with their order, and everyone leaned back while she filled the table with the various dishes. They began to dish up.

"I would think that Adele would let us know if there was any trouble back there," Terry said. "It's her job as your groundskeeper to make sure that people aren't trespassing on your property."

Erin nodded. "Yes… but I just got the feeling… she knows more than she says. She always does. She keeps her own counsel. But I wondered the other night whether she knows that someone is camping out back there. And maybe she doesn't want to tell anyone."

"Why not? If someone is squatting on your property, you need to get them off. You don't want to be liable for anything that happens to them while they're living on your land. If one of the kids has an accident or eats poisonous berries… you don't want to have to deal with that."

"But it wouldn't be my fault."

"You want to get sued and find out?"

Erin frowned and ate her Chinese food slowly. While she didn't want to kick someone who was in need off of her property, she also didn't want to be held responsible for something just because it was done on her property. She tried to balance the two against each other.

"And there's adverse possession, too," Willie put in.

"What's adverse possession?"

"It means that if someone squats on your land, and you allow them to, then they can claim that the land has become theirs."

"They can claim a property just by squatting on it?"

"What do you think all of those people out there are trying to do? They can't afford to buy land, but if they can squat on it for long enough, they can take it over."

"So when you kicked Ryder off, is that why? Because you didn't want them to be able to take it over?"

"I don't like people crowding me or trying to jump my mineral claims. They can start pulling ore out of one of my mines long before they can claim adverse possession." Willie sliced the meat off of a chicken wing with sharp, decisive strokes of his knife. "And no one is taking ore out of my mines but me."

Everyone was quiet for a few minutes, eating their own meals and considering the conversation. Erin caught Terry looking at Willie, his eyes sharp and discerning. Erin was sure that he still considered Willie a suspect. He was happy to sit there listening to Willie talking about adverse possession and his mines, stacking up the motives that Willie had to get Ryder off of his property permanently.

He'd tried telling them to leave once and Ryder had come back. Even when Willie kicked them off again, they had only gone a couple of roads over when they set up camp again. Was it because they still wanted access to Willie's property?

"That cave... were there minerals there?" Erin asked.

"There are minerals in every cave. That's what caves are made from," Willie countered with a smile.

"I know. I mean... precious metals or diamonds or anything like that. Why was Rip interested in the cave? Is there something worth mining there?"

Erin thought back to the way the cave and the property had looked the day that she and Vic went out there. There was no sign that Willie had been mining, as far as she had seen. She hadn't gone inside the cave, but if Willie were taking minerals out of that mine, he had to move them, and Erin hadn't seen any tracks in the dirt. No wagon or cart or truck.

"That's not any of your business," Willie told her matter-of-factly.

Erin nodded her agreement.

CHAPTER 31

"We didn't really talk much about your day," Terry murmured to Erin as they cuddled that night, getting ready for sleep. "How did your visits go?"

"Good. I got in to see Mary Lou and Joshua. They're... coming along, I guess. I wish Josh was doing better, but I guess you can't expect him to recover right away from something so traumatic. Everyone keeps saying, 'kids bounce right back,' so I kind of expected him to be back to his old self again. But... I should know better. I've seen trauma and how it can affect people. Even kids."

Terry nodded, snuggling her close. "That makes sense. We like to think that a negative experience is just that, something that happened that we can just move on from. But it isn't always the case. It still changes us. Maybe a little, maybe a lot."

"Yeah. I want to give Josh a hug and tell him that it is all going to be okay. But he's not my kid. I can't do that. And... I don't know how he's going to be. How hard it is going to be to get over the hump. Some people... don't ever recover."

"Does Mary Lou have him in therapy? She really should."

"I don't know. She didn't bring it up and I would never ask."

"Well... keep an eye on him. You're right, sometimes it's too much for people. If that's the case for Josh, we need to make sure he gets the help he needs before he does something to harm himself."

"Yeah. That would really be terrible."

"It would." Terry rubbed Erin's back and shoulders. She turned a little to give him better access.

"Anyway. So that was Josh. And then there were the Fosters."

"A happier visit. How are they holding up with the new baby?"

"Everything seems to be good. Peter is helping out with the little kids as much as he can. She sent him to the store today to pick up some things for her, and he did a good job at that."

"You don't sound like you approve."

"I hope I didn't sound that way with her, but I think she could see that I was… uncomfortable with it. I guess… I'm just a bit paranoid about things like kidnapping. The things that could happen to him on the way over there. I know Bald Eagle Falls is a safe place, but… nowhere is completely free of bullies and pedophiles…"

"No. Unfortunately not. But walking to the store and back during the day… that should be pretty safe for him."

"As safe as anything," Erin said. She yawned and stretched, tensing and then relaxing all of her muscles. "Safe as houses."

"Just like you're safe here," Terry reminded her. He put his arms around her again, his breathing long and even.

"Yes." Erin closed her eyes. "So many babies this year. Are there always so many babies?"

"Who has babies?"

"The Fosters, the Ryders, Adrienne, that other family out there. Everybody has babies." She sighed. "Except us."

Terry took in a sharp breath. Then he seemed to be holding it, to have stopped breathing altogether. Erin pried her eyes open to look in his direction. She could see his face in the dark, but it was only a pale oval in the darkness. No features.

"What's wrong?"

"You just said that everybody has babies except us."

"Yeah."

"Are you… wanting a baby?"

"No. I don't think so. I don't know. I don't think I'm really mother material. I think all of those years in so many different homes kind of put me off of families. Kids can be such a bother, you know."

"Well… so they can. They can interfere with a lot of plans, tie you down, cause a lot of heartache. But people still choose to have them."

Erin turned over and snuggled into Terry's chest. "You don't have to worry. I'm not making any kind of decision."

"If you're thinking about having kids, I'd like to at least hear about it."

"Not really. Just when I see or hold someone else's baby, I always feel this sort of… tug. Just hormones, I guess. Biology. The drive to perpetuate the species. I start to wonder what it would be like. Think that maybe someday…"

Terry breathed in and out a few times, waiting. "Someday…?"

"Maybe. But not yet."

"Okay. Go to sleep now."

"I am." Erin closed her eyes again and drifted off.

She and Vic had talked off and on a few times over the next day about the various homeless families they had encountered so far, speculating on their plans, how they were going to survive, and if they needed help or would even take it if they did.

After getting home from the bakery, Erin decided that she needed to take the bull by the horns and find out where Adrienne's family was staying. Or at least to make sure that they weren't squatting in her woods.

Terry was working a shift with the police department, so Erin left a note on the kitchen table saying where she was going, and headed out the back, through the gate, into the trees.

It was easier for her to navigate now than it had been when she had first arrived and had explored the woods. It had seemed so vast then, and she didn't know one area of the woods from another. The intersecting footpaths or animal paths had all looked the same to her, as had the trees and other vegetation.

But she knew her way around now. She knew the shapes of the different trees, the clearings, the berry bushes, and the pathways that connected them all. She didn't need a map, she knew where everything was, and no longer got lost if she didn't keep an eye on the sun and the direction she was traveling. It only took her a few minutes to make her way to Adele's cottage. She didn't know for sure that Adele would be there, but she didn't usually head out on her ramblings until the sun started to go down, so there was a good chance she would still be at home or close to the cottage.

She heard a crow cawing overhead and looked up, trying to identify whether it was Skye. Maybe he was the early warning system that someone was approaching the house. When Erin reached the cottage, Adele opened the door.

"Erin, come in. What can I do for you?"

Erin entered but didn't sit down at the table. She looked around at the room, her eyes taking everything in. Were there more possessions there than there usually were? Fewer? Was anything out of place?

Adele followed Erin's gaze, and her lifted eyebrow gave her an amused appearance.

"Well? Can I get you something?"

"No. I'm sorry. I just wondered... The other day when you came by, we talked about people hanging around lately, about the homeless or indigent..."

"Yes...?"

"I wanted to check with you. They're not camped out here, are they? In these woods?"

"There's lots of space," Adele said, not answering the question.

"Yes, I know. And I really don't want to have to search it all myself. I know that everyone needs somewhere to live, but... I could be liable for anything that happens on my land."

"What is going to happen?"

"I don't know. I can't predict. Things go wrong. People have accidents. Hurt each other. I don't want something to happen that I'll be held responsible for."

Adele stared out one of the small windows, considering. Her non-answer had actually been a pretty big giveaway. Yes, of course they were camped out in Erin's woods. Like Erin, Adele did not want to have to kick them out. She wanted a way out of it.

"Do you really think anyone would hold you responsible?"

"I don't know. I guess they could sue me, and then the court would have to decide how much of it had been my fault. How much money I had to pay for what happened. I don't really want to have to pay anything. The bakery is stable financially right now, but if something were to happen and I had to pay thousands of dollars in reparations… I'd go under. Auntie Clem's would be gone. I don't know what I would do. I guess I would have to sell the house and this land."

Erin let Adele think that part out to its final conclusion. If Erin sold the land, then Adele would be out a home as well.

"Or look at what's happened to Willie. Someone gets killed on his claim, and he's the prime suspect."

"No one would hold you responsible just because a murder happened on your land."

"I've been a suspect before. I don't like the way it feels."

Adele snorted and nodded. "Have to agree with you on that one."

They were both silent for a while. Finally, Adele spoke. "I'll get them to move on."

"I'm sorry."

Adele nodded. "That's just the way life works. What is it the Christian scriptures say? He who has the most will get more, and he who has the least, it will be taken from him?" She sighed. "I have always thought that very unfair."

"Me too," Erin agreed.

CHAPTER 32

"*D*o you think I should talk to them?" Erin asked. "I could explain that it was my decision, not yours, and… I want to do more for them, but I don't know what. I've told everyone I can that they can come to the bakery for food; I need to get rid of day-old baking anyway. But they're all so proud. They say they take care of themselves."

Adele shrugged. "I don't know if it will make any difference whether you or I tell them. It is my job. And as far as finding them somewhere else to live, or feeding them your leftover bread, I can't help you there. I don't know the best way to help people trying to make it on their own. I guess… just offer and then step back. See what happens down the line."

Erin nodded. "I worry about the children especially. It's one thing for the parents to decide that they don't want any help and that they're going to live on land that isn't theirs, but the kids didn't choose that. They don't choose to go hungry and or live like vagrants."

"So, what should happen?" Adele asked gently. "Send them off to foster care to families who will take care of them properly?"

"No." Erin sighed. "I know there aren't any easy answers. I just want to take care of them."

"Like I said, you have a soft heart. That's not a bad thing, but it is uncomfortable. Like having a paper cut on your index finger. It's always brushing against something."

Erin nodded. It was an apt comparison. Would it be better not to have a soft heart, so that it wouldn't be as uncomfortable? She would have to be a different person altogether. She would no longer be herself.

"I think I'd like to talk to them. I want to... be able to explain and let them know that I'll help in other ways if I can. I just can't be worried about what might happen with them on my land."

Adele described to Erin where the family was staying. They were practically in Erin's back yard. Erin laughed ruefully and headed back toward home.

"Thanks, Adele. I appreciate it."

"I know I should have told them right away not to camp on your land. I should have told them it was private property and to leave."

"Maybe you have a soft heart too," Erin teased.

"Not a good thing for a groundskeeper. I need to be tough, not be swayed by every sob story."

"You shouldn't beat yourself up either. You haven't been swayed by every sob story. This is the first one, isn't it?"

Adele nodded. Erin wondered whether it were true. Had there been others that she hadn't known about? Maybe not squatters, but people that Adele had let stay overnight, or to have a quiet campfire together because they weren't bothering anyone? Or inviting her friends over for a midnight pagan ritual? Erin hadn't kept an eye on the property, trusting that Adele was doing her job and keeping everyone else off. Maybe Erin needed to be more aware of what was going on right under her nose.

In a few minutes, she was at the edge of Adrienne's camp. She had neglected to ask Adele if there were a Mr. Adrienne around. Or if she needed to be concerned about sneaking up on people who might be armed. She really should have at least weighed the risks and considered all of the facts before she decided to shoo them out.

For a moment, she considered just returning home and seeing whether Terry was back and could go along with her. Or going back to get Adele or telling her the next day to just go ahead and inform them herself, as Erin had chickened out.

But she didn't want to be a chicken about it. How hard was it to tell a woman that this was private property and she would have to find somewhere else to camp? There was a whole wilderness outside of Bald Eagle falls to choose from.

Erin took a deep breath to center and fortify herself. Then, she moved into the clearing where Adrienne and the children sat around an empty camp stove, warming their hands. The smell of hot dogs hung in the air. The children's eyes went to her immediately. A couple of the kids jumped up, ready to run for it. Adrienne shifted the baby in her sling and looked at Erin with tired, defeated eyes.

"I'm sorry," Erin said. She tried to swallow a lump in her throat.

"We have nowhere else to go tonight," Adrienne said. "It would take more than an hour to break camp, and then it will be dark, and the children should be in bed sleeping."

"In the morning, then," Erin said. "When everyone is up, you can get started... you should have time to find somewhere else."

"You make it sound so easy. You have no idea."

"I haven't had to do anything like that myself," Erin said. "I believe that it's going to be hard. So get a good night's sleep now, worry about it in the morning."

Adrienne wiped at her face with the back of her hand and Erin realized with horror that she was crying. Adrienne had seemed so hard when they had talked earlier that Erin hadn't expected this. She thought that Adrienne would just tough it out and not show Erin how she felt about it.

Or maybe that was planned. Perhaps she was hoping to break Erin down with her tears.

"Mama!" One of the children hurried over to her and threw his arms around her. "Why you crying? It's okay. Don't cry." He used a corner of the baby sling to wipe the tears away.

"I'm just tired," Adrienne told him. "You know how it is when you're so tired that every little thing makes you sad. I'll be fine. You guys need to start getting ready for bed."

"We don't hafta go?"

"Not now."

The little boy looked at Erin. "It's the nice cookie lady," he said. "She's nice."

"Yes. She's trying. Now hop to it. Where's your toothbrush?"

The little boy crawled into one of the tents. Erin noticed that it wasn't a zippered nylon tent, but heavier canvas with snaps. Maybe army surplus. Maybe a hundred years old. Erin hadn't ever seen one quite like it before.

"You heard me," Adrienne told the other children. "It's time to get ready for bed."

One of the girls took a child of indeterminate gender by the hand to take him into the tent and begin their bedtime routine. Another older girl sat there at first, looking across at her mother, not budging.

"You too, Hope," Adrienne said. "No staying up late tonight. You need lots of sleep to give you energy tomorrow."

"We don't have anywhere to go," Hope said seriously.

"We'll work something out."

Hope scratched at a fraying hole in the knee of her pants. She sucked her thin cheeks in, looking worried. "Aunt Ann would take little Jeffey and Samantha. She said she would."

Adrienne said nothing.

"And what about Bell? She said if I could help with chores, maybe I could stay there." Tears started to track down Hope's face. She wiped them away, but couldn't make them stop. "I don't want us to be split up."

Adrienne held out an arm toward her. Hope crawled around the cook-stove into her mother's arms. Adrienne gave her a hug and kissed the top of her head.

"We're not going to split everyone up. We'll figure something out."

"Ike had to go live with his grandma."

"I'm not going to send you to live with anyone else. Okay? You just relax. Get a good sleep tonight so you can help me in the morning. We need to break down the camp and get everything packed. I need help with that. You know how the little ones get underfoot."

Hope sniffled and nodded. "You aren't going to take them to Aunt Ann?"

"No."

"Like Ike?"

"No."

"He was sick, and they had to send him to his grandma to get better."

"That's right," Adrienne agreed. "But you're not sick, are you?"

"No. I'm as healthy as a horse." Hope puffed her chest out. "I never get sick."

"Then I need you right here with me to help me out."

"Okay."

"Now, go get ready." Adrienne looked over at the tent. They could hear giggling and bickering intertwining as the children got themselves and each other ready. "Tell the others to knock it off and get in the beds, or there's gonna be trouble when I get in there!"

Hope laughed and crawled into the tent, where she repeated the threat loudly. There was silence for a moment, then whispers, and, before long, they were all giggling and playing together again.

"Thank you for giving us the night," Adrienne said.

"I'm so sorry that I can't let you stay here."

"I know. I didn't think you would. But it would have been nice if it had worked. The kids could walk to school. It would be so nice to be so close to everything."

"What will you do?"

"Homeschool, like usual. Find somewhere farther out… where people won't be as likely to bother us."

"Out where the others are? Jenny and the other families?"

Adrienne shook her head. "No… maybe for a day or two until we sort something out. But I couldn't live out there. Not where…" She dropped her eyes and swallowed.

Erin understood. Not where Rip had been killed. It didn't feel safe to Adrienne. The others might have decided to overlook the tragedy, but she couldn't.

"We'll find somewhere else," Adrienne said.

"Do you have a husband? Someone to help you?"

"Sometimes," Adrienne said with a shrug. She didn't offer any more. Maybe, like Rip, her husband was not reliable, taking off to gamble or pursue other vices.

Or maybe he was gone looking for work. Or employed in a work camp hours away. Erin shouldn't judge someone she'd never even heard of by the same standards as someone as self-destructive as Rip Ryder.

CHAPTER 33

*A*t home, Erin didn't tell Terry about the family living in the woods or the fact that she had put them on notice that they had to leave. It was her property, and she wasn't required to report trespassers or squatters to the police. She had taken care of it on her own. Without Adele's or Terry's help. Although she felt terrible for having to do it, she was proud of herself for having the strength to just go ahead and do what she knew had to be done.

There was more to Erin Price than met the eye. She wasn't a shrinking violet. Wasn't just a baker or a business owner. She was the type of person who stepped up and did what needed to be done.

But she was glad it was done and out of the way and hoped that Adrienne would just quietly move her family out of the woods without Erin having to do anything more about it. She knew that squatters could be hard to get rid of. Sometimes a person had to get the police or courts involved to get them off of the property. She really hoped that Adrienne would not be like that.

Instead, when she and Terry sat down to relax and visit for a while before bed, she asked him about Jenny. She had inquired before, when they had been at the restaurant with Vic and Willie, but the conversation had not gone in the direction she had hoped.

"How was Jenny Ryder when you told her about her husband?" she asked. "I wonder if I should go out there again… see if there is anything I can help with. I feel bad, her being alone with a new baby and all of those kids. It can't be easy for her."

"I'm sure it isn't. But I'm not sure she would accept any help, even though your intentions are pure. People don't like it when you poke your nose into their business."

"I know. But how was she?"

Terry considered what he could tell her. "She was… not as emotional as I expected. But that doesn't mean anything. Everyone has their own way to deal with grief. Some people weep and wail, and others nod and go on as if you had told them what time it is. Neither one tells you how close they were or how they are really feeling."

Erin nodded. "And you don't know how they are going to act after you're gone… or after a few days when it starts to sink in."

"Exactly. Someone like Jenny Ryder, who has led such a hard life, will be used to dealing with opposition and not showing any sign of weakness. So I wouldn't expect her to bawl her eyes out in front of me. I would have expected more… but that doesn't mean anything."

"What is she going to do?"

"I couldn't tell you."

"How is she going to be able to manage? With those kids and a new baby and no breadwinner? What is she going to do?"

"I am not privy to her life plan. Maybe she has a business we don't know about. Knitting. Reading audiobooks. Writing web content. Just because she doesn't own land or a house, that doesn't mean that she's necessarily destitute. Some people like to live off the land. Not to put all of their hard-earned cash into real estate."

Erin hadn't thought about that. She was only assuming that they were poor because they were homeless and because the children looked skinny and were not well-dressed. But they could just as easily be burning off a lot of energy playing outside, and their clothes reflected that fact. Or Jenny didn't see the need to get expensive new clothing when they were living out in the sticks and just bought whatever she could get cheaply at a thrift store. Or she was given clothing by other members of the community.

"She could be like the millionaire rancher," Erin said. "He walks into a store in blue jeans, with manure on his boots, and everyone assumes he's just some kind of laborer. When he might own half the county and likes working with his hands."

"I doubt if Jenny is a millionaire rancher."

"But she could be anything."

"Yes, exactly."

"Do you think… what did she say to you about the remains? I assume if you're done gathering all of the evidence you need, she has to claim the remains if she wants to bury or cremate him."

"Or she can *not* claim them and leave it to the county to dispose of them."

"Is that what she's going to do?"

"She didn't say specifically. I told her she could contact the funeral home in town and they would help her with the arrangements and request his remains… but she didn't say if she was going to. Just thanked me. There really wasn't much for me to do. She didn't want to talk about Ryder or what might have happened."

"Not at all? She must have said something."

"I had my questions… but she wasn't too inclined to answer. I got only grudging answers as to how long it had been since she saw him last, where she thought he had gone, and so on."

"I gathered from what she and the others said that they figured he was off drinking or gambling. Or maybe off with another woman. They weren't terribly complimentary about him."

Terry nodded. "Yeah. I don't think she had an easy time with him. Some people say that a marriage certificate doesn't make a difference, but I think in a case like that… a marriage certificate would at least say he was committed to the relationship. And the lack of one showed that he wasn't."

Erin nodded. And what about her relationship with Terry? They hadn't ever talked about getting married, rarely even alluded to it. She knew that as far as the Baptist ladies were concerned, she was committing a sin by having a relationship with Terry without being married to him. She had been the temptress who had come into Bald Eagle Falls and led the most eligible bachelor into sin. While Terry was not a regular churchgoer, he was a Christian, and therefore a good catch for the young women in the church.

Where would their relationship go? Erin wasn't sure. But if she'd been entertaining the thought of having children with him, she thought she would want to be married first.

"Were all of Jenny's children Rip's? Or was she with somebody else before?"

Terry cleared his throat. "That didn't come up in the conversation. She wasn't very inclined to talk as it was. I think that if I was to start off with questions like that… I might not have gotten any answers to the rest of my questions."

Erin laughed. "I suppose asking a woman who her children were fathered by might not start you off on the best foot."

Terry took a drag from his beer, nodding slightly in agreement.

"She had… how many? Five? Including the baby?"

"I didn't ever get a really good count. They were running around and playing games. And who knows if all the children were even hers. I think the families there kind of watch whoever's kids happen to be over. They're camped close enough together that the kids can mix."

Erin got the inkling of an idea. She frowned, thinking about it for a moment, and then reached for her planner to start jotting down a list.

"Uh-oh," Terry intoned. "What is it now?"

"No, it's nothing. I was just thinking that before when I was trying to give them food, I said that I thought they didn't have enough to eat. That they were too poor to be able to look after themselves."

"Yes…?"

"What if I took over a care package, but it wasn't because they need food, but because they just lost their father and husband. Or almost-husband. People take each other food when they've lost someone. Casseroles, desserts, things for the funeral, food that they can just warm up so they don't have to think ahead or do any work in the beginning, when it is so hard and they might be entertaining guests."

"Ah. So you think you could take food over there and say it was for the funeral."

"Right. And people take food to mothers with new babies too. To cut down on the amount of work they need to do. And Jenny has both. She's lost Rip and she has a new baby. If anyone needs a lighter load, it's her."

"Maybe you've found your way around the pride thing."

"I hope so. And I was thinking—it was because of what you said—that if I can get a load of food to Jenny, that with the other kids coming and going, *they* can get enough to eat too. There will be too much for just the Ryders. If their community really does take care of each other, then they'll distribute the food around the rest of the families, so that everyone gets some, and no one is singled out as being more needy."

"So, what are you writing out?"

"Just… what I think I should take out with me."

"You're not just going to take all of your day old out with you?"

"Well… no. I have some in the freezer, plus whatever is left over tomorrow, but I might want a few extra little things too… just to make it a little easier. And maybe if I pick up a few things from the grocery store…"

"You'll end up crossing the line. From a thoughtful gift to making them feel like it is charity."

"Oh." Erin sighed. "Okay. I'll scale back. Not too much. Do you think… if I mention it to the ladies who come to the bakery, some of them might contribute too?"

Terry considered this, his fingernails scraping across his five o'clock shadow. "I don't think very many of the church ladies feel like the squatters are… part of the flock. But if you mention it to them… maybe make the assumption that they would behave in a properly Christian manner toward the needy whether they are members of the congregation or not… I think that the guilt would probably ensure that you got a few donations."

"Good." Erin nodded. Over the next couple of days, there should be a good number of the ladies coming in to stock up for Sunday dinner. Most of them liked to have soft white rolls to go with their roast beef dinner or whatever their traditional family meal was on Sunday. She could go out to see Jenny after the ladies' tea on Sunday, assured of having a good amount of food for her and the other families in the settlement.

"Don't forget about refrigeration," Terry warned. "If you overdo it on the casseroles, they are just going to spoil. Those families don't have refrigeration."

"Oh. Okay. Yeah. I wouldn't have thought about that. I'll encourage the ladies to donate foods that are shelf-stable, if they can."

"Cream of mushroom soup will be better for the squatters in the can than in a casserole."

"Right. And it's less work for the church ladies." Erin smiled. "Win-win."

∼

Erin managed to work the homeless families into casual conversations with her customers over the next couple of days. It was fairly easy to bring them up, with the shocking news of Rip's death. It was still at the top of people's minds, and all Erin had to do was talk sadly about the family Rip had left behind. His destitute widow and fatherless children, including a newborn. So sad, and she hoped that a lot of people would help out, showing a lost sheep that they cared.

"How many children are there?" Lottie Sturm demanded. "We should get their names and ages to put on the prayer list."

"Oh... yes. I can find out," Erin agreed. "I guess... when I'm out there...?"

"We should know before you go out," Lottie disagreed. "We should be praying that the spirit will move them when they receive our gifts. That their hearts will be softened and open to the promptings of the Holy Spirit so that they recommit their lives to him."

Erin swallowed. She nodded her agreement. "Sure. Of course. But, um... how am I going to find that out before I go out to see them? They don't have a phone, I can't reach them that way."

"Talk to the school. You explain what it's for, and they'll give you the names and ages of the children."

"I don't think they go to the school. They're outside the city, and I think they probably homeschool. It would be too far for them to drive in every day."

"Well then, you can still go to the school for their records."

"If they homeschool..."

"They have to register with the school district," Lottie said with a firm nod. "That's the law. If they don't, they risk getting in trouble for the kids being truant. They don't want trouble with the police and the school district."

"Oh. I didn't know they did that. Okay. Do I just... you think the office would give me that kind of information? Isn't it confidential?"

"Not if you ask the right way," Lottie assured her confidently. "You're not asking for anything confidential—just first names and ages. You don't need last names, or marks, or what grades they are registered for, or birth-dates, or any of that kind of thing. Just first name and age. Everybody in the community already knows that information, so it can't be confidential. They're just making things easier so that you don't have to go to all of the other families and say, 'Are any of your kids the same age as any of the Ryder kids? And what are their names?' They're just collating the information for you. That's all."

Erin laughed. She had a feeling that the school might see it differently, but she could at least try. If the school couldn't help, then maybe she could talk to the Fosters and to Adrienne. Between the two families, they would probably know the names of all of the Ryder children.

CHAPTER 34

*A*s it turned out, dealing with the school was easier than she had expected. Instead of going into the office, she called up Vice Principal Fitzroy, whom she had coordinated the bake sale with. He had been perfectly happy to help. After alternately cursing and cajoling the computer for a few minutes, he had managed to make it give him first Jenny's full name, and then those of each of her children's.

"They're not all school age yet," he told Erin. "But the district registers them with early childhood learning in situations like this, so that they can evaluate whether any interventions are needed and we know who is coming up before they are in first grade. It's important with families like this who are..." he dropped his voice confidentially, "indigent. Less likely to be seeing doctors or public health nurses. If you have a child in need of early language intervention, and you don't find out about them until they are six, well that just won't do. It's *early* language intervention. And it isn't so early if you wait until they are six or seven."

Erin made noises of agreement. She was afraid that if she asked anything, Vice Principal Fitzroy would tell her all of the family's confidential issues, and she didn't want to know them.

"So the oldest child's name was..." she prompted, hoping to get him back on track.

Fitzroy read off the name of the oldest child, age eight, and went down the line to the two-year-old. Erin wrote each of them down.

"And then she has a newborn," she added. "I don't know his name."

"Oh, does she have another one?" Fitzroy asked. "We'll need to get his details. I don't suppose you could do me a return favor…?"

"I'll do my best," Erin promised. "Thank you for everything."

Terry offered to go out to see Jenny again with Erin, but she knew that Jenny probably would not take too kindly to her bringing a policeman with her. Terry had done the death notification, so it wasn't like she wouldn't know that he was on the police force.

Instead, she went with Vic in Willie's truck, like they had done the previous time. It was quicker this time, since they knew where Jenny was. At least, Erin hoped that she had stayed in the place and had not run away or gone deeper into the woods with her children. Erin found herself holding her breath as they went down the last road, straining for a view of the children and the tents. When they came into view, she nearly cheered aloud. She let out her breath.

"Good, then. That's good. She's still here."

Vic nodded her agreement. The children stopped playing to watch the truck pull in, and then went back to their games. They had seen this truck and these women before. It wasn't novel enough to end their game.

Jenny was lying on a blanket on the grass with her sleeping baby snuggled up to her, the dappled shadows from the trees overhead swaying back and forth over the baby's bare skin.

Wasn't it bad for him to have sunlight directly on his delicate skin? The UV rays couldn't be good for him. It wasn't direct summer sun, but still… Erin would have thought that you had to be more careful with a baby. Keep him wrapped up to protect his skin.

Jenny opened her eyes and watched them approach, but did not get up or invite them to come any closer.

"Hi," Erin greeted cheerfully. "I don't know if you remember us. We were here the other day and…"

"Of course I remember you," Jenny growled. "I don't get a lot of women coming in from town to harass me."

Erin got closer. She didn't like towering over Jenny, so she set down her bulky box and sat down on the ground close by, watching Jenny and the baby. "We're not trying to harass you. We just want you to... be a part of our community."

"Well, I'm not, am I?" Jenny challenged.

"You are. A bunch of the ladies have sent you some supplies. Because of your—Rip dying, and you having a new baby. One of those things that they do to help out members of the community going through life's challenges. I'm sure you know how these ladies are always making casseroles and desserts when there is a funeral or a new baby born. They know how hard it can be to have to cook on top of everything else."

Erin looked at Vic, hoping for some help, but Vic just nodded that she was doing fine and didn't contribute anything.

Jenny looked at Erin suspiciously. "The church ladies sent casseroles," she said. "Because of Rip dying? They hated Rip."

"I don't think they knew Rip well enough to hate him. Besides, that wouldn't be very Christian." Erin delved into the box and pulled out a can of soup. "I told them that I didn't think you had any way to refrigerate or freeze casseroles, so they should send foods that were easy to prepare and eat that didn't have to be refrigerated."

Jenny's eyes went wide, and the children stopped playing, instantly aware of the food.

"There are a few things in here that will have to be eaten pretty quickly," Erin admitted. "Not everything is shelf-stable. But you can eat those things first..."

"Sometimes we put things in a cold stream to help keep them chilled," Jenny offered. "I mean... not casseroles, but fruit and vegetables... drinks..."

"What a great idea. I would never have thought of that." There were probably a lot of things that Erin wouldn't have thought about. Not until she was actually out in the wilds and had to think up things that would help her to survive.

Jenny nodded slowly. She propped herself up on one elbow. The baby stirred and made little mewling sounds, then settled again and was quiet. Erin gazed at him.

"What's his name?"

"Little Ike. After his granddaddy."

Ike seemed like a strange name for a baby. But they would probably call him by some nickname until he got older. Peanut. Boo. Junior. He'd grow into his own name eventually. The baby was tiny. Erin could hardly believe that he was big enough to be out of the hospital, but she knew that he had to be a couple of weeks old.

"What day was he born?"

Jenny's brows drew down, and a V wrinkle appeared between them.

"How much did he weigh?" Erin went on, trying to demonstrate that she was just asking all of the normal questions that someone would ask about a new baby, not being nosy.

Jenny stroked the top of his downy head with one finger. "The third," she said finally. "And… we didn't weigh him right away. I don't have a scale out here. But we took him to the doctor last week, and they said he was five pounds."

"So he's really small. Was he early?"

The other woman was still frowning at Erin, not liking all of the questions. "Maybe a little. I usually have small ones. Thank goodness," she rolled her eyes, "I don't know how I'd manage to squeeze a bigger one out!"

Erin laughed. "I've heard people say that bigger ones are easier, but I don't know how that could be true."

Jenny put her hand over her lower pelvis. "Ouch. No, I think that's just a story."

"You didn't have him at the hospital, then?" Vic asked. "Just by yourself? Did you have a midwife?"

Erin looked again over the little camp. Had Jenny had the baby out there? In a dusty tent, with no doctor around? What if something had gone wrong? What if she had been in trouble or the baby had not been breathing when he was born?

"I had a friend," Jenny said cautiously. "Women have been taking care of other women having babies for centuries. There's nothing wrong with that."

"That must have been scary," Erin suggested.

"He's not my first baby. Maybe for my first one, I'd want a midwife or to be close to a doctor, but I've had a few before." Jenny looked around at her other children, who had resumed playing.

"I suppose."

Jenny shifted the baby, snuggling him up against her body. "He had a bit of jaundice. They get yellow, you know. The ones that are little are more likely to get it. In the hospital, they put them under special lamps. But the sun is just as good. The doctor said that was just fine, as long as he's not in direct sun for too long. Just getting lots of sunlight on his skin helps break down the yellow stuff."

So it wasn't bad for him to be lying there with the sunlight filtering through the trees onto his bare skin. It was actually good for him. Erin felt a little guilty for assuming that it was bad and that Jenny didn't know how to take care of him properly. She had lots of kids. Lots more experience than Erin did. Of course she knew what she was doing.

Erin studied Jenny's face. She looked tired. What did Erin expect? Jenny had too many responsibilities, all of those children, a newborn, and her husband had just been murdered. Anybody would have been gutted by such an experience.

She tried to identify what else she saw there. Jenny's expression was guarded, not liking these women who came to her home expecting her to answer questions and receive their gifts graciously. They should leave soon, let her rest as much as she could.

But there was more than that. She also looked… haunted. Erin didn't know how else to classify the emotion that lay underneath everything else. Like she had seen too much and wanted to be finished. Maybe it was depression? Postpartum? That could be devastating to someone with as many responsibilities as Jenny.

"Do you have someone to help you out?" she asked. "Maybe someone who could take the kids for a little while to give you a break."

"Who would take all of these?" Jenny scoffed, nodding toward them. "Besides, they help me out. The older ones."

"But maybe someone could take a couple of the little ones for a few days. Or a few families could help…"

"Farming them all out to different homes? They belong here, not anywhere else."

"I didn't mean permanently. Just for a little while, until you have things sorted out."

Jenny lay her head down on the blanket again. "I want my kids close to me. You don't know what it's like…"

She had just lost her husband. Of course she wanted her children to be with her, not taken away. They were a comfort to her. They were the only ones who understood what it was like for her to lose Rip.

One of the small children approached them. She stood on her tiptoes to look down into the box without getting too close to Erin. "Can I put the food away, Mama?"

"Yes. Go ahead. If you don't know where something goes, just leave it in the box."

"Is there food goes in the stream?"

"I don't know what's in there. Stay away from the stream right now."

She nodded and got closer. Grasping the edge of the box, she pulled it, sliding it away from Erin toward the tents. It took a lot of hard work for her to pull it over the bumpy ground to the kitchen tent, but she persisted and got it there. When a couple of the other children approached to see what was in the box, she chased them away.

"Selena is a good little mama," Jenny said distantly. "She's always so good with the others."

"She must be a real help to you."

Erin watched Selena pull items out of the box and stack them onto various shelves or corners in the kitchen. She placed the perishables on the table.

"We should be getting on our way and letting you rest. Will you please let me know if you need anything? The church ladies have added you and the children to their prayers lists. I don't know if you are religious or that means anything to you. But I'll give you my number, in case you need something."

"Really?" Jenny raised her brows. "That's nice of them. I never thought those ladies would care anything about us. Not the way they turn up their noses at my kids. We don't need anything," she shook her head, "so you don't need to come out here again."

Erin pushed herself to her feet. "Okay." She had done all she could. "You take care, then."

CHAPTER 35

"*Y*ou've done everything you can," Vic commiserated when they were on the highway again.

Erin let out a long sigh. "I know. I can't think of anything else I could do. I want to help them all out... but what else am I supposed to do?"

"Nothing. You've done everything. You've gone above and beyond."

"Those kids. They deserve better. And Jenny..." Erin shook her head. "She looks so sad. This should be a happy time in her life, just bringing a new baby into the world. But look at what she is facing. Husband murdered. No home. Living out in the middle of nowhere. Six other kids."

"She looked so tired and sad," Vic agreed.

"I just want to hug her. To take all of the kids out for ice cream. To make it all right again. But it's not. Who knows how long it will take for things to turn around for them. If ever."

"I know."

They drove on for a while.

"You know, if you really think that those kids are in danger, or not getting enough to eat, you should call social services," Vic said.

Erin's heart pounded painfully. She couldn't do that to Jenny and her children. Erin knew what it was to be stuck in the system. She wouldn't do that to all of those kids. Unless...

"I don't want to do that. I don't think it's to that level yet... I don't think..."

"Then... you'll just have to let it go. You've done everything else that you could. If you think that Jenny can't take care of the kids, then you need to make a report. But if you think she's doing okay, you'll just have to let her do it her own way."

"There should be lots of berry bushes around there. And other wild foods. There's fresh water. Fish. Birds. Rabbits. Even if Jenny doesn't hunt, they keep saying that the families care for each other, that the community will step up. So they'll all help her when our food runs out."

"There won't be berries for a couple more months," Vic said. "But the rest of that... yeah. Maybe Willie and I will take a couple of hunting weekends and drop some game off for them."

"If they would take it."

"They will if they're hungry enough."

They covered a few more miles before Erin spoke again, so frustrated, her heart feeling like it was being wrung like a wet sponge. "What if one of those kids gets hurt or sick? What are they going to do?"

"Drive them into the city. Go to the hospital there. The same as if a child in Bald Eagle Falls got really sick."

"But they don't even have phones. Or computers to look up symptoms to decide if it is something serious or not. They can't do anything. And what if Jenny is hurt? She injures herself chopping wood or picking up the baby, or scalds herself making breakfast. Who is going to help if she's too badly injured to drive herself?"

"We can't make those decisions for her, Erin. She has to think about it herself, figure out what risks are reasonable. I don't know what else to say. It's true of anyone in town, too. We can't control what people are doing in their own houses. Whether they are cutting something the wrong way, or pouring lighter fluid on a fire, or stepping out into Main Street without making sure there isn't any traffic first."

"Step in front of Beaver, and that could be the end of it," Erin muttered. She laughed bleakly, but there was no joy in it. She didn't snap herself out of her funk with the joke.

"Yes. There's danger everywhere, and we can't do anything about the people who decide to take risks that we wouldn't take. Jenny might think that you're taking stupid risks by living in town, where there are people living practically on top of you. Working in the heat every day. Getting up before the sun just to bake bread for people. Even just making gluten-free products when only a tiny percentage of your customers have celiac disease. She'd think you were stupid, risking your business for such a small segment."

"She'd be wrong."

"Yes. She would. You're running a profitable business and providing an important service. That was the right choice for you."

Erin nodded. "I guess everybody makes different life decisions. But mine don't affect any children. I don't have to worry about whether my kids can eat based on my choice of gluten-free or regular bread. When it's your kids, you have a bigger responsibility. You're not just choosing what you prefer."

"I agree. I'm just saying you can't take it to heart. There's nothing you can do, and she's allowed to make her own choices. If it's not endangering the children, maybe it's time to just let it go."

"Okay. I will."

~

Erin was not prepared to have Lottie Sturm show up on her front steps. She found the woman difficult enough to deal with when she came to buy bread at the bakery. She was constantly complaining and correcting other people. If Erin was not around or paying attention, she would start preaching at Vic or railing about the evil choices of modern-day youth. She had been warned more than once to mind herself while she was there, but if she thought she could get away with something, she would.

Erin opened the door and didn't know what to say to Lottie. She forced a smile and nodded at her, waiting for her to state her business.

"We've been praying over those poor Ryder children," Lottie explained, fluttering the paper that Erin had given her at the ladies' tea that morning. Had she been praying ever since then? And who was 'we'? Erin knew that Lottie was good friends with Cindy Prost, who was Bella's mother and another difficult-to-manage customer. Were she and Lottie praying together? Or was it a whole covey of the Baptist ladies? It had been a long day, and Erin was sure their knees must be tired and their mouths dry if they had been praying all that time.

"That's so kind of you," Erin said. "I saw Jenny this afternoon, and I told her that you were. She seemed… it seemed like it meant something to her."

"It should," Lottie agreed in a firm voice. "I came by to find out if you had any information on the baby? I understood that you were going to get its name and birthday as well."

Erin nodded. "Yes. Of course. It's a boy. Ike. And he was born on the third."

Lottie fished in her purse for a pen. Erin knew she should invite Lottie in to make it easier for her to juggle things, but she didn't want to have to entertain the woman any longer than was absolutely necessary. She waited while Lottie got the pen out and then lay the paper flat against the door to write the information. She frowned and shook her head.

"No, I've already got an Ike, age five."

"Well… that's what she said. Maybe the school got something wrong."

"You wouldn't have two Ikes in the same family."

Erin had been in foster families where there were two children with the same name. But that was foster care, not a family naming two of their children the same thing.

"Well… it does happen sometimes. People give their children the same name, but they go by a second name or a nickname. Like… George Foreman and Michael Jackson."

Lottie rolled her eyes and shook her head. Erin didn't want to hear her rantings about the people Erin had picked as examples. "Maybe they're both named after a grandfather, or it's a family name. Vice Principal Fitzroy wouldn't necessarily know if the boy who went to school went by… I don't know, Charles instead of Ike. He just gave me the first names of the kids that showed up on his records. That's different than actually knowing the kids and what their preferences were."

"I suppose that's it," Lottie said. She wrote the information down with a scowl. "I don't know how we're supposed to pray for two separate children with the same name. We have to have some way of differentiating them."

"You could say 'Ike who is six and Ike who is a baby,'" Erin suggested. "But isn't your God all-knowing? So he would know even if you called them both by the same name. He wouldn't even need names."

"You need their names," Lottie argued. "That's how you do a prayer list. You have to have names."

Erin shrugged and shook her head. "Well, now you have the names."

Lottie muttered something under her breath and turned away. Erin waited until Lottie was at the bottom of the steps and quietly closed the door behind her. She let out a whistle and didn't know how else to react. Laugh at Lottie? Call Vic and tell her about the conversation? She felt silly and giddy and knew that she had probably been up for too long and needed to go to bed.

"Holy cow," she said aloud to herself. "I do declare!" She giggled at herself.

⁓

Erin was restless knowing that Terry was on night shift. He had been doing mostly afternoons since he had gotten back from his leave, which was good for all of them. She didn't worry much about that. Because of his brain injury and insomnia, the sheriff had promised not to put him on nights. But Terry had since recovered from his constant headaches and insomnia. The sheriff had decided it was time to put him back into the rotation. The others had had to cover all of the night shifts, and Terry said it was time for him to start pulling his weight again.

He'd been doing really well, but she couldn't help worrying that it could set him back again. The doctors had said that he needed to get a good night's sleep if he were going to recover fully. They called for good sleep hygiene habits, which Erin knew meant going to bed and getting up at the same time every day. Not working various different shifts that meant that he had to sleep during the day sometimes and the night others.

Because of their schedules, Terry was just getting home as Erin and Vic were having their morning tea. After kissing him good morning, Erin gestured to the kettle. "Did you want some?"

"No, I'll make my own beverage, thanks." Terry went to the fridge and pulled out a beer. He said that one beer before bed helped him sleep better than any of the other sleep aids the doctors had prescribed. And it wasn't like he was getting drunk. He was very good about keeping it to one drink. Doctors said that was healthy. Erin's experiences with men who did drink too much colored her perception. She tried to remain nonjudgmental and not to let it make her anxious. She knew that Terry was not a drunk and rarely ever had more than one drink in a day.

She smiled at him and turned back to Vic, relating to her the visit from Lottie. Vic nodded, grinning.

"You never know what people are going to name their kids in backwoods Tennessee. I've seen families where all of the brothers and first cousins have the same given name." She giggled. "They're all named after granddaddy and great-granddaddy, of course. So they all have different nicknames, and you have Big Ike and Little Ike and Slim Ike and Red Ike…"

Erin shook her head. "Lottie acted like I must have gotten it wrong. But I wrote everything down right there when Vice Principal Fitzroy was giving it to me, and you heard Jenny say that the baby's name was Ike, right?"

"I did."

Something tickled at the back of Erin's brain. She considered, trying to nail down what it was.

"What?" Vic prompted.

"No, I'm just… trying to remember… something…"

"Don't try too hard, I can see the smoke coming out of your ears…" Vic teased.

"You do not! It's just that I've heard the name Ike before."

"I'm sure you have."

"No. Recently. Just the last few days."

She tried to run through the various different scenarios. One of Jenny's children had mentioned Ike before; she must have been talking about Big Ike. Or was it someone else?

"Oh, no. It wasn't," Erin corrected herself aloud. "It was Adrienne's daughter."

"Adrienne's daughter is named Ike too?"

"What did Willie put in your cornflakes this morning? You're in a silly mood!"

"I don't know. Just trying to keep things light, I guess. I don't want to be sad and solemn all day. Yesterday was too serious."

"Yeah. It was." Erin wanted to move on too. She looked at her watch. "Well, we'd better get going. I guess I'll see you later," she told Terry. "Have a good sleep."

"I will," he agreed. He gave her another kiss, and she and Vic headed out.

CHAPTER 36

*E*rin continued to puzzle over what she only half-remembered from the visit to Adrienne. She talked it through with Vic in the afternoon lull.

"I'm sure it was Adrienne's little girl that talked about Ike. Something about... Ike had to go with Grandma, something like that."

"So it must be like I said. A bunch of the first cousins are all named after Grandpa Ike."

"Then Adrienne and Jenny must be related." Erin frowned, thinking it through. "Adrienne never said that she was related to Jenny. But if their kids were first cousins, then wouldn't that mean..."

"That Adrienne and Jenny were sisters. Or maybe sisters-in-law."

"They're both blond and slim," Erin said slowly. "But they really don't look like each other."

"Sister don't always look similar. Or like I said, they could be in-laws. Or it could be Great-Grandpa Ike, and Adrienne and Jenny are cousins. Or even further back than that. Sometimes these names get recycled over and over again with every generation."

"Maybe I should talk to Adrienne again. She was a lot easier to talk to than Jenny. Not that either one was easy, but Adrienne was grateful to me for letting her stay on the property for the night, so maybe she'd be more likely to talk to me again. I don't think Jenny is going to."

"But why talk to either of them again? They're living their own lives and it really isn't anything to do with you. Why keep bothering them?"

"I just… want to know." Erin didn't want to put into words what she was thinking, not even to herself. She wanted Adrienne to agree with Vic's suggestion. It would give a nice clear answer to the problem with the names. That would make Erin feel better and then she would be able to go on without worrying any more about it.

"Well… we'll go look for her after work, then," Vic agreed. "Do you know where she moved to? Or if she moved like you asked her to?"

"I didn't check… but I haven't smelled their cooking again, so I don't think they're close by."

"Or maybe they just moved downwind."

"Well… I guess. But Adele knows that I told them to move on, so she wouldn't let them camp on the property again."

"Unless she did."

Erin rolled her eyes. Adele had allowed them to stay there to start with, even though she knew it was her job to make sure that no one trespassed on Erin's private land. It was a possibility.

"I don't think she's still there. I bet she moved back out of town, over where the others are staying. Somewhere close to them, anyway, where they won't be bothered."

"Well, we'll go check," Vic promised.

They closed up as quickly as they could without unbalancing the schedule for the next morning. Some of the batters that they normally mixed the night before and left soaking overnight could be made the next day without too much change in texture. And Erin could hold over a few muffins and loaves from the day before to let the batters soak longer, and make them a little later in the day than usual. Just so they could get out a bit early to go talk to Adrienne. She might be close by, or she might have moved back toward where Jenny and the others were.

Erin went into the house to drop off a couple of things, startling Terry.

"You're home early!" He held his hand over his chest, eyes wide, and laughed at himself.

"Just a few minutes," Erin admitted. "I'm just going to put these things down. Vic and I are going to take Nilla out for a walk."

Terry looked at her, eyes narrowed. Erin kept her face blank. They *were* going to take Nilla out. It wasn't a lie.

Terry nodded. "Sounds good. That will probably be good for him. Work off some of that extra energy."

"Yeah. He hasn't exactly settled down as much as Vic would like!"

"It's a crime that dog was not properly trained while he was a puppy. I realize that there's a big difference between terriers and shepherds," Terry looked at K9, "but a dog has so much more potential when it is properly trained. You add to and encourage its natural abilities. That little dog could be an asset if he was trained, instead of a little whirlwind of destruction whenever there's no one looking after him."

Erin nodded her agreement.

"But Vic's doing her best, and the dog training people said that it's still possible to properly train an older dog. It just takes longer and is more of a challenge."

"Well, I hope it starts paying off soon. Vic shouldn't have her property torn apart just because she did a nice thing and rescued a dog without an owner."

"Yeah." Erin inched toward the back door. She wanted to make use of as much of the daylight as they could.

"And you don't want it destroying the value of that apartment or the yard. Vic won't be here forever and if you want to rent it to someone else after her, you don't want to have to strip the whole thing out and start over."

"She's not leaving any time soon…"

"Maybe not. But you can never be sure. She won't necessarily tell you if she and Willie start looking at a bigger place. Or decide that Vic should move into Willie's house."

Erin frowned. Vic was out in the back yard with Nilla, waiting for Erin. Erin didn't want to think of her ever leaving the loft apartment. It would be so strange living in Bald Eagle Falls without Vic close at hand, coming into the kitchen in the morning, the two of them going into work together…

"I didn't say she was leaving," Terry said apologetically. "Just that you don't know when it could happen."

"You're right. I've got to go. Back in a bit."

CHAPTER 37

*N*illa was excited about being outside and being allowed to go into the woods, which were usually off limits. He didn't seem to understand the constraints of the leash and kept getting himself tangled around tree trunks and in the underbrush. Erin was frustrated at their slow progress. It was going to take forever to search anything but the areas closest to the house with him charging around like a Tasmanian devil.

"I'm just going to run ahead and see if she's still at the same site as she was earlier," she told Vic.

If Adrienne had moved farther away but was still in Erin's woods, it would take time to locate her, and Erin wasn't willing to wait for the crazy little powderpuff.

"Okay. Sorry about this. We'll catch up as soon as I can get him untangled. I guess the woods were not such a great idea when he still hasn't gotten the idea of heeling."

"Yeah, it's okay, I just want to check."

Erin picked up her pace and hurried toward the corner Adrienne had been camped in before. Erin had soon left Vic behind and was on her own. She felt a little anxious and uncertain, but she knew the woods and there was no danger. Adele patrolled it for any unsavory characters. Any wild animals would be more afraid of Erin than she was of them. At least, that was what Terry said. Mostly, the big predators didn't come right into the town.

She looked around quickly and kept moving. Keep moving and making noise, and they would run away before she even saw them. Animals were afraid of humans.

Except when they weren't.

As she used the game trails and looked for the place Adrienne had camped, she couldn't help thinking of the squatters' children playing in the trees right out there in the wilds. A predator might never consider taking a grown adult, but a child, small and light, was easy to drag off... what if something was hungry, or wasn't spooked by the sounds of the children playing? What if it went closer for a look, and saw the young prey scampering around completely unprotected? Even worse, what if the children were back and forth between the camps, through the woods on their own, so that no adult knew which children were where? It could be hours before someone realized that a child was missing. Especially if they didn't have phones to connect with each other.

Erin was spooking herself. By the time she reached Adrienne's abandoned campsite, she was jumping at every branch blowing in the wind and the noises of squirrels or rabbits in the bush. She turned a circle, looking around the clearing and waiting for her heart to settle back into a normal rhythm.

"Adrienne? Are you here?" It was obvious that she wasn't, but Erin still wanted to make sure. Willie had said that Ryder, even when told to move on, had only moved a short distance away, believing that he was no longer on Willie's property. Adrienne might have moved her camp and assumed that Erin would not look any farther than the clearing.

Erin looked at her watch. It wasn't getting dark yet, but it was getting closer to sunset, and she knew they would lose the daylight quickly. She hadn't brought her big flashlight with her and had not planned to search in the darkness.

She called a few more times, circled around the outside of the clearing looking for any sign that the little family had just dragged their gear to the next likely spot. But she couldn't see any indication of what direction they had gone.

Vic caught up to her, panting a little and keeping Nilla on a very short leash to keep him from getting tangled again. "No Adrienne?"

"No. I don't see her around here. She must have gone out to where the others are." Erin sighed. "Do you think we could go out there tonight? It's going to be getting dark by the time we get out there."

Vic studied her. "It's not that urgent."

"I know." But to Erin, it was. "But do you think we could anyway? Otherwise, we have to wait until tomorrow, and she could have moved farther away. It's possible that she's already gone."

"And it's just as possible that she's staying with the rest of the families out there. Especially if they are all related. If Jenny is her sister, she's not going to be so quick to take off. They could help each other out trading off babysitting so that they can get work or errands done. And to keep the kids close."

Erin nodded. But she worried there were reasons for Adrienne or Jenny, or both of them, to run away and get out of Tennessee, or at least far away from Bald Eagle Falls. Vic shrugged.

"If you want. Sure. We'd better move it, because like you say, it's going to be dark soon. Not only that, but we're going to want to get some sleep tonight."

Erin breathed a sigh of relief. She supposed she could have gone out there by herself, but she was much happier if Vic went with her.

They retreated to the house as quickly as they could. Nilla started prancing excitedly around the truck, and Vic laughed. "I guess someone likes going for a ride." She opened the driver's side door, and Nilla leaped up into the seat like a cat. Erin wouldn't have guessed that he would be able to jump so high.

"I'll just let Terry know that we're going out."

Vic raised her eyebrows. She had a pretty good idea that Terry was going to ask questions about the necessity for the sudden trip out looking for the family.

Erin went into the house through the back door and retrieved her purse from under a sleepy orange cat. "Vic and I are going to run some errands. Won't be too long."

"Where are you going?" Terry called from the bedroom.

Erin ignored the question and hurried back out. Vic was in the driver's seat, tapping on her phone, and looked surprised to see Erin.

"That was quick."

"Just needed my purse. I don't want to... waste any time."

"Okay. Off we go."

They avoided further discussion about why Erin felt such a burning need to go talk to Adrienne. Erin didn't want to explain what she was thinking, in case speaking it made it true. She knew it was magical thinking and not logical, but she still found herself irrationally superstitious sometimes. She just wanted to be proven wrong. Then no one would know how close she had come to believing the worst of someone.

"Which property do you want to go to first?"

"I guess... Willie's. He hasn't been out there the last day or two, right? So he wouldn't know if she was camped there. We know they've used it before."

"I wouldn't think they'd want to camp there when someone has been kicked off already. And since... Rip died there. People tend not to want to hang around places where relatives died."

"It's the closest property, so we might as well check it out first."

Vic couldn't argue with that. So they went to the property the Ryders had previously camped on.

The clearing that Jenny had used was not occupied but, in looking around, Erin saw that there was a small group of tents on the other side of the fence. She recognized the army surplus tent.

Erin and Vic got out of the truck. Nilla raced around crazily, yipping and running in fast loops.

"That dog is possessed," Erin laughed.

"Just happy not to be cooped up in an apartment," Vic said.

With the noise the dog was making, Adrienne couldn't very well be unaware of their arrival. She walked around from the back of one of the tents with a pot in her hand. She looked from Erin to Vic, angry.

"We're not on your claim. You can't kick us off."

"Whoever owns this land could," Vic pointed out reasonably.

"Nobody owns this land. No one cares that we are here."

Vic shrugged. "Maybe not. We're not here to kick you out anyway." She tilted her head toward Erin. "We just wanted to talk to you."

"Talk to me? Fine, go ahead. Talk to me."

Erin cleared her throat. It was awkward to begin. She hadn't planned on the meeting being so confrontational. She thought she and Adrienne understood each other. Adrienne had known that Erin didn't want to kick them out. That she had been nice to them and given the kids granola bars. If she'd had a chance to talk to Jenny, she knew that Erin had brought plenty of supplies for the little settlement. But Adrienne wasn't happy to see her, she was defensive and resentful.

"I'm sorry. I didn't mean to upset you. I just want to talk."

"So, talk."

Erin cast about for how to start. "When we were talking before, then one of your kids said something about Ike. Is Ike one of your kids, or…?"

Adrienne's eyes were narrow and suspicious. "No, I don't have an Ike." She shrugged. "Why?"

"It's nothing, I guess. It just seemed like there was more than one Ike around, and it was confusing."

Adrienne stared at her.

"Does Jenny have one named Ike, then?" Erin asked, as if she didn't already know the answer.

"She might."

Erin knew that Adrienne and Jenny were close enough to know the names of each other's children. What did she know that she was hiding?

"Her older boy, his name is Ike, right? He's eight?"

One of the children piped up, a little boy with dark hair peeking out from behind the tent. "No! Ike is five, like me!"

There were giggles from other children, out of sight. Adrienne whipped around to look at him. "Samuel Andrew, do you want a hiding? Quit listening in on other people's conversations and go play. All of you. Go on. This is just boring grown-up stuff. Go find some skipping stones."

There was the sound of little feet running away and more giggles. Samuel stood up taller where he had been hiding so that Erin could see more of him. His bottom lip stuck out. "But it's true. Ike is five."

Adrienne swung the pot that was in her hand. Not to throw it at him, but drenching him with the water that it contained. At least, Erin hoped it was water. Samuel yelped and ran away. Adrienne lowered the pot and looked at Erin, the corner of her mouth twitching. Vic burst into peals of laughter. Erin tried to keep a straight face but was unable to stop a huge grin from splitting her face.

After the tension that had dominated the conversation, it was a huge relief to laugh at little Samuel getting soaked by his mother. The three of them just shook their heads and laughed, relaxing for the first time. Adrienne set her pot down on the ground.

"I declare... when I was a young 'un, I thought my parents knew everything, including how to raise a family. It is *terrifying* to think that they didn't have any better idea than I do now. You're just winging it every day. Right, wrong, you have no clue." She gave a single laugh. "Don't ever have children."

"It looks very... challenging," Vic said, still trying to smother her giggles.

"And it's twice as challenging as it looks. Or a hundred times. Hundreds of little decisions every day, and I don't think more than half of them are right. It's a wonder any of them survive childhood." She sobered suddenly and looked away.

Death wasn't funny. Not when their community had been touched by it so recently. Soaking a pouting child with water was funny. Thinking about their deaths was not.

"Sorry," Erin said, though she wasn't sure what she was actually apologizing for. For reminding Adrienne about what had happened? For coming out and bothering her again, when they just wanted to be left alone?

Sorry for all of the challenges that had brought Adrienne to that place.

Adrienne sighed. "There has been so much going on. Too much, I think. We're all feeling it. I know you've been trying to be kind and helpful. It's just come at a really bad time, and we're not very trusting of outsiders. You want to be nice, but you don't know how disconcerting it is for us to deal with this behavior."

"With what? With being nice?"

Adrienne nodded, then wrinkled her nose and scratched her ear. "When you're not used to it... when all you're used to is people ignoring you, or chasing your kids off, or shouting at you to get a job... then having someone go against all of those conventions and treat you like a real person... I don't know what to do with that. I'm sure it's the same for Jenny. We're just waiting for the other shoe to drop. To find out what's really behind all of this nice behavior."

Erin nodded slowly, understanding. She knew how anxious she would get at a foster home that she'd only been at for a few days, trying to discern where the dangers were. She would be very off balance until she figured out the rules and the personalities of a new place.

"Well, I'm sorry," Erin said, tongue in cheek, "for being so nice."

Adrienne smiled and nodded. She looked in the direction the children had run. "I think I'd better check in and make sure that they're staying together and no one has fallen into the water. You ladies... can get on your way."

Erin and Vic nodded and headed back toward the truck.

CHAPTER 38

*A*s they walked toward the truck, Erin looked back over her shoulder toward Adrienne and the tents. Adrienne was soon out of sight, walking into the trees behind the tents to check on the children—or to escape Erin's and Vic's prying eyes.

Vic called Nilla to her and struggled for a minute to get the leash back on him. "You've had your fun now, it's time to settle down to go home."

Erin looked in Adrienne's direction once more.

"Can we look at the cave again?"

Vic raised her brows in disbelief. "You want to go see a cave?"

"Well… yes. Not to explore it. Just to see it again, and think."

"Why?"

"Why are they camped so close to it? Why do they care about being close to the cave? I mean, Rip wanted to mine it, if Willie is right. But he's gone now. Is Adrienne going to mine it? Her husband, if he shows up again? Why does she care about being close to it?"

"I don't know." Vic shrugged. "I think it's more that she wants to be close to the rest of the settlement, not that she wants to be close to the cave."

Adrienne had said that she would not stay there for long; she didn't want to be close to the place where Rip had been killed.

"But if she and Jenny are such good friends, why isn't she on the other side? Closer to Jenny? It would be farther away from the cave, but that doesn't really matter. Does it?"

Vic shrugged and led the way toward the cave again. The sky was getting dark, and she grabbed a flashlight out of the truck before heading into the bush. Erin tried to ignore the thumping of her heart. She wasn't afraid of the dark. She didn't even have to go into the cave. She just wanted to go over there again, to think about it, and to try to understand what appeal it had other than the possibility of mining minerals.

It seemed like it was farther away than it had been the first time Vic had taken her to it. Maybe the dimness made things appear farther away. Maybe it was her anxiety that made it feel like it was taking longer to get there. She started to worry that Vic had taken her in the wrong direction or walked by it, missing it. But then she saw the rock face, glowing dimly in the falling dark. Vic ran her flashlight along the wall. Nothing appeared to be any different from the last time they had been there. Nothing seemed to be wrong or out of place. Erin followed Vic to the mouth of the cave.

"Come in with me," Vic suggested.

"No, I can't."

"I don't want to go in there myself. If you want to figure out what Adrienne is here for, you need to come in with me. You're the one who wants to see."

"You can just take pictures, like last time."

"Showing you a picture on a little tiny screen isn't going to give you a sense of what it's like in there. And anything smaller than my head isn't even going to be visible on the screen."

"I can't go inside a cave."

"It's been a long time since you were hurt," Vic said reasonably. "Nothing is going to happen to you in here. We go in, we take a look around, and we come out. There isn't anyone else here that's going to bother us. No one knows that we're here, so it isn't like they might have set a trap for us. There isn't going to be a cave-in here."

Any of those things could happen. Erin didn't believe that it was safe to walk into the cave and then back out again. Her experiences had taught her otherwise.

"Vic. Can't you just go have a peek?"

Vic held the flashlight toward her. "Why don't you take the light and go in first, so that you can see everything. You won't be afraid if you can see."

Nilla was scratching around, sniffing at all of the plants and rocks at the cave entrance. He scraped at the dirt with his back feet and then strained toward the cave to go inside and investigate. The furry little beast didn't even have enough sense to be scared.

"Nilla. Let's go back to the truck," Erin called.

Vic shook her head. "Not yet. Come in and see what it is you were looking for. I'll let Nilla in first and then you'll know there's nothing to be afraid of."

"Just because he doesn't have any sense?"

"No. Because if there was anything to be afraid of, he would get eaten first."

Erin laughed.

"Come on." Vic motioned Erin toward the cave, and pressed the flashlight into her hand. "Turn on the light."

Erin did.

"Shine it into the mouth of the cave."

Erin got a little closer and shone the light inside. It was a strong light and lit up the interior well. Just a lot of rock. No one lurking inside. The floor of the cave was sort of sandy. There wasn't a lot of loose rock. The walls were jagged, glistening in the light and throwing odd shadows.

The entrance 'room' was large and, with the light on, it didn't seem that dangerous.

"Send Nilla in," she told Vic.

Vic gave a laugh and did so, letting Nilla off of the leash once more. She didn't have to tell him to go in; he was already straining to explore it. Erin crept in after him.

"I don't know if this is a very good idea."

"You're not going to know until you try it. I don't think it's that bad. Nothing is going to happen."

Vic followed close behind her. Erin felt comforted rather than crowded to have Vic on her heels.

"To the right?" she asked.

"Yes."

Erin followed the curve of the walls, finding her way through open spaces and then smaller crevices. But none of them were too small. She didn't have to crawl on her belly. They were, of course, large enough for a man to get through. Because Rip had gone in there, and the police had gone in there. They would only have to duck or to turn sideways.

There were a couple of places where Vic needed to show her where the passage was but, in a few minutes, Erin could hear the musical tinkling of the underground stream as it flowed over the rocks and then dribbled into a pool. Erin stepped into the larger room, like a dwarfen hall. She shone her flashlight around, looking for anything out of place.

"You see?" Vic said. "Just like my pictures. Only better."

Erin kept shining the light all around them, right up to the farthest corners of the room. She took a couple of steps toward the pool. She was determined not to go too close to the water. She didn't want to see the horror that Vic had seen that day when Willie had taken her there spelunking even in her mind's eye.

"Get closer," Vic urged.

Erin shook her head. "This is close enough."

"There's something in there."

Erin closed her eyes. It was dark. She opened them again. She didn't want to be in the dark. But she didn't want to see what was in the pool, either. Another body? A blind white fish? She didn't want to know what it was. Not at all.

Vic got closer to the pool. "Give me the light, then."

Erin shook her head. The light was hers. No one else was going to get control of it.

"Then shine it over here," Vic insisted.

Erin shone it at the pool without getting any closer, keeping her eyes averted from it. Vic bent over. She laughed. "Well, I don't think it's anything you need to worry about," she said.

Erin looked reluctantly over to Vic. A fish, then? A cave salamander? Something harmless, but undoubtedly slimy and gross.

"What is it?"

"A fridge."

"What?" Erin frowned and squinted toward the pool. There was no big, square, white fridge. She would have noticed something like that.

"They're using it as a fridge." Vic dipped her hand into the flowing water. "It's freezing cold. Must come from snow runoff higher in the mountains."

Erin shuffled closer. There were bottles of juice, some condiment jars, a few items that were weighted down with rocks. Jenny had said that they used the stream to keep things cold. Erin had assumed she meant an outside stream. But the cave would be better. Fewer animals around. Maybe they couldn't smell any food smells once the items were in the water.

"These are some of the things that I gave Jenny."

"Then it looked like your plan worked. She did share it with the others in the community who needed it."

Erin nodded. She was still worried about looking into the pool and imagining Rip's remains there, but she was curious about seeing the crime scene, sterile as it appeared to be. She looked around the cave slowly.

"So… they think that Rip was hit somewhere over there," Erin waved at the opposite side of the cave, "and then dragged into the pool."

"Yeah. The blood they found and the rock were over there."

"The rock?"

"Uh… the murder weapon," Vic said, looking embarrassed. She had been careful before not to say what the weapon had been, not wanting Erin to have to picture it.

"A rock. So… it wasn't a premeditated murder. He wasn't shot or stabbed. Someone picked up what was already here, in the cave." There were a few loose rocks of various sizes around the cave. "It was spur of the moment. Anger or maybe self-defense."

"Yeah, that would fit."

"Two people… who knew and trusted each other."

"Maybe," Vic was less confident in that answer.

"Would you go into a cave with someone you didn't trust?"

Vic considered this. "No," she agreed finally. "I guess I wouldn't."

Erin sat down on a large rock, considering. "The Ryders had already been using the cave. Willie had tried to kick them out a couple of times. Jenny said they used the stream as a fridge."

"Right. They knew about the cave, the stream, and the pool. Rip was going to mine it. Jenny was using it to keep food from spoiling."

"But there wasn't any food in it when you found… him."

Vic shook her head. "No. But they might have run out of perishables. They wouldn't get too many things at a time that needed to be refrigerated. They might have eaten everything they had purchased. All of the foods that might spoil."

"Is it possible that Jenny didn't know that Rip's body was in here?"

They were both quiet for a long time.

"Maybe… she had the baby and was still too sore to come this far," Vic suggested.

"The baby was born on the third. What day did Rip die?"

"You'd have to ask Terry what they have it narrowed down to now. I know it was around that time, but I don't think they have an exact date."

"So… she had the baby, Rip disappeared and she didn't look for him? And didn't come in here for anything?"

"No. Why would she? If she knew they were out of food, she wouldn't come here for that. If she thought that Rip had taken off on her, then why would she come here? She would assume that he was in town or the city, not that he was lying in a cave somewhere."

Erin got up, walked to the opposite side of the cave and back again. She tried to connect everything up in her head.

"He was too big for one of the women to move him."

Vic agreed immediately. "He wasn't a featherweight. She would be pulling someone almost twice her weight, with lots of friction with the floor to slow her down. And why even do that? Why move him at all?"

Erin went over to the stream and the pool and prodded at the rocks.

"How big was the rock that was used to kill him?"

Vic considered them, measuring them in her mind against what she remembered before the police had taken over the scene. "Maybe… like that one," she said, tapping one with her toe.

Erin handed Vic the flashlight. She bent over and picked the rock up, testing how much it weighed, how easy or hard it would have been for a woman a little bigger than she was, used to outdoor chores and wrangling children, to lift and use as a tool. It was heavy and awkward, but would not be impossible for her to use, especially not if she were angry. If Rip had confessed to infidelity or gambling away their last cent, Jenny could have been very angry.

"But she was pregnant," Vic pointed out. "I don't know if you could do that if you were pregnant."

Erin lowered the rock, then tossed it back in the direction of the tumble of rocks she had taken it from. It landed on a different side, and Erin could see something scratched into it. She got closer, squinting, to make it out.

CHAPTER 39

$\mathcal{J}$KE

It was in large, untidy letters.

Maybe the child himself had scratched it in. Five-year-old Ike. Erin stared down at it, her mind whirling, trying to put everything together in a way that made sense.

"What is it?" Vic asked, bending down and shining the light on it to read it herself. She looked back at Erin, baffled. "What?"

"I don't think he could have scratched that in himself," Erin said, arguing against the first thought that had occurred to her. "These are really hard. It's not like writing with pencil and paper. And he was only five."

Vic picked up a smaller rock from the ground of the cave and tried to imitate the scratchings on the rock that Erin had dropped. Her attempt was not very effective. Her scratchings were fainter than the ones on Erin's rock.

"No... I don't think a five-year-old did that," she agreed.

"What are you doing here?"

Erin shot to her feet, startled by the sharp voice. They both whirled around to face the doorway to the cave, the only direction they could go if they wanted to get out. A man stood blocking the passageway, shoulders broad, a shotgun in his hands. The man from the settlement. Wiseman.

Vic swore under her breath. Erin saw her hand twitch in the direction of her bra holster, but it was going to be too awkward to get at. She wouldn't be able to draw her weapon with the man already holding his shotgun on them.

"We're just looking around," Erin said lightly. "We wanted to see where it was that Rip died. Just... curiosity."

He didn't believe a word she said. "You've already seen it."

"Well... Vic did," Erin admitted. "But I didn't."

He looked back and forth between them. "Why couldn't you just go away and stay away? How many times did we tell you? You weren't invited. You were told to leave. Why couldn't you leave us alone?"

"I wanted to help," Erin said lamely.

"This is helping? Prying into our business? Sticking your nose into something that was none of your business?"

"No... I mean... this wasn't part of it. This was just... trying to understand in my head what had happened. It didn't make sense."

"And now you've gone and screwed things up."

Vic looked down at the rock Erin had dropped, and at her attempt to replicate it. "Is this... a headstone? Is that what it is supposed to be? A grave marker?"

He shrugged one shoulder, not admitting it and not moving the gun an inch away from them.

"Because five-year-old Ike died," Erin said. "Is this..." She looked at the pile of rocks in and around the pool. "Is this where he is buried?" She moved her feet away a little, not liking the idea of standing on or near his grave.

"No, not in here. We couldn't leave him in here. She couldn't."

"Jenny?"

He just gave her a hard stare and didn't answer.

"Then this is where he died," Vic suggested. "That's why the marker is here."

The rocks, the pool, the cold food just out of reach.

It would be a temptation for a hungry child. A child climbing over the rocks, over a slippery wet surface, trying to reach a bottle of juice or a package held down with a large rock. So easy for him to slip and fall and either hurt himself or end up in the water. Maybe a child alone, separated from his siblings, following his daddy. Or sneaking away when Rip was supposed to be watching him. Maybe Rip had been too drunk to understand the danger or the need to watch him closely.

"So Rip… that's what made Jenny so angry? She blamed him for Ike… getting killed?"

"I wasn't part of that conversation," Wiseman growled, "but I can imagine how it went. I didn't get here until it was too late. Too late for either of them to take anything back. And if you think I would ask her to explain exactly what had happened, you're crazy." He stared at the pool, then looked up from it and gazed at the blank wall of the cave as if he could see a movie playing there. "She was in trouble herself. Saving her had to be the priority."

"Saving Jenny?" Vic shook her head. "From what?"

"She went into labor," Erin guessed. "Lifting that heavy rock. Trying to drag Rip's body. Maybe picking up Ike's."

"She was in a bad way." His voice was gravelly. "I had to get her out of here. Away from *him*. But she wouldn't leave her little boy behind. Doubled over with pain, and she still had to carry him." He swallowed, his Adam's apple moving up and down as he tried to keep his voice steady. "She had to save her boy." He saw the questions in their eyes and shook his head. "It was way too late for him."

Vic rubbed at the corners of her eyes. "Poor Jenny. That poor woman."

Wiseman walked toward them. The gun was still pointed loosely toward them. He toed the other rocks with his boot. He turned one over and found what he was looking for. On the reverse side, this one was scratched too.

RIP

Rip? Or was it R.I.P.?

Either way, they were both gone. Jenny's son and her husband. Both killed in that cave.

CHAPTER 40

"Why did you leave Rip in here?" Vic demanded, sounding angry. And maybe she was. Angry that they had just left the body there for her to find. To inhabit her nightmares, maybe for years to come. "If you took Ike out of here to lay him to rest, why couldn't you do the same for Rip? Why leave him here, in this pool?"

Wiseman didn't look at Vic. He was looking at the pool, where he had disposed of the body.

"Have you ever tried to move a man of that size? A dead weight? Do you know how long it would have taken to get him out of here, even with help? I could barely get him over here, pulling and rolling him. I couldn't have gotten him all the way out. And even if I could, why would I? He was stupid and careless and caused his own son's death. Why show him respect? Why give him any dignity in death?"

He circled partway around the pool, like the restless pacing of a bear in a zoo cage, looking down into it and seeing what only he could see.

"So yeah, I dumped him in there. I weighted him down. I cut him. Cut into his flesh so that the fish would be attracted to him faster. After they were finished with him, it would have been easy to move his cleaned bones out of here. To throw them in a trash heap or burn them. Get rid of every last bit of him." His lip curled into a sneer, disgusted with Rip.

Wiseman was no longer between Erin and Vic and the exit. Erin gave

Vic a nudge and started to shuffle toward the passage. It wasn't exactly covert. With the bright flashlight in her hand, every move Erin made was magnified, the light and shadows jumping around the cave walls. She was feeling closed in. Trapped in a cave again. She didn't want to find herself in the bottom of a pit, or injured and blinded by the dark, tied up and trying to find her way around a maze of tunnels. Her heart was in her throat.

No matter how casual and relaxed she tried to appear, Wiseman couldn't help but notice their intention to leave. The shotgun came up, pointing toward them.

"Where do you think you're going?"

"We're going home," Vic said. "Don't you think there has been enough killing here? You don't want two more bodies to dispose of. Especially when one of them is the girlfriend of a Bald Eagle Falls police officer."

"What?" His eyes flicked from Vic to Erin and back again.

"Yeah. You really want Officer Piper looking for you? I don't know how hard they're looking for Rip's killer, and they don't even know about Ike, but if Erin and I disappear, you think Piper won't move heaven and earth to find out what happened to us? And you already know my boyfriend, don't you?"

"I don't know anything about you."

"You didn't recognize the truck outside? Willie kicked Rip out of here twice. He never talked to you? Told you to stay out of this cave?"

Wiseman's finger tightened, starting to squeeze the trigger. Erin's heart was in her throat. Vic's arguments were not helping. They were pushing Wiseman in the wrong direction, making him panic. He would wipe out anyone who knew anything. Anyone who could identify him or knew anything about his role in the cover-up.

"You aren't guilty of murder," Erin told him, her voice squeaking upward so she sounded like a doll playing a recording of a faked child's voice. "You didn't have anything to do with Ike's or Rip's death. Just with disposing of the body. That's all. You don't want our blood on your hands."

The muzzle of the shotgun wavered but didn't move away from them. His finger on the trigger did not relax.

"Go," Vic murmured. "He's not going to be talked down. Just move."

Erin agreed. She jumped to the side, then turned her back on Wiseman and zipped toward the entrance as quickly as she could over the rough ground, trying to ignore the disorienting play of the light and shadows cast by the flashlight. She knew Vic was right behind her. She couldn't look back or she would slow down or freeze up.

Wiseman shouted at them to stop. Of course they didn't. The thunderous blast of the shotgun filled the cave, echoing. Erin couldn't help looking back to see if Vic had been hit. If Wiseman had killed her friend…

Vic was still moving, her face white. "Go, go, go!"

Erin needed no more urging. Wiseman called after them again, swearing. Following them.

Erin heard Nilla yipping wildly.

Nilla. She'd forgotten all about the annoying little white puffball and, apparently, Vic had too. But they couldn't stop with Wiseman in pursuit. Nilla would have to follow them, to find his own way out. At least he was a much smaller, faster target than either Erin or Vic.

Erin couldn't breathe. The walls closed in around her as she left the large cave and had to slide sideways through the passageway, watching the rocky ceiling to make sure she wasn't going to hit her head on some outcropping. She couldn't get any air. She could barely see through a black haze in her vision, even with the flashlight still firmly in her hand.

Wiseman yelled, not in anger but in pain. Erin looked back, but she had left the big room and of course she could no longer see what was going on there. Nilla was barking and growling, a different note in his voice. He must have gone after Wiseman.

Nilla had always been such a coward when threatened by Willie; Erin would never have guessed he would have the courage to attack a man. She sucked in a deep breath and kept going, trying to get out before Wiseman could resume his pursuit. Nilla had given them a bigger head start, but they weren't out of danger.

Erin moved as quickly as she could. In a few minutes that seemed like hours, they were running through the trees, back toward Willie's truck. Erin's lungs burned. She was not a runner and she had put on a couple of pounds in the time she'd been working at Auntie Clem's. She was still slim and had been working on tai chi, but she was not exactly fit.

As they got within sight of the truck, she heard Nilla yipping again, and the dog caught up with them, then burst past, barking excitedly to be let into the truck. By the time they reached it, he was pacing impatiently, wondering what was taking the two-legs so long to get there. Erin and Vic didn't say anything, both puffing and trying to catch their breaths.

They jumped into the truck without a word. Nilla hopped into the back seat of the cab. They slammed their doors shut.

Vic started the truck and shifted into drive, which auto-locked the doors.

As they pulled out, spraying gravel and clumps of grass and weeds, Erin saw Wiseman emerging from the trees, limping after them, shouting, still carrying his shotgun.

She ducked, hoping he wouldn't shoot the truck, and held on to the dashboard as Vic floored it over the washboard surface of the little-used road.

CHAPTER 41

Of course, it wasn't all over. Erin realized as they sped back toward Bald Eagle Falls that she had another firing squad to face. She was going to have to tell Terry what they had found so that the police department could follow up properly. And they had tipped off someone who had been an accomplice after the fact in the murder and who would probably go straight to Jenny to let her know that Erin and Vic had figured it all out.

"Oh, great," Erin muttered.

Vic looked over at her. She opened her mouth to ask what was wrong, then closed it again, nodding her head. "Uh… yeah. Officer Piper."

"He's not going to be happy."

"What did you tell him when you left?"

"Just that I was going out to take care of some things."

Vic considered, staring at the highway stretching out ahead of them. "I think you should call him."

"It would be easier to explain face to face."

"Yeah, but if you call him, then you can explain and not have to be there to take the fallout right away. He can hang up and be mad for a while, but when he sees you, he'll be calmed down."

"Like when we went to Whitewater Falls to find Joshua."

"Right. He was mad at first, but by the time he got out there, he was just happy that everyone was okay. And Terry can get out here faster to deal with *him* if you don't wait."

Erin nodded to herself. Vic had a point. She did a few of her tai chi breathing exercises and took out her phone. She tapped her speed dial for Terry. She wasn't sure whether she wanted him to pick it up right away, or whether to hope he was tired out from working and had fallen asleep so it would go to voicemail. But if he didn't get the message right away, then she'd have to call the sheriff or someone else in the police department and explain to them. She wasn't sure that would be any better. Then Terry would want to know why she hadn't talked to him first.

"Erin? Is everything okay?" he asked as soon as he picked up.

"Why wouldn't everything be okay?" she countered.

"You left here in such a hurry and didn't say what was going on. I didn't know if something was wrong or you just wanted to get to a sale before it closed." His tone was teasing, but had an edge to it as well. Like he hoped it was just something innocent that they could joke about, but was afraid that it wasn't. And of course he was right.

"We're fine," she said to start with. Reassure him of that first. Help reduce the tension. "We—Vic and I—went out to the cave. I wanted to see something."

She left out the part about going to see Adrienne first. That wasn't what had gotten them in trouble, but Terry would think that it was. He would accuse her of sticking her nose where it didn't belong, all that stuff that she'd heard before.

"To see what? You won't even go inside a cave."

"I did!"

"You went inside?"

"Yes. I really did. And it wasn't as bad as I thought it would be. And nothing… there wasn't a collapse and I didn't get hurt."

"No. You see? I told you it would be okay. And next time, it will be easier because you'll know that it is safe. That something bad doesn't happen to you every time you go into a cave."

"I still don't think I'm going to do it again."

"We'll see," he said with good humor. "So… did you see whatever it was you wanted to know about?" The police had already processed the scene, so of course he didn't see what she could have learned from the cleaned-up murder site. He thought they had found everything there was to find, but he had been wrong.

"Well, actually, yes."

"Which was what?"

"The families over there, the Ryders anyway, they were using the cold water in the stream and pool for refrigeration."

"How do you know that? There wasn't anything like that in it when we were there."

"They cleaned it up before anyone found Rip's body."

"I suppose they didn't want to be questioned, so they didn't want there to be any indication that any of them had been in the cave."

"Yeah."

"That's tampering with evidence, but I don't think anyone is going to prosecute them for it."

"There's more than that. That's just how it started."

"How what started? You think that is somehow related to Ryder's death?"

"It was. In a roundabout way."

"You're going to have to explain it to me. Are you on your way back? You can tell me all about it when you get home?"

"We're on the highway right now, on our way home. But I think I should tell you everything right now. You're not going to want to wait."

"Wait for what?"

"Well… you need to go out there…"

"Exactly what did you find out?"

Erin took a couple more deep breaths. "Promise me you won't get mad."

"Erin."

"I just don't want you to blow up."

"Just tell me. The more you say things like that, the more anxious I get."

"It had to do with the baby being named Ike."

There was a pause. "We talked about that. There are a lot of reasons that they might have named the baby Ike."

"But we didn't talk about one of them. That sometimes, a family gives a baby the same name after a previous sibling dies. It happened a lot in Clementine's genealogy that I've been reading. Sometimes a family would have two or three babies named the same thing, because the first few died in infancy."

"Yes, that's true. I don't see it happening very much anymore, but I'm sure it still does happen sometimes."

"Especially with families with long traditions. Like we were talking about, where they want to carry on grandpa's name in every generation…"

"So are you telling me that they had a child named Ike who died, and that was why they named the baby Ike?"

"Yes."

"Only… when did he die? I thought he was registered with the school. Did the school just register him automatically and didn't know that he had passed?"

"He just died recently. Right before Rip."

There was silence on the other end of the phone. Erin pictured Terry grabbing his notebook and pen to start jotting down notes, realizing that Erin had actually discovered something important to the case.

"Tell me what you know," he instructed. "When did the other Ike die?"

"The same day as Rip."

"You think it had something to do with Rip's death?"

"Yes. I think it was the motive for his murder."

Another pause as Terry apparently wrote notes to himself. "What do you think happened?"

"Something happened in the cave. Rip was supposed to be watching Ike, or maybe he was drunk and he did something stupid. Whatever it was, Ike died there in the cave."

"What makes you think that?"

"We found a rock in there with his name carved on it. A makeshift tombstone."

"A rock could be carved with his name for a lot of different reasons. He could have done it himself. Kids like to write or carve their names into everything."

"But he didn't. There's a man in the settlement, his name is Wiseman, and he confirmed it. That Ike died. And Jenny… she's the one who killed Rip. Because he killed their son."

"It would have taken a lot of strength to lift a rock of that size and bring it down with enough force to do the damage that was done."

"And you don't think a woman would be strong enough? You hear about them lifting cars when their children are in trouble. You don't think that a woman used to living and working out there in the wild, chopping wood and stuff like that, couldn't lift a rock?"

"She was very pregnant at the time. That was either right before or right after the baby was born. It isn't that I can't see a woman being able to lift a heavy rock or to kill her husband in a fit of rage or grief. Just… in that condition… wouldn't she be risking harm to the baby? Or to herself, if she'd already had the baby and happened to tear something with the strain?"

"I don't think she was thinking about the consequences. She just acted. She was so upset, she just picked it up and…" Erin didn't finish the sentence. Maybe if she didn't say it out loud, she wouldn't see it in her head. She wouldn't have nightmares about what Jenny had done.

"And this Wiseman, he is a witness? He says this is what happened?"

"Yes."

"We'll need to get someone out there to talk to him, then."

"I think you should get someone out there soon. Or… he won't be out there anymore. And neither will anyone else."

"Because you had to go and put yourself in the middle of it," he sighed.

"We just went to see the cave. We didn't know that anyone saw us and would follow us in."

"You're lucky he didn't do anything to try to shut you up."

Erin didn't say anything.

"He didn't do anything, did he?"

"He had a shotgun. He was threatening us. He fired it, but we're okay."

"Tell me Vic didn't shoot him."

"Vic didn't shoot him."

Beside her, Vic snorted. "He got the drop on us, Officer Piper," she said loudly so that he would be able to hear her. "Or I might have!"

"So… what? He just let you go?"

"Nilla attacked him. Distracted him and slowed him down enough that we could get away."

"Nilla? So that little ball of fur is worth something?"

"You're not allowed to badmouth him anymore. Not after that."

"I guess not. I'm going to have to revise my opinion of him."

"Me too. He was a good dog." Erin looked over the seat at Nilla, who wagged his tail excitedly, tongue lolling out in a wide doggie smile of satisfaction. Erin chuckled. "Yes. Good dog!"

"So…" Terry drew her attention back. "How bad is this? Did he follow you? You figure he'll run, and Jenny with her family?"

"Yeah. That's why I wanted to call you and let you know before we got home. You might want to… rally the troops."

"Yep. Going to have to. I'm still doubtful about whether Jenny Ryder would have been able to do that. We'll need to ask the medical examiner's opinion on height and whether a woman— a heavily pregnant one especially—would have the strength to do it."

"Go ahead. But I think that's what happened. And that's what Wiseman said. Baby Ike was born after that. She went into labor that day, probably because of the exertion, or her mental state, whatever. I think he was probably a bit premature; he's very small and jaundiced."

"It's possible. I can also see, with one child dying and another being born the same day, her being superstitious about naming him the same thing. Sort of a reincarnation thing."

"They're Christian. Christians don't believe in reincarnation, do they?"

"Not officially, no. But that doesn't stop some of them from believing in it, or believing in old superstitions about death and rebirth. I've known a lot of people who have been able to hold competing beliefs. They don't really see the conflict, even if you point it out to them."

"Huh. Well, it kind of makes sense. One child replaces the other. Maybe it brings her a little bit of comfort."

"I'd better go. You guys are on your way straight back here, right? And no one is following you?"

Erin looked behind them, watching for any vehicle that might be in pursuit. She'd been forced off the road once before, and she didn't want to think about it happening again.

Vic shook her head. "I haven't seen anyone following," she said. "I've been watching."

Erin reported this back to Terry.

"Good. I'm going to hang up. You guys stay safe. If you think there is a problem, call me back."

"If Jenny did do it… if she killed Rip in a fit of passion because her son had just died… will she be able to get out of it and not have to serve prison time?"

Terry's voice was gentle as he answered her. "I'm not a lawyer, Erin, but no, I really don't think so. Even with manslaughter, she's still going to have to serve some time. Maybe she has a family member who can help look after the kids while she's in prison."

Erin swallowed, a lump in her throat. "Okay."

"I'm sorry, Erin."

"I know."

CHAPTER 42

*I*t was anticlimactic going back to the house. Everything was quiet
and peaceful. Terry was already gone. The animals were there.
There were no playing children or men with shotguns. Vic promised to stay
with Erin. If Willie got back, he could join them, but Erin didn't have to be
alone.

She tried practicing her tai chi, hoping that would help her to unwind
and relax. But the sadness pressed down on her. All of those children having
to go live with someone else. Maybe being split up. Maybe having to go
into foster care if there weren't any relatives around to take care of them. She
felt the weight of it on her own shoulders. She had been the one to pursue
it, to put the puzzle pieces together and sort out that it had been Jenny.

If she had known when she started where the clues were going to lead,
she wouldn't have pursued it. She would rather they just left Jenny alone
and let her go on taking care of her children. What justice would be served
by putting her in prison? It wouldn't change the fact that Rip was dead and
her children fatherless. It wouldn't bring big Ike back. It would leave the
children scattered in various homes, with no mommy and daddy and no
continuity. They would all be better off if Jenny could just continue taking
care of them.

"You were worried about them before," Vic pointed out, reading Erin's
face as she tried to work through her forms and resolve her feelings. "You

were afraid of the children not getting enough to eat, getting enough super-vision, getting the education they need out there in the woods. So now… maybe they'll go somewhere that they can have those things."

"But if they had to choose between those things and their mama, they would choose to stay with their mama."

"Well… probably. You can't know that for sure, but kids don't always know what's best for them. Just because they want to be with Jenny, that doesn't mean it's the thing that's best for them."

Erin breathed out in time with her movements. "Yes, it is."

Vic looked startled. "It is what?"

"It is the best thing for them. To stay with Jenny. I don't have any doubt."

Vic watched her movements, frowning. "Really? You really think that's the best?"

"Yes. I've seen how being taken away from their parents hurts kids. Especially when it's for something like not being able to provide for them. Not having enough food in the house, or a job, or not having a place to live at all."

"They don't take kids away just because their parents are poor."

Erin stopped and looked at Vic, raising her brows.

"Well, they don't, do they?" Vic insisted.

Erin continued her tai chi movements. "All the time."

Erin couldn't sleep. She lay there awake in the bed, lonely and craving Terry's body next to hers and his comforting arms around her, but knew that he probably wouldn't be home before she got back up for work.

She had told Vic and Willie to go home. She didn't need them to stay up with her. She was safe enough with the burglar alarm and her trusty attack cat. If Wiseman had followed them back, he would have done some-thing right away, while Terry was still away, so Erin wasn't worried about it.

She lay there by herself, worrying, thinking about all of those children being ripped away from Jenny while she was taken off in a police car in handcuffs. It was horrible to think about. All that much worse because it was Erin's fault.

She heard the door open. Terry didn't call out to her, assuming that she would be asleep, but she heard the familiar, comforting sounds of him locking the door and rearming the burglar alarm and of K9 panting and his claws clicking on the kitchen floor. She rolled over on the bed, waiting for Terry to come in, but he didn't check in on her right away, so she eventually put her feet on the floor and went out to him.

"Oh!" Terry startled when he saw the movement out of the corner of his eye. He touched his chest lightly, taking a deep breath. "You're up. I didn't think you would still be awake."

"I couldn't sleep. Not thinking about those children. A newborn, Terry. He won't even remember her."

"Erin."

She waited for the platitudes. For him to reassure her that it would all work out for the best, and that Jenny had to face justice for what she had done. He didn't say anything and, eventually, she looked at his face. "What?"

"She was gone."

Erin swallowed and waited for more information. Jenny was gone? Did that mean she had escaped or that she had killed herself—and maybe taken all of her children with her? She looked up into Terry's face. He put his hands on her shoulders, warm and comforting.

"She and Wiseman and the rest picked up and left. We've got APB's out on them, but I'm not confident that we'll be able to find them again. They got a head start on us, and we don't know by how much or what direction they went in. They could be out of the state already, or they could be deeper into the wilderness. If they've driven out of state, they'll probably have dumped their vehicles or stolen new plates. I think it's pretty certain that we won't be able to find them again. Tracking people who are largely invisible... it's dang near impossible."

Erin hugged herself to him, putting her cheek to his chest. "I know I shouldn't be happy about that. I should want you to catch her. But I don't. I want her to be able to raise her children."

"It will be a hard life. Kids who spend their whole lives on the run don't have it easy. But it isn't like they had it easy up until this point anyway. Or that it would have been easy for them if she had still been there when we got there."

"I'm glad you didn't have to take them away from her."

"To tell the truth, I am too. I don't think any of us were too disappointed."

"Even Stayner?"

Terry chuckled. "Even Stayner. He's not such a bad guy, Erin. Just a little rough around the edges."

Erin snorted. "A little."

CHAPTER 43

*E*ven with Terry in bed with her and knowing that Jenny had managed to escape with her children, Erin still couldn't sleep. She knew that Terry wasn't asleep either. He was still, but she could tell by his breathing pattern and the tension in his body that he was lying awake. She turned around to face him and snuggled up.

"You should take one of your sleeping pills," she told him.

"Nah. I'm fine. If I don't get much tonight, I'll sleep better tomorrow night."

"I don't want you getting sleep-deprived…"

He knew that the lecture was coming. "I won't. I'll take care of myself. I'm just saying that one night won't be the end of the world. Same as for you."

"If I took a pill, I wouldn't be able to get out of bed when it was time. Vic can, but they just knock me for a loop."

They both just breathed for a while, cuddled up together, knowing that they weren't going to be able to get to sleep. They had too much on their minds.

"Erin."

"Mmm-hm?"

"When you talked about how many women were having babies the last few weeks…"

"Yes?"

"You mentioned us. That we weren't."

Erin rubbed her eyes. Her heart started to race. "What about it?"

"Do you want to?"

"Have a baby?"

"Yes," his voice was patient and amused. "Do you want to have a baby? Us together."

She wasn't sure how to answer him. If she said no, he would be hurt and think there was something wrong with them as a couple. If she said yes, then she'd have to deal with the extra pressure, and she wasn't sure whether it was the right thing or the right time.

"I don't know," she said finally. "I thought... maybe someday. But I don't know for sure I want to have a baby. And I'm pretty sure that... now isn't the right time."

He kissed her forehead. "Okay."

"Is it? That doesn't upset you?"

"No. I just wanted to make sure we were on the same page."

"And we are?"

"I'm okay with waiting to see. But when you mentioned it... I didn't want you pining away after a baby or deciding you wanted one but afraid to let me know."

"No, not yet." Erin pressed her face against him. "Sometime, maybe... but not yet."

Did you enjoy this book? Reviews and recommendations are vital to making a book successful.

Please leave a review at your favorite book store or review site and share it with your friends.

Don't miss the following bonus material:
Sign up for mailing list to get a free ebook
Read a sneak preview chapter
Other books by P.D. Workman
Learn more about the author

Sign up for my mailing list at pdworkman.com and get Gluten-Free Murder for free!

PREVIEW OF WHAT THE
CAT KNEW

CHAPTER 1

*R*eg Rawlins climbed out of the car and stretched, her muscles cramped after being in the car all day. According to the dashboard readout, it was a few degrees warmer than it had been in Tennessee. Added to that, it was humid and the air felt muggy. She could smell the ocean. She'd heard that all points in Florida were within sixty miles of the ocean as the crow flies. She was looking forward to spending some time swimming and looking for seashells. She'd always wanted to live near a real beach. A warm, sandy beach.

"Witch!" accused a homeless man sitting on the sidewalk with a cardboard sign. He had long, scraggly hair and a beard, streaked with gray, and he was missing several teeth. His clothes were ragged, and even though he was a few feet away, Reg could smell his unwashed body.

She gave him a scowl, but didn't turn away. His reaction interested her. She was dressed for the part she intended to play—headscarf, heavy jewelry and hoop earrings, a long, flowing peasant dress—so it was not unexpected that he would notice her and comment on her getup. But he had gone with *witch* rather than a fortune-teller or medium, which she thought was an odd choice. She wasn't wearing a pointed hat or black robe.

"What makes you think I'm a witch?" she demanded.

"All redheads are witches!" he informed her.

"Ah." Reg's red hair was all done in cornrow braids, which hung free around her face rather than being wound up under her headscarf. She liked the effect. And she liked the way the braids felt when she turned her head and they all swished back and forth. She ignored the homeless man and looked up and down the boardwalk.

She liked the atmosphere of Florida. Laid back and relaxed, not like in Tennessee where she had visited Erin. There had certainly been some uptight ladies there. She didn't regret leaving, though she was sad things hadn't worked out with Erin. Erin had been a lot more fun when they were kids. She'd grown up too much and become a stuffy old woman instead of the lost child she'd been when they had lived with the Harrises and then again when they had both aged out of foster care and had run a few cons together. Now she was grown up and mature and responsible, no longer interested in Reg's ideas.

"You don't know what you're missing, Erin," Reg murmured, looking around at the blue sky and the green vegetation, the tang of salt hanging in the air. Swimming in Florida was going to be nothing like a dip in the ocean in Maine. Miles of sandy beaches, warm water, and not a care in the world.

She gathered up her braids with both hands and pulled them back behind her shoulders, letting them fall again.

"There somewhere good to eat around here?" she asked the bum.

People looked at her oddly as they passed, and Reg didn't know if it was because of her outfit or the fact that she was talking to a non-person.

"Only if you like seafood!" the man cackled.

Luckily, Reg did.

"You should go to The Crystal Bowl," he told her. "That's where the witches gather."

Reg pursed her lips, considering him. "The Crystal Ball?"

"The Crystal *Bowl*. Get it?"

"Where is The Crystal Bowl?"

He gestured down the boardwalk. "Yonder about two blocks. Big sign. Can't miss it."

Reg had been told that Florida, and Black Sands in particular, was *the place* for psychics and mediums but she hadn't expected there to actually be enough of a community to warrant a restaurant of their own. She was glad she'd picked Florida over Massachusetts; she'd had enough of New England to last her a lifetime.

The Crystal Bowl had satisfyingly dramatic decor and furnishings. Blacks, reds, and golds combined into a rich tapestry of mysticism, lit by flickering candles which were actually tiny electric lights. East met West in a sort of a cross between an opium den and a carnival fortune-teller set. They worked together in harmony rather than clashing.

The patrons of the restaurant, however, were disappointingly normal. Shorts with t-shirts or light blouses, sunglasses propped on foreheads, everybody looking at their phones or calling across the room to greet each other. No sense of mystical decorum.

The sign said 'please wait to be seated,' but Reg walked across to the bar counter and selected a stool.

The bartender was spare, his skin too pale for a Floridian. He obviously spent too much time in the restaurant out of the sun. Either that or he was a vampire.

"Afternoon," he greeted, adjusting the spacing between the various bottles on the counter and turning their labels out.

"Hi."

"Don't think I've seen you here before."

"No, just flew in on my broomstick."

He eyed her. "Wrong costume."

Reg grinned. "Good. The old bum down the street said that I was a witch, and I was afraid I'd gotten it wrong."

"It's the red hair."

"So I hear. Mediums can't have red hair?"

"Mediums can have whatever they want. So what will it be?" He gestured to the neat rows of bottles behind the bar and the chalkboard on the wall behind them.

Reg looked over the options. Should she establish herself as someone with exacting and eclectic tastes? A connoisseur? Someone who was obviously unique and memorable?

But she wanted the bar to be somewhere she could let her hair down, not where she had to always be playing a part.

"Just a draft," she sighed. "Whatever is on tap."

He nodded and grabbed a beer stein. He filled it and placed it neatly on a coaster in front of her, pushing a bowl of pretzels closer to her. Something nice and salty to encourage thirst.

"So, Miss Medium, your name is…?"

"Reg Rawlins." She figured she was okay using the name, even though that was what she had used in Bald Eagle Falls. She didn't think any charges would follow her all the way to Florida. It wasn't like she was going to be filing taxes under the name.

He gave a nod. "Bill Johnson."

Reg took a pull on her beer. It had been a long drive and she was glad to be able to relax and recharge her batteries. Thinking of figurative batteries, she decided she'd better check her actual battery. Reg pulled out her phone and checked the charge. Not too bad. It would last her a couple more hours, and maybe by that time, she would have settled somewhere. She launched her browser and tapped in a search for lodgings. There were plenty of hits for short-term rentals. Lots of vacationers. Finding somewhere permanent might take a bit longer, but at least she'd have a place to hang her hat. Or her headscarf. And plug in her phone.

"You need a place to stay?" Bill asked, obviously recognizing the website.

"Looks like there are lots of options."

"Sarah Bishop is looking for a tenant. She's easy to get along with. You two would probably hit it off."

"Oh?"

Bill looked around the room. "She's not here yet. She often shows up for supper. If she doesn't, I can give her a call and let her know you're interested."

Reg raised an eyebrow. "You don't know me from Adam. What makes you think I would hit it off with Sarah Bishop or that you can recommend me to her?"

"Let's just say… I'm good at reading people. And I would know you from Adam, given that Adam was of the male persuasion."

Reg considered pointing out that there were plenty of men who could pass as women or had transitioned from one to the other, but decided that antagonizing him wouldn't be the wisest thing for her to do. So she took a sip of her beer and didn't challenge him.

"Okay. Well, I'd appreciate that. Being able to move in somewhere long-term right away would be a real plus. Thanks."

"No problem." He moved away to help another patron.

Reg continued to browse through the lodging listings to get a sense of what costs to expect for rent and what her options were if she didn't like Sarah Bishop's place. It could be a dump. Sarah Bishop could be Bill's sister or ex and he just wanted her off of his back. He had been pretty quick to offer his help and judge Reg worthy as a tenant for his friend.

Someone took the stool next to Reg's, and she looked up to see who it was. A strikingly handsome man. Thirty-something, short hair slicked back from his face to show off a widow's peak, a stubbly beard that at first glance made it look like he had forgotten to shave for a couple of days, but on a more careful examination was painstakingly trimmed. His eyes were dark but glowed almost red in the dim lighting of the restaurant, reflecting the red furnishings and wall coverings. Add a cape, and he'd be perfect to cast as a vampire.

He gave her an enigmatic look. Almost smiling, but not quite. A smirk. She thought he was going to greet her as Bill had, recognizing her as a stranger and asking who she was. But he merely inclined his head slightly and waited for his drink, which Bill brought over without being asked. Obviously his 'usual.'

"Reg Rawlins, Uriel Hawthorne," Bill said, making a gesture from one to the other by way of introduction.

Great choice of name. Reg was impressed. Still, Uriel said nothing, just threw back his shot and watched her.

"Nice to meet you," Reg said, thrusting her hand out to shake his, forcing him to acknowledge her presence.

He left her hanging for a moment, not moving to take her hand, and then finally responded, taking her hand in his in a soft, caressing gesture that made her immediately want to pull back. But she set her teeth and gave him a warm smile. She gave him one more squeeze before letting go and pulling back again.

"A pleasure to meet you," Uriel returned. "Are you thinking of joining our little community?"

"Well, we'll see how it goes," Reg said with a shrug. "I'm new in town and I've never been part of... this kind of community before. I've always just been on my own."

"There is something to be said for that."

Reg raised her eyebrows in query.

"Setting your own rules, doing your own thing," Uriel said. "No one with preconceptions as to how things should be done."

"Right." Reg nodded. Rules, in her opinion, were made to be broken. She wasn't about to buy into a social construct that tried to control her activities.

~

"Ah, here's Sarah," Bill said, hovering near Reg.

It took her a moment to remember who Sarah was and why she should care. Sarah was the landlord looking for a tenant.

Reg turned, following Bill's gaze. She was looking for a woman of around her age, since Bill had said that he thought she and Sarah would hit it off. But she didn't see anyone who fit her preconception.

Bill gave a little wave, and a woman nodded to him and corrected her course to join him at the bar.

She was an older woman, at least in her sixties, with a round face, bottle blond hair that curved around her face, and wire frame glasses. She looked like a friendly grandmother, lips pink with freshly-applied lipstick, a flowered shirt, pink slacks, and flat white sandals. She smiled at Bill.

"Good evening, Bill. How are you today?"

He nodded and didn't bother to answer the greeting. "Sarah, meet Reg Rawlins. She has just arrived in town and is looking for accommodations."

"Oh!" Sarah's face lit up. "Well, my dear, isn't that wonderful! I just happen to have a cottage that I am trying to rent out! Would you join me for dinner?" She motioned to the tables in the dining area. "I'm afraid I can't manage bar stools these days."

"Sure," Reg agreed, sliding down from hers and taking her drink with her. "That would be nice."

She didn't bother saying goodbye to Uriel, irritated with his distant, disinterested manner. Sarah led her to a table which was probably her regular, as there didn't seem to be any problem with her seating herself instead of waiting to be seated. She smiled and chatted with some of the other patrons as she made her way to her seat.

"Sit down, sit down," she encouraged Reg, as if Reg had somehow been holding her back. "Reg? Is that short for something? Where did you come from?"

"Regina. I've lived all over."

"Well, that's a pretty name. Did you pick it, or was it already yours?"

Reg laughed at the question. "I was saddled with Regina, but I picked Reg."

"Very nice. I like it. And what do you do?" She made a little gesture to indicate Reg's costume. "You read palms? Tarot?"

"A little of everything. Mostly, I talk to the dead."

"Oh." Sarah nodded wisely. "That's a good gig. Have you been doing it for long?"

Reg studied the woman, not sure how honest to be. She wasn't sure whether she should be open about being a medium or a con. Both paths seemed equally treacherous.

"I've always had… certain tendencies… gifts, if you like…" she said obliquely. "I'm just testing the waters now… seeing whether this is something I should pursue…"

Sarah nodded. A waitress came over and handed them menus, introducing herself and showing off a couple of rather long canine teeth when she smiled. Sarah took no note, and barely gave the menu a glance. She'd obviously been there enough times to know what she wanted.

"What's good?" Reg asked, glancing over the offerings.

"The seafood is fresh. Other than that… burger and fries… I wouldn't try anything too adventurous."

"Good to know."

After placing her order, Reg leaned back in her seat, looking Sarah over.

"How about you? Did you retire to Florida, or have you always lived here?"

"I've lived lots of places, dear. Florida is good for my old bones. As for retiring… maybe someday, but not yet."

"What is it you do?"

Sarah raised her brows, as if surprised that Reg didn't know. Was she supposed to have guessed? Did Sarah think that Bill had told her?

"Well, I'm a witch," Sarah said, as if it should have been obvious.

"Oh." Reg sat like a lump, with no idea what to say or how to respond. Sarah had turned the tables on her. Reg was used to provoking a reaction from other people. She liked to dress up and to say extravagant things to see how people reacted to her different personas. This time she was in the hot seat. "Oh. I guess I should have guessed." Reg threw her hands up in what was both a shrug and indicating their surroundings. "After all, we are in the Magic Cauldron."

Sarah blinked. "The Crystal Bowl."

"Whatever. This is a witch hangout, right? So of course that's what you are."

"I thought you knew. You didn't just wander in here of your own accord, did you?"

"There was an old bum down the boardwalk... he called me a witch, and he pointed me this way. So, yes... I knew... It's all just a bit much." Reg looked around the restaurant. "I mean, *everyone* here can't be a witch."

"Of course not," Sarah agreed. "We have people of all different spiritual and paranormal persuasions. Witches, warlocks, wizards, mediums," she gave Reg a nod, "fortune-tellers, healers... people who are gifted and people who are seekers."

"Okay, then." Reg looked around at the patrons and shook her head, having a hard time believing that they were all running the same con. "And there isn't too much competition for the same... customers?"

"Some people think Black Sands has gotten too commercial, and some people complain it has gotten too crowded. But for the most part... people are willing to live and let live. We are peaceful people."

"Uh-huh."

Sarah launched into a lyrical description of the town and its more inter-esting citizens. Reg tried not to sit with her mouth open as she listened. The waitress eventually came over with their meals. Reg hadn't realized how hungry she was getting, but when the platter was placed in front of her, she suddenly realized she was famished.

"This looks lovely," she told the waitress, not expecting to be getting a beautifully plated fish at the offbeat witches' diner. She dug in immediately, taking several delicious bites before looking at Sarah to ask her if she was enjoying her food.

Sarah's eyes were closed and her hands hovered over her plate as if she were warming them in the steam rising from the food. Reg turned to look at the waitress, but she was already gone. Reg looked uncomfortably at Sarah, wondering if she should follow suit.

Sarah's eyes opened, catching Reg staring at her.

"Uh..." Reg fumbled. "Amen?"

Sarah nodded slightly. Then she started to eat.

"It really is good," Reg said. "Really nice."

"I wouldn't eat here all the time if it wasn't," Sarah agreed. She patted her stomach. "I wouldn't have to worry so much about my waistline if I was cooking for myself!"

She was plump, but in a grandmotherly sort of way. Reg couldn't imagine her skinny; it just wouldn't have fit. Adele, Erin's witch friend back in Tennessee was tall and slender, and that worked for her, but it just wouldn't work for Sarah.

"So why don't you tell me about this cottage of yours?" she asked. "Bill seemed to think that we'd be able to come to terms."

"He's very empathic," Sarah said. "He reads people."

"Ah. Of course." It made sense for a bartender. Reg had known her share of good and bad barkeeps.

"It's just a little two-bedroom," Sarah said, answering Reg's question. "But it's just you…?"

"Yes. No dependents."

"So you could use one room as your bedroom and the other as an office, and still have space for entertaining in the living room."

"Right," Reg agreed. She hadn't thought about seeing clients in her home. She wasn't sure she wanted anyone to know where she lived. If they didn't like what she had to say, they wouldn't know where she lived to confront her. She had thought she would go to them, do readings in their own spaces. She could read a client a lot better if surrounded by their own things. People gave a lot away by the way they lived.

"It's separate from the main house, so we wouldn't be on top of each other. We can each keep our own hours. That can be a problem with night people and day people mixing. The kitchen is small, really just a prep area. You could come use the big kitchen if you needed to do any major baking or entertaining. I really don't use it that much."

"I don't expect I would either. I don't do a lot of my own cooking."

"You see? You'd be perfect. You wouldn't be complaining to me that there's no oven. It really does have everything you really need."

"Well, maybe we could go see it after dinner, and talk business."

"You're going to like it just fine. I can tell."

As Reg wasn't that picky, Sarah was probably right. If Reg didn't like it after a month or two, she'd have a good idea by that point of where to look for somewhere better. It wasn't a long-term commitment.

Which was good, because Reg Rawlins didn't like long commitments.

CHAPTER 2

*C*old, clammy fingers traced across Reg's face, awakening her in the wee hours of the morning.

She sat bolt upright, her heart racing. She looked quickly around her, trying to remember where she was and who was there with her. A chaotic childhood had conditioned her to be instantly awake and ready to fight. Strike fast to protect herself and escape to somewhere safe. But there was no one else in the room. Maybe the roof leaked and a drop of cold water had traced its way across her cheek.

She touched it, but it was dry, with only the memory of those icy fingers lingering behind.

Reg listened for a long time, hearing the lap of the waves in the distance. It was a restful, peaceful noise, and gradually the slamming of her heart slowed to its normal rate, though it was still pounding too hard to get back to sleep.

"There's no one here," Reg said aloud, very quietly. "You're perfectly safe, Reg. No one is going to hurt you."

It was comforting to hear those words.

When she was a kid, therapists had told her social worker and foster parents she had PTSD, and that was the reason for much of her unwanted behavior. It was nonsense, of course. Reg had never been in a war or terrorist attack. She'd never been kidnapped. Sure, she'd grown up rough, but a lot of kids had. And Reg was good at adapting. You couldn't call a few nightmares PTSD just because it was the fashion.

She listened to the waves for a long time. It was growing light as she drifted off to sleep again, still not sure what had awakened her in the night.

When she got up in the morning, it was with the clear plan to get a cat. She needed a cat. It would be a good prop. Witches had cats or other familiars. People instinctively felt that people who owned pets were kinder and more trustworthy than those who didn't. And it would give her a little company, without having to resort to having another person around the house. Reg liked company, but she liked having her own space.

A cat was the perfect idea.

Reg giggled to herself at the pun. A purrfect idea.

She checked addresses on her phone, thinking about what else she would need to buy in order to settle into her new living space. The fact that it came furnished was a bonus. She packed and traveled light and was used to operating on a shoestring. A fully-furnished cottage was a level of luxury she wasn't used to.

She picked up groceries and the basics she would need to care for a cat before going to the pound, patting herself on the back for thinking ahead and realizing that she wouldn't be able to do the other shopping once she had the cat in the car. She'd have to go straight home, and she wouldn't want to just abandon the poor critter there to go run errands.

At the animal shelter, self-styled as a pet sanctuary, before she was even allowed to look at the animals, Reg had to fill in a bunch of paperwork indicating her willingness to take care of a pet for the rest of its natural life and to follow all of the rules that the shelter set forth, such as not declawing a cat.

The place was noisy and smelly. Every effort had been made to make it a nice place, comfortable and humane for the animals, but it still stank. Reg thought about Erin. She probably would have run out of there puking, she was so sensitive to bad smells. Reg wasn't sure how she even managed to keep pets of her own, what with having to change litter and clean up after any accidents. They hadn't been allowed pets when they had lived with the Harrises, but Reg had seen enough examples of Erin reacting to human smells and accidents that she had no doubt she'd have difficulty cleaning up after animals.

There were old cats and tiny kittens and everything in between. Orange cats and tabbies and calicos. Short hair and long. Unlike the dogs, most of the cats didn't interact with the people walking by their cages, but simply slept, curled up in the corners of the cages. Occasionally, one of them would open its eyes or lift its head for a moment, but mostly they just continued to sleep.

She had thought she would be tempted by the playful younger kitties, but she thought of them keeping her up all night and wasn't sure that was what she wanted.

Maybe getting a cat had just been an impulse. Buying a pet was one of those things you were never supposed to do on impulse.

There were good reasons for getting a cat, but there were reasons not to as well. It might be noisy and wake her up nights. Have hairballs. Scatter litter and shed all over the house. It might jump up on the counter and get into things. Get out of the house and run out into the street.

It was probably a bad idea.

Reg looked into the next cage. The black and white cat raised his head, then climbed out of the nest of blankets in the corner, stretched, and walked up to the front of the enclosure.

"Hey, cat," Reg murmured.

He sat up tall and gazed at her, serious and still. Reg poked her finger through the bars at him, hearing a voice in the back of her head warning her never to poke her finger into an animal's cage. Even a hamster would bite you if you stuck your fingers through the bars. But just like she had ignored the foster mothers who had warned her not to do dangerous things, Reg ignored the voice in her head.

The cat's nose twitched as he caught her scent. For a minute, he just sat there. Then he leaned forward and took a step closer, touching his nose to her finger, and then rubbing his cheek against it. She felt his teeth brush over her finger as he rubbed. She scratched under his chin.

"Hey, you like that? Does that feel good?"

He rubbed against her and started purring a deep, satisfied rumble.

One of the shelter workers walked up.

"Wow, you connected with the tux!"

Reg looked at her. The girl was a teenager, maybe sixteen or seventeen, blond, with round cheeks. "The tux?"

"See, he's black with a white chest. Like he's wearing a black tuxedo and white shirt. So we call him a tuxedo cat."

"Oh, that's cool."

"And he has two different colors of eyes, too. I love that."

Reg looked at him and realized he had one green eye and one blue. "I guess that means he's special."

"I think he is." The girl poked her finger through the bars to try to scratch the tuxedo cat as well, but he only rubbed against Reg's finger. "He's been pretty depressed since he was brought in. His owner died and he hasn't really clicked with anyone. We've tried to play with him and to get him interested in things, but he's been so sad, pretty much all he'll do is sleep. He barely even eats."

In direct contradiction to her words, the cat stopped rubbing against Reg's finger and went over to his food bowl. He sniffed at the food, then began to eat, crunching the kibble.

Reg laughed.

"Well, he wouldn't!" the girl protested. "It must be you. Maybe you remind him of his owner."

Reg watched the cat. "What do you know about her?"

"Her? He's a he. A boy."

"No, I mean his owner. What do you know about her?"

"Oh. Well, he's also a he. A man. Don't really know much about him, just that Tux must have really been attached to him."

If she were going to get a cat, then it was obviously going to have to be that one. None of the other cats had shown Reg any interest at all, and she hadn't been particularly attracted to them. She clicked her tongue, thinking about it, and the noise made the cat turn his head to look at her again. He left his food bowl and again walked to the front of the cage, purring.

"I guess... this is the one," Reg said.

At least he was a short-hair, so he wouldn't get too much fur scattered around the cottage. And he seemed very quiet and sedate, not like a kitten that was going to jump on her face in the middle of the night and keep her awake.

"Oh, good!" the girl exclaimed. "I'll go get Marion, and she can help you with the adoption."

"Okay. Sure."

Reg waited there, scratching and quietly communing with her cat until the older supervisor approached to talk to her about the process.

If Reg had been expecting to just walk in and get a cat and walk out ten minutes later, she was sadly mistaken. Even the intake had taken longer than ten minutes. Apparently she needed counseling, needed to be walked through how to care for a cat, all of the things that could go wrong, budgeting for food and vets, what to do for behavioral issues, and on and on.

Reg had a headache by the time they were done and was ready to just pack it in and go home without a cat. But that would make the hours that she had been there wasted time, and she wasn't going to waste her first full day in Florida. Half of her groceries were already sitting spoiling in the car, and she wasn't going to walk out of there empty-handed.

Marion finally decided that Reg was ready to go and took the tuxedo cat out of his cage and settled him into a cardboard box, transferring the furry blanket he had been sleeping on into the box as well.

"That will help him transition, having something that already smells like home with him. Now you be sure to call if you have any questions about his care. Normally I would recommend that a first-time pet owner start out with a smaller animal, like a hamster, but... that tux needs a home badly, and he seems to like you."

Reg watched Marion close the box securely, and then took it from her. She didn't want to stand there discussing it any further. She wanted her cat home.

~

The *Reg Rawlins, Psychic Investigator* series is a spin-off from the *Auntie Clem's Bakery* series that follows the exploits of Erin's foster sister.

What the Cat Knew, Book #1 of the *Reg Rawlins, Psychic Investigator* series by P.D. Workman can be purchased at pdworkman.com

ABOUT THE AUTHOR

Award-winning and USA Today bestselling author P.D. (Pamela) Workman writes riveting mystery/suspense and young adult books dealing with mental illness, addiction, abuse, and other real-life issues. For as long as she can remember, the blank page has held an incredible allure and from a very young age she was trying to write her own books.

Workman wrote her first complete novel at the age of twelve and continued to write as a hobby for many years. She started publishing in 2013. She has won several literary awards from Library Services for Youth in Custody for her young adult fiction. She currently has over 60 published titles and can be found at pdworkman.com.

Born and raised in Alberta, Workman has been married for over 25 years and has one son.

∽

Please visit P.D. Workman at pdworkman.com to see what else she is working on, to join her mailing list, and to link to her social networks.

∽

If you enjoyed this book, please take the time to recommend it to other purchasers with a review or star rating and share it with your friends!

facebook.com/pdworkmanauthor

twitter.com/pdworkmanauthor

instagram.com/pdworkmanauthor

amazon.com/author/pdworkman

bookbub.com/authors/p-d-workman

goodreads.com/pdworkman

linkedin.com/in/pdworkman

pinterest.com/pdworkmanauthor

youtube.com/pdworkman

Lightning Source UK Ltd.
Milton Keynes UK
UKHW020138230422
401939UK00003B/249